T-R-O-U-B-L-E

"Here's the thing," she continued, leaning over the table. "I . . . oh, God, okay. Listen. Don't laugh."

"Okay."

"I want you."

Well. He didn't know why she thought he would laugh at that. Spit his wine out in surprise, maybe. But definitely not laugh.

"But I'm leaving."

"O . . . kay?"

"So I don't want you to get too attached."

"Okay." There seemed to be something wrong with his vocabulary.

"You seem like a nice guy, that's all."

"Thanks?" he said, because that sure didn't sound like a compliment.

"And despite what people say, I'm not a total monster. I don't want to hurt you. But . . ."

"But?"

"But I can't get over this urge to climb across the table and jump you."

"Check, please."

Falling *for* Trouble

SARAH TITLE

ZEBRA BOOKS
KENSINGTON PUBLISHING CORP.
http://www.kensingtonbooks.com

ZEBRA BOOKS are published by

Kensington Publishing Corp.
119 West 40th Street
New York, NY 10018

All Kensington titles, imprints and distributed lines are
available at special quantity discounts for bulk purchases
for sales promotion, premiums, fund-raising, educational
or institutional use.

Special book excerpts or customized printings can also be
created to fit specific needs. For details, write or phone the
office of the Kensington Sales Manager. Attn.: Sales Depart-
ment. Kensington Publishing Corp., 119 West 40th Street,
New York, NY 10018. Phone: 1-800-221-2647.

Zebra and the Z logo Reg. U.S. Pat. & TM Off.

First Printing: July 2017
ISBN-13: 978-1-4201-4185-6
ISBN-10: 1-4201-4185-6

eISBN-13: 978-1-4201-4186-3
eISBN-10: 1-4201-4186-4

10 9 8 7 6 5 4 3 2 1

Printed in the United States of America

ACKNOWLEDGMENTS

When I was twenty-six, I moved from a cool person's post-collegiate life in San Francisco back to my hometown, which is very small. I was saving for grad school and living with my parents and lying about watching movies all night with my "friend," Alex, who was a poet. (We weren't watching movies. We were smooching. Which I'm sure they knew.) One day, while I was barist-ing, my high school English teacher came into the coffee shop and said to the student he was with, oh, here's Sarah Title, she gave the student-at-large speech at graduation just like you're going to! And the look of horror on the kid's face, that he would someday be an old lady working in a coffee shop when he thought he was living a life of such promise . . . Of course, I did have a purpose, but he didn't know that. Anyway, that experience was pretty much the catalyst for this story. So thanks, Mr. Dunn and Unnamed Student, who hopefully has found lots of success.

Like a lot of librarians, I grew up in my local public library. The Halikarnassus Public Library is very inspired by the Lee Memorial Library in Allendale, NJ—though, let's be real, I took a lot of liberties. But all the good parts, those are like Lee Memorial.

I feel like my books are as much about finding home as they are about finding love. As someone who seems to enjoy a regular state-to-state move (or as a masochist . . . not sure which), I am very grateful to the people I call home, no matter where they are geographically. Trish, Marsha, Toni, Dana; Brock; Maureen; and Tom, Amy, Mary Ellen, and Brian. And my parents. Hi, parents! Ignore that stuff about movies.

And thank you to Alicia Condon from Kensington who continues to be my biggest champion (except for my mom—hi, Mom!), and without whose insights these stories would not be. Thank you also to Louise Fury from the Bent Agency who is taking me places, baby.

It's a rough time to be a woman in America, but I hope, if you're reading this (and even if you're not, but you won't know that if you're not reading it, will you?), that this story brings you a little laughter and respite and hope that you'll find the place you were meant to be.

Prologue

Peggy checked the clock one more time.

She really was pathetic. Not pathetic, she told herself. A woman of routine. She'd retired last spring from her forty-two years at Halikarnassus Middle School—did she really expect herself to undo decades of routine in a year?

Still, she would like to know what it was like to sleep in.

She looked down at Starr, her ragamuffin little poodle who was another part of the reason she couldn't sleep in. "You and your old-lady bladder," she scolded, without much heat. Starr barely lifted her head from the cushion on the kitchen chair that was closest to Peggy's.

Peggy had a whole list of things to do, none of which were particularly setting her world on fire. She had promised to make some zucchini bread for her pregnant neighbor, she needed more laundry detergent, she had to make appointments for both herself and Starr at their respective groomers.

She was just biding her time.

She wondered if Joanna was up yet. She was in LA, so it was unlikely—more likely that she hadn't gone to bed yet. Raising that wild granddaughter of hers had earned every gray hair Peggy meticulously covered up. Peggy still had a hard time thinking of Joanna as an adult, capable of living on her own. Not that Joanna was incompetent, she was just . . . stubborn. Sometimes too stubborn to do the right thing.

Peggy never should have let that girl take guitar lessons.

Oh, sure, it channeled her rebelliousness into something more creative, but now her only grandchild was living across the country pursuing a career that did not come with a 401(k). A rock musician. If Joanna's mom could see Joanna, well, she'd probably blame Peggy for getting her guitar lessons in the first place.

Peggy reached for her phone—a smartphone, thank you very much—and debated sending Joanna a text. Last night had been a big night for her. Her band, Bunny Slippers, was opening for . . . well, Peggy couldn't remember. Something to do with pennies? It wasn't really her style of music. Of course, neither was Bunny Slippers, but those songs kind of grew on a gal. They were all about kick-ass females, as Joanna would say. None of that sappy love garbage.

Which was so very Joanna. That made Peggy even more proud, that her baby was making it big being nothing but herself. Peggy was nervous when Joanna started talking about signing to a major record label—she had visions of shady, predatory A&R men taking advantage of an all-girl rock group. She knew this was sexist, but she couldn't help it. Joanna was her baby girl; she'd always be protective of her. But their new manager seemed to have the band's best interests at heart, and he got them on this tour with the Penny . . . somethings. What were they called?

Oh yes, the Penny Lickers.

Absurd.

But very, very popular.

Peggy really wanted to call Joanna to see how the first show had gone. She'd just send the text, and if Joanna was up, she'd call her back. If not, Peggy'd talk to her after her thrilling day of postretirement errands.

She looked up at the clock again.

Finally.

"Come on, Starr. Time for a walk!"

No matter how brightly Peggy said that, Starr always attempted to bolt when the leash came out. She was fast for an old lady, but so was Peggy, and she had ten pounds of squirmy fluff in her arms and leashed in no time. They were running a little late. Peggy hoped she hadn't missed him.

This is so very wrong, she said to herself as she shut the front door behind her, which was the same thing she told herself every morning. She waved to Doris, next door, who was watering her flowers, and to Carla across the street, who was at her mailbox, which was a little obvious.

Still, she couldn't blame the woman.

Peggy coaxed Starr down the steps and onto the short path through her front yard, once again amazed at the torque the ten-pound dog could produce when she was faced with something she did not want to do. Starr was just deigning to slowly climb down the stairs when he turned the corner.

It was wrong, surely, to build her morning around

the daily opportunity to ogle the new library director in his running shorts. She would never stand for this kind of behavior from a man toward a woman. And yet, every morning, she joined the other women in the neighborhood to wave and smile at Liam Byrd.

Sometimes he stopped to chat, bouncing up and down on the balls of his feet while they talked about books or about Joanna. Liam was quite the music aficionado. He knew more about the music she grew up with than she did, and he was always asking after Joanna's career. He told her that he had bought the newest Bunny Slippers album. He said he liked it, although his face told her otherwise. Such a nice young man.

Lately, he hadn't been stopping, just waving and jogging on. Poor boy was stressed. The town council was giving him headaches about his budget. Peggy'd like to give the town council a headache. But then she'd watch Liam run on, and she found it hard to be mad at anyone for a good while after that.

Today looked like it was going to be just a waver, which was just as well, because Peggy's phone was vibrating in her pocket. She reached for it while offering Liam her brightest smile. Then Starr apparently decided she *did* want to go on a walk after all, because she started barking and following Liam (not that Peggy could blame her). Except that in her stubbornness, Starr had wrapped herself around Peggy's legs, and Peggy's attention was divided between her phone and Liam's shorts, which left nothing for her balance, so when Starr took off, Peggy didn't stand a chance.

She went down.

Hard.

Oh, Lord.

Peggy opened her eyes to see the cloudless spring sky, then Liam's flushed face.

"Peggy? Peggy, are you all right?"

She was fine, she wanted to tell him. Just embarrassed. But she found she couldn't catch her breath, and she thought she might be having a heart attack but it wasn't her chest that hurt, it was her leg. Oh, Lord, she'd never felt such pain before in her life, not even when she gave birth to Joanna's father. Liam's sweet, concerned face swam in front of hers, and she heard Starr barking and someone talking about an ambulance, which she hoped was not for her because she was fine; it was just a little breath-stealing, paralyzing pain in her leg; there was no need to make such a fuss.

"Peggy? Stay with me, okay? The ambulance is coming," Liam said, and he was such a dear. She really should stop objectifying him like that. She should tell Doris and Carla to back off, too. Especially when he was being so nice to her, even if she didn't really need it. She wanted to tell him that, and to get on her feet to go into the house and ice her leg and maybe find something to drown her shame in. She started to do that, but as she tried to sit up, her leg moved and the look on Liam's face told her that she had said out loud the curse words she was thinking. Then his face started to darken, and so did the sky, and then she didn't feel a thing.

Chapter One

"Jo? Joey Green?"

And that, in one frustrating nickname, was the reason why Joanna Green never came back to Halikarnassus. The fact that it was a nosy little town with one bar and few people worth drinking with, she could deal with. It was more the fact that everyone in town seemed obsessed with the Joanna she had been in high school—a screwup and a hell-raiser and a general bad influence. She hadn't been home in years, and that one nickname made it abundantly clear that no one was going to try to get to know Joanna the Adult.

Not that Joanna the adult was any less of a screwup. Hell, that was why she was standing in the airport, waiting in baggage claim for the suitcase holding all of her worldly possessions (with the exception of her guitar, which she would never, in a million years, trust to baggage handlers).

Coming home as an abject failure with your tail between your legs was one thing, Joanna thought.

Having to explain that failure to a bunch of people who didn't expect anything more from you was a new level of humiliation she wasn't sure she could deal with. *Just keep an eye out for your suitcase,* she told herself. *You don't have to talk to anyone. You just need to grab your bag, convince a cab to take you all the way to Halikarnassus, and hope that Granny is home to lend you cab fare.*

Totally an adult.

"I thought it was you!"

Joanna could no longer ignore the persistent nostalgia at her elbow. A young woman in an enormous gray scarf was looking at her expectantly. Joanna tried to place her . . . she looked vaguely familiar . . .

"Oh my gosh, you don't remember me. Skyler Carrington?" Scarf Girl gave her a hopeful look.

"Holy crap, Skyler? I thought you were like . . ." The last time Joanna had seen Skyler, Joanna was getting in big trouble for making her cry because she wouldn't let her play with her very expensive guitar. Skyler had been what, five? Seven? She was ten years younger than Joanna, a fact that had caused Trina, Joanna's best friend and Skyler's big sister, a minor adolescent breakdown because they now knew where babies came from and she didn't want to think about her parents doing *that.* Of course, once Skyler was born, Trina was ruthlessly protective of her sister, who was, frankly, a brat.

Skyler had been three. Or five. Or whatever. That was a long time ago. She was probably much less bratty now. And wasn't that why Joanna had avoided coming home? Because she knew people would only see her as she had been back then? Pot and black kettle and all that.

Back then Joanna was a foul-mouthed, rebellious, broke teenager. Now she was . . . well, she wasn't a teenager.

God, how depressing. She'd left town to shake off the image everybody had of her, only to find that the reason they had that image was because it was who she was.

Except that now she was old. And Skyler Carrington was as tall as she was.

And Skyler Carrington was leaning forward to give Joanna a hug. "Trina's not going to believe this! What are you doing here?"

"Just, uh . . ." Skyler Carrington didn't need to know the whole sad, sordid story, and it made Joanna feel a little better that news of her epic failure had not reached Halikarnassus yet. At least, not the airport two hours from Halikarnassus. "Just visiting."

"Granny! How is Granny?"

"Good, fine." She hoped, anyway. She hadn't spoken to Granny in a few days, despite Granny's best efforts. But Joanna knew she would just want to hear all the details of the big concert, as she called it, and Joanna wasn't ready to go there yet. Or ever. Granny probably wouldn't ask any questions when Joanna showed up unannounced on her doorstep, right?

God, she wasn't just a failure. She was a delusional failure.

And Skyler was looking at her expectantly. "What are you doing here?" Joanna asked. "Love the scarf."

"Oh my God, I just finished a semester in France. I'm, like, so not used to speaking English! And everyone here is so . . . American!"

"You'll get that, what with being in America," Joanna suggested.

"I'm just having, like, culture shock. Literally everything in France is, like, so much better. I can't even with this." Skyler waved her hand around.

Joanna couldn't even with the baggage claim, either. She also couldn't with this kid having adventures in France while Joanna had been working hard, making music, then throwing it all away in one stupid night. Skyler had probably done more in her teenage life than Joanna had in her . . . more than teenage life. They both talked big; this kid had actually done big things.

Fortunately, the baggage carousel started to move and, as if the gracious gods of Joanna's hometown shame were looking down upon her struggle to keep it together in a conversation with her old friend's formerly bratty toddler little sister, her suitcase came out first.

"Well, this is me. Nice to see you."

Skyler reached forward to help Joanna with her suitcase. "Are you going to be home for a while? Trina is going to die when I tell her I saw you."

Joanna pretended not to hear. She just waved and lost herself in the crowd, dragging all of her worldly possessions behind her.

"You okay back there?"

Liam looked in the rearview mirror long enough to see Peggy weakly wave a hand at him, then turned back to the road. He was not entirely comfortable driving her car, but his ancient Sentra didn't have a very roomy backseat, and when Doris had called to instruct him to pick Peggy up from the hospital, those instructions included figuring out a way to enable Peggy to elevate her leg on the drive home.

He wasn't entirely sure how he, of all of Peggy's friends in Halikarnassus, was chosen to pick her up from the hospital.

Not that he thought of saying no. Not even for a second. He'd been there when Peggy fell, and he still felt responsible for her broken leg, despite everyone's reassurances to the contrary. It wasn't his fault her dog was crazy and her phone rang. But she always came out of the house to wave and chat with him when he went on his morning run. If he didn't run, she wouldn't have come out.

So picking her up from the hospital was literally the least he could do.

Then he discovered that Doris intended for him to drive Peggy's car.

And he understood why the responsibility had fallen to him.

Nobody wanted to drive Peggy's car. It ran fine, great, even, especially considering its age. But it was massive. It was the kind of old-person car his grandparents used to drive. It didn't suit Peggy at all. She was old, sure, but not, like, *old* old. Not like grandparents old.

Although, he supposed, she *was* grandparents old, since she had a granddaughter who wasn't that much younger than he was.

The mysterious Joanna Green, whose music he knew from his post-college punk days. The girl could wail on the guitar. She could beat a lick into

submission and get up for more. He was half in love
with her the first time he heard her play with the
Slutty Brontes, a kick-ass post-punk riot grrl group
that made him want to break things, in a good way.
He was heartbroken—way more than he should have
been—when they split up. But then she formed
Bunny Slippers and they were . . . well, they were
loud. But it was kind of like when he found out Dave
Grohl had been the drummer for Nirvana. Sure, the
Foo Fighters were great, but they weren't Nirvana.

Liam couldn't believe that he now lived in the
town she grew up in, that he was friends with her
grandmother, and that he waived overdue fines for
people who knew her back when she was just starting out.

Not that anyone else was that impressed with her
talents or her success. The general opinion about
Joanna Green in Halikarnassus was that she was
nothing but trouble, and an inadequate granddaughter to boot.

He wondered if she knew about Peggy's broken
leg. Last he'd heard (not that he stalked her, but the
mayor's wife had an inexplicable habit of keeping
him informed of Joanna's movements), her band
had signed with a major label and was touring with
the Penny Lickers.

This made him love her a little less.

Which probably wasn't fair. He knew he was a
music snob, and he shouldn't begrudge anyone
for making a living. But the Penny Lickers? Widely
acknowledged to be the twenty-first century's most
boring rock band?

"Is there a reason you're driving so slowly?"

Peggy was half sitting, her head held up by a stack of pillows and a matching set elevating her broken leg. Liam had managed to wrangle the seat belt around her, but still. He wanted to be careful.

Also, he wasn't entirely sure where the outside of the car ended, and he was deathly afraid of taking out an innocent side mirror.

"Just being careful," he said with a smile.

"You and your careful," Peggy teased. At least she was teasing him. She must not be in too much pain if she could still tease him.

Then he heard a snore from the backseat, and he was reminded of the copious amounts of painkiller the hospital had given her.

"Oh, Peggy," he said, and she snored in response.

As he continued his crawl to her house, pulling over occasionally to let other cars pass, he admitted his selfish hope that Peggy would be well enough to attend the next town council meeting. She, like a lot of the older Halikarnassians, didn't have a very high opinion of their mayor, Hal Klomberg Jr. His father had been mayor for years before he finally retired, and though everyone voted for Hal Jr. thinking he'd fulfill his promises to follow in his father's footsteps, nobody seemed to appreciate the job he was doing.

Liam hadn't lived in Halikarnassus for most of that—he'd moved to town after the election but before Mayor Klomberg Jr. decided a course of fiscal responsibility was the only way to get the town out of the financial mess it was in. As far as anyone knew, the town wasn't in a mess. Sure, the economy wasn't great, but Halikarnassus had never depended on manufacturing like so many of the towns around them.

It seemed Mayor Jr. had a fetish for cutting budgets. The library was next on his list.

Or it had been, until Peggy and her self-appointed White-Haired Old Ladies stepped into the fight.

"The last council meeting . . . .that was a classic," he told his sleeping passenger. "Although I'm glad Councilman Weber cut off your time. While I'm sure everyone would have enjoyed watching you take Mayor Klomberg over your knee, I'm pretty sure you would have been arrested."

Of course, if she'd been in jail, she wouldn't have been rushing outside to greet him, and she wouldn't have broken her leg.

"We're in a mess, Peggy." He needed his staunchest defender. Mayor Klomberg's plan was to cut the library's budget in half. Half. It wasn't an exorbitant budget to begin with, but Liam had dutifully worked on a plan to deal with the eventuality. It involved cutting hours and giving up on new books and, worse, firing a lot of people who'd worked at the library for a long time.

"Damn Junior," Peggy muttered.

Okay, so maybe she wasn't as asleep as he'd assumed. It was just as well, he thought as he slowly, carefully, pulled into her driveway. He had bigger things to worry about than library budgets. Like how he was going to get Peggy inside.

Chapter Two

Joanna sat in the backseat of the Carringtons' car, between the triumphantly returned Francophile Skyler and the Great Dane, Max. Max needed to stick his head out the window, Mrs. Carrington explained when she ushered Joanna into the middle seat. Seeing the amount of slobber flying past the window took some of the sting out of sitting in what felt like a built-in booster seat. Riding with her knees under her chin was a small price to pay for a free—and slobber-free—ride from the airport.

Between the highway wind, the blaring French pop music, and the shouted conversation among the three Carringtons, Joanna was having a hard time focusing on anything other than holding onto the front seat as Mr. Carrington switched lanes with reckless abandon. She remembered that about him now. If there was a way to drive faster, he would take it, no matter how green his middle-seat passengers got.

Of course, her greenness wasn't just from the bad driving.

"I can't get over how sweet it is that you're coming

home to take care of Peggy," Mrs. Carrington said from the comfort of the front seat.

Joanna squeezed her hands together. The truth was, she had had no idea that Granny had been in the hospital, which made her feel like a monster. Joanna had seen the missed call from Granny's cell when she was at LAX. She hadn't felt up to talking to her, explaining to her that due to her stupendous badness, she had destroyed the first good thing to come from her musical career. She knew she'd have to do that eventually, but Joanna foolishly thought doing it in person would be easier.

No, she hadn't. She just wanted to put it off for as long as possible.

She'd spent her last dime on the baggage fees that came with her one-way ticket. Her plan was to show up on Granny's doorstep with a big "surprise!" and a plea for cab fare. She totally took it for granted that Granny would be there. Granny was good like that.

Now, even though Granny had foiled Joanna's plan, she still provided a convenient explanation for why Joanna was back. Not at all because her career had blown up in her stupid face. Nope, she was home to play the dutiful granddaughter that nobody in town really believed she was. This made her feel like an opportunist in addition to being a bad grand-daughter.

Well, nobody had to know the truth. Her heart-lessness could be her little secret, tucked away where her soul used to be, before she sold it to rock and roll.

Joanna would feel a lot better about it if she wasn't sick with worry.

"I haven't talked to her in a bit," Joanna said,

Sarah Title

hoping she sounded casual through her gritted teeth. "How's she doing?"

"Of course, you've been on the plane. She's coming home from the hospital today. Doris Sampson arranged one of those care calendars for meals. She must not have known you were coming home."

"Nope. I wanted it to be a surprise." Ha ha, surprise.

"Well, I'm glad you were able to tear yourself away from that rock-star life." Mrs. Carrington giggled.

She really giggled.

Joanna turned to Skyler to commiserate over Mrs. C's persistent un-hipness, but Skyler was asleep, her chin tucked into her enormous scarf.

"I used to tell Peggy, I can't imagine what I would have done if Trina had followed in your footsteps. You were always such a troublemaker! Trina could never keep up with you!" Mrs. Carrington's laugh sounded a little forced.

Joanna reminded herself that she should be grateful for the free ride from the airport. Not that she'd had much of a choice—Skyler had trapped her in a bear hug (she had always had a bit of hero worship for Joanna, that kid), then dragged her over to her parents, who battered her with questions she tried to avoid. Mrs. Carrington had always looked at her with a vague sort of pity. That poor girl, her parents ran off, nobody but her and her grandmother in that old house. Still, that pity made Mrs. C much more forgiving of Joanna's bad behavior (just acting out, she explained). Teenage Joanna had enjoyed watching the conflicted look on Mrs. C's face as she tried to maintain her self-appointed reputation of being a cool mom while also protecting Trina from a girl who was clearly a terrible influence.

Hey, Joanna didn't put that joint in Mr. C's night-stand drawer.

Sure, she took it up to Trina's tree house and taught her how to smoke it. But it wasn't Joanna's fault that it was there in the first place. Besides, Trina was not as innocent as Mrs. C thought she was. Whose idea was it to drive to Schenectady to sneak into frat parties? Who made out with her math tutor while her parents were watching television in the next room? Who decided to perform the uncensored version of "Add It Up" by the Violent Femmes at the eighth grade talent show?

Okay, that one was Joanna's idea. But still.

Poor, deluded Mrs. Carrington.

So, back at the airport, when the Carringtons embraced her (literally) and insisted on giving her a ride to Halikarnassus, Joanna's guilt at her spoiled, misbegotten childhood ways made her resist. She wasn't going to Halikarnassus, she insisted. Even though her grandmother was currently on her way home from the hospital, the Carringtons asked. Once her panic-induced deafness subsided and her blood was flowing normally again, Joanna quickly changed her story. Yes, she was going to nurse Granny and her broken leg, why else would her only next of kin be at a nearby baggage claim.

And since Granny might not even be home yet—thus making it impossible for her to loan Joanna cab fare—a ride with the Carringtons would be much more convenient. All she had to do was swallow her pride.

Much more convenient, she reminded herself as Mr. Carrington cut off a school bus and sped down the exit ramp toward Halikarnassus.

And just like that, Joanna was back.

If riding in the backseat of the Carringtons' car wasn't enough to make her feel like a kid, the long county road leading to Halikarnassus brought back memories so visceral, Joanna could practically feel the baby fat growing back. Each shrub was familiar. There was the house with the picket fence that people kept running into when they took the turn too fast. There was the shabby-looking cottage that made national news with its over-the-top Christmas lights.

No matter how much she tried to fight it, this place was home.

"Trina always had the talent, though," Mrs. C continued, oblivious to Joanna's tumultuous flashbacks.

She was right. Trina was the best drummer Joanna had ever worked with, not that she knew it when they were dicking around with their band in high school. She just knew she had a best friend who liked to make noise as much as she did. But then Trina went to college, and Joanna went to LA, and Trina fell in love with an insurance agent and bought a house in town and had a couple of kids.

Meanwhile Joanna was off living the high life, drinking cheap beer and sleeping on the floor of the band's van, until she managed to destroy the one big break she had that would have shown all of Halikarnassus that she was not the royal fuckup they'd all assumed her to be.

Her thoughts were interrupted by a familiar sound coming from the radio. The Carringtons' top-shelf satellite radio was programmed to the easy rock station which, to Joanna, was just elevator music with electric guitars. Sure enough, it was everyone's dad's favorite band, the Penny Lickers.

The song was almost over, but Joanna recognized it. It was the one about the guy who was telling his girlfriend's dad that the girl was too good for him, that he would break her heart, to tell her to stay away, except that the guy really loved the girl, and the dad saw that, and he was like, *hey, listen, buddy, just do the best you can, it's all we men can ever do.*

A really charming song. Whenever she heard it—which was way more often than she wanted to— Joanna felt really bad for the daughter.

"And that's the latest from the Penny Lickers, who're out on tour now," the DJ said with enthusiasm that didn't sound entirely genuine. "It's a great show, go out and catch them if you can."

Joanna should have been on that tour. She didn't want to be, she was sure of that. But that didn't explain the little pain in her chest every time she realized what an opportunity she had squandered.

"Speaking of a great show, did anyone see them kick off their tour? Apparently there was quite the kerfuffle with the opening band, what were they called, Jimmy?"

"Bunny Slippers," came the voice from the booth.

"That's right, Bunny Slippers. Cute girls. Too bad their guitarist—"

Whatever the DJ was going to describe was mercifully drowned out by Max's impassioned howling. Joanna wanted to kiss his slobbery face. Instead, she watched as Mr. Carrington slowed down—barely—to pull into Granny's driveway.

"This brings back memories, huh?" he said as he put the car in park. "I haven't dropped you off here in, what, fifteen years?"

More like ten, but Joanna didn't feel like correcting him. She was just sitting between a sleeping teenager and a slobbering dog, taking in the sight of Granny's old familiar car, the rosebushes on either side of the three steps that led to the blue front door. If she disliked it so much, why was her heart giving off little bursts of excitement?

She was just tired, that was it. And dejected. And useless. And, well, home. She climbed over Skyler, who grumbled in her sleep, and took her suitcase and her guitar from Mr. Carrington, and headed up to the front door.

She was home. And Granny needed her.

Wouldn't she be surprised?

Peggy did not have enough counter space.

She also needed a bigger fridge, and maybe a second freezer.

Liam looked helplessly around Peggy's kitchen at the stacks—literally stacks—of casseroles in containers of varying size and disposability. Each was labeled with the contents, the name of the cook, and instructions regarding the return or recycling of the dish.

It was a marvel of neighborly efficiency. As far as Liam knew, none of this had been here when he'd left to get Peggy from the hospital an hour ago. Of course, he'd been intercepted at the front door by Doris, who had Starr unhappily on a leash and who handed him Peggy's spare set of keys and went on her way. For all he knew, the neighbors had been delivering this stuff all night.

He liked that about Halikarnassus. People took care of each other. They knew each other, and they looked out.

Maybe if he rearranged everything she already had in the fridge. He could make it work. It was just like a really complicated game of Tetris. Casserole Tetris. He could do it.

He had his arms full of a head of lettuce and individual yogurt containers when he heard the front door open.

Starr, who, last time he checked, had been curled up next to Peggy's shoulder, came charging through the house, barking her head off and scaring the crap out of him. He bobbled the yogurt and heard a "holy shit, what is that?" from the front door.

He dropped his bounty into the sink—good enough for now—and went out to at least prevent Starr from escaping. Before he greeted Peggy's guest, he scooped Starr up, and like clockwork, she stopped barking. She did, however, take a suspicious sniff in the direction of the woman standing at the door.

She had jet-black hair, a guitar strapped to her back, an enormous suitcase at her feet, and a look of utter confusion on her face.

She stepped back off the porch, looked at the front of the house as if confirming that she had the right address, then stepped back up. She looked even more confused.

"Is this still Peggy Green's house?"

"Yes," Liam answered, trying to figure out where he knew this woman from. Maybe a library patron? Although surely he would have remembered if she'd ever been to the library. She was like his teenage fantasy come to life: rock-and-roll looks and a bad attitude. Plus a guitar.

Ah. A guitar.

"Joanna?" Peggy hadn't said anything about expecting her granddaughter, but then, Peggy hadn't been saying much since she broke her leg. Mostly just snoring.

"Who're you?" Probably-Joanna's look went from confused to suspicious.

"Oh! Right. Hi, I'm Liam. I'm a friend of your grandmother's." He bobbled Starr and held his hand out to shake, but she just brushed past him, lugging her guitar and that huge suitcase with her.

"Is she here?"

"Yes. She's resting. She, ah . . . she didn't mention that you'd be coming."

"It's a surprise. Is she all right? I mean, broken leg and all . . ."

"She's fine. Well, she'll definitely be laid up for a few weeks, at least, but the doctor said everything checked out okay. I have a bunch of prescriptions I was going to get filled for her . . ."

"Is that your dog?"

Liam looked down at Starr, who was still giving Joanna a suspicious look.

"No . . . this is Peggy's dog. Starr?" Liam knew Joanna didn't visit much—or at all—but she didn't even know Peggy had a dog?

"*That's* Starr?" Joanna asked, in a way that suggested Peggy had not accurately conveyed the concentrated power and attitude that was Starr.

"Is she in her room?" It took Liam a second to realize she meant Peggy, not Starr. Because Starr was clearly not in her room, since she was squirming under Liam's arm. He just nodded, and Joanna turned and walked down the hallway. Starr wiggled free and followed her. He heard a sharp bark, followed by an "Oh my God, my baby!" from Peggy; then the door closed.

Liam should go. Peggy's granddaughter was home, and although she didn't look like the warm, caretaker type, clearly she was here to do just that. Why else would she be here? Peggy once told Liam that Joanna had sworn never to come back to Halikarnassus again. Too boring, too claustrophobic, she said. It was kind of sweet, her breaking her vow like that.

Not that Joanna looked sweet.

He should leave them to their reunion and let Joanna take care of her grandmother. He could run and get the prescriptions filled, or, well, he definitely didn't need to buy groceries. The least he could do was figure out how to get all this stuff into the fridge, he thought. He opened the fridge and channeled his internal Tetris master.

Chapter Three

"Oh my God, my baby!"

So much for making a quiet entrance, Joanna thought, then stumbled out of the way as the angry fluffball streaked past her and jumped up on the bed. When Granny had told her she'd adopted a sweet little poodle, Joanna was expecting something, well, sweet. This dog glared at her from behind Granny's hip.

"Hey, Gran," Joanna whispered, though she didn't know why. Granny sure wasn't whispering. It was just that she looked . . . delicate. Joanna wasn't used to seeing her delicate. Until that dreadful moment in the airport, she couldn't remember ever thinking of Granny as mortal.

Granny reached her hand out to Joanna, and she came into the room, standing awkwardly by the edge of the bed, holding Gran's hand.

"Don't be so silly, I won't break," Granny said, and tugged on Joanna until she was sitting at her side. The fluffball growled.

"No offense, Gran, but you did break."

"Oh, hush, Starr," Granny told the dog, ignoring Joanna's comment. The dog let out a quick, sharp bark, then walked in a tight circle and lay down.

"Sorry about that. She's very protective of me," Granny explained.

More than I am, that's for sure, Joanna thought.

"She is a ferocious guard dog," she said. "Much tougher than she looks."

"Lie down. Looking up at you like that is hurting my neck."

Joanna did as she was told—for once—resting her head on the edge of Granny's pillow. She pulled her legs carefully onto the bed so as not to disturb the complicated pyramid of pillows her broken leg was resting on. Joanna shouldn't have worried, though. As soon as her head hit the pillow, she was swamped by memories of lying, just like this, with Gran in the middle of the bed, Joanna next to her, acting like she was just going to lie there for a minute, Gran letting her pretend that she didn't need the comfort.

"Are you really here?"

"Yes, Gran. I'm really here."

"I've been taking a lot of pain medicine. Things are a little fuzzy."

"It's really me."

"You got here fast. I should break my leg more often."

"Hmm." Joanna would relay the whole complicated tale later, when Granny was clearheaded. Although, she thought, maybe she should do it now, when Granny wasn't sure to remember.

Granny lay back, her eyes closed. "The dog was a retirement present."

Joanna lifted her head a little to look at the bedraggled poodle with a bad attitude. "Some present."

"From one of my students. Do you remember the Taleses?"

Joanna thought. The name sounded familiar. But then, this was Halikarnassus. She probably knew them.

"Sure."

"Amber Talese was in my last Humanities class. She volunteers at the animal shelter, and she said when she saw Starr, she knew we were meant to be."

"Are you sure that was a compliment?"

"Well, I've gotten quite used to her, the ornery thing."

"You've got a thing for ornery ladies," Joanna said.

Granny pulled Joanna's hand up and kissed it.

"Does it hurt?"

"My leg? Like hell."

"I'm so sorry, Gran."

"It was my own stupid fault. I was trying to do too many things at once. I'm old now, you know."

"Don't say that. You still have all your beautiful blond hair," Joanna said. It was an old joke between them, how they each had such naturally beautiful hair, when the truth was, they both spent way too much time and money on hair dye. It was one of the most important lessons Gran had taught her.

"I like this," Granny said, fingering the pink streaks in the underlayer of Joanna's hair. They were all that remained of the Bunny Slippers makeover, the first time Joanna had had her hair dyed by someone other than a friend in a tiny bathroom. She wasn't ready to let go of the black, but Jeff insisted on "softening her up a bit."

That was the first sign that Bunny Slippers was headed in a direction she did not want to go.

"So what really happened?" she asked Granny, unwilling to go into the history of her pink hair. That was a little too close to the real reason she was home.

"It's embarrassing."

"More embarrassing than me getting caught sneaking food to the neighborhood feral cats?"

"That wasn't embarrassing, that was sweet."

"Yes, but I had an image of badassery to uphold."

"And Doris did throw a fit. She was sure those cats were tearing up her garden."

"Well, Doris never did like me much."

"Oh, hush, now," Granny said. But Joanna noticed she did not contradict her. That was Granny, ever diplomatic. And that was Joanna, ever disliked by the respectable citizens of Halikarnassus.

Not that she was bitter about it.

"Tell me," Joanna urged, trying to get her mind off her own unlikability.

Granny heaved a mighty sigh that made Starr look up. The dog uncoiled and walked closer, resting her head on Gran's shoulder.

"About a year ago, we got a new library director."

"Whoa. Did Mrs. Pratt die?"

"Not funny, young lady. No, she retired like all us old people do."

"God, you're not as old as Mrs. Pratt."

"No, actually she's three years younger than me."

Joanna remembered Mrs. Pratt as old and stooped and gray-haired and mean. There was no way she was younger than Granny.

"Well, the new director is the nicest young man. Liam. He's from Boston. He's done wonderful things for the library. It's changed so much since I used to take you to summer reading when you were little. You should stop over and see it. How long will you be here, anyway?"

Joanna didn't know the answer to that question, but she was pretty sure her time in Halikarnassus would be brief and library-free. "What does the nice young library director have to do with your broken leg?"

"I'm telling you, it's embarrassing."

"Granny, you're making me think he did something to you."

"No! No no no. It's just that, well, he's so young and handsome. And I may be old, but I'm not dead yet, you know? Oh, God, this is humiliating." Granny let go of Joanna's hand to cover her face.

"Gran, tell me." Joanna really could not imagine what Liam and his handsomeness had to do with Granny's accident. If Joanna was going to seek angry vengeance, she needed some more specifics.

"He's a jogger," Granny said through her hands. "And every day he follows the same route through this neighborhood."

Joanna waited, confused.

"All of us ladies like to wave hello to him. To be neighborly."

"Okay . . ."

"He wears the most adorable running shorts."

Oh my God.

"Gran. Did you trip and fall because you were ogling the library director's legs?" She tried very hard not to laugh because her granny was in pain. She tried, really. But in the end, she couldn't hold it in.

"Oh, stop!" Granny said, but she was laughing, too. "I wasn't just ogling. I was also taking Starr out and I got tangled in her leash," Granny gasped between laughing fits.

"Granny!"

"You can't tell him! Promise me."

Joanna couldn't imagine a situation in which she'd be called upon to tell the library director anything, let alone that her grandmother was perving out on him. "I promise."

"Oh, sweetie. It's good to have you home."

"I missed you, Gran." That was the truth, even if it wasn't actually good to be home.

"I miss you, too, my love. Oh, Lord, I'm pooped. All I've been doing is lying here."

"You need to rest, Granny. Heal and stuff."

"You're right. I'm going to have a little snooze. You won't be gone when I wake up, will you?"

"No, I'll be here." She wasn't sure for how long, but she could stick it out through one nap. Probably.

Okay, definitely. She had nowhere else to go.

"And when I wake up, you'll tell me why you're really here." It wasn't so much a question as it was a demand. But then Granny closed her eyes and the dog snuggled closer, so Joanna just slid off the bed and tiptoed out of the room.

Liam still had his head in the fridge when Joanna came out of Peggy's room.

"So, should I worry about who you are?" she asked.

He hit his head on the shelf on the way out. Rubbing his sore noggin, he turned to face Joanna Green, Prodigal Granddaughter and Slightly Intimidating Rock Star.

"Hi. I'm Liam. I'm a friend of your grandmother's," he said, even though he was pretty sure he had said the same thing when she came in. He stuck out his hand for a friendly shake. She didn't take it.

"Liam the Librarian?"

"Uh . . . yup." He hated when people called him that. That's what his friends back in Boston used to call him. It drove him nuts. He always felt like they were laughing at him when they said it.

Joanna wasn't laughing, but she was definitely looking him up and down.

"Hmm," she said, and Liam looked down to make sure his fly was closed. "So, Liam the Librarian," she said, taking a seat on one of the bar stools at the kitchen island. "What are you doing in Granny's fridge?"

"Oh, uh, right. So, folks have been bringing by food. A lot of food."

"Of course. The Halikarnassus Hunger Force. They come by with food and condolences, but really they just want to stick their noses in your business."

"That's a very Lizzy Bennet thing to say."

She looked confused.

"From *Pride and Prejudice*? When she comes back from her trip early because Lydia's run off with Wickham and the neighbor lady comes to visit her and she says—"

"I know who Lizzy Bennet is."

Ah, so she wasn't confused. Just not interested in literary allusions and bad jokes. He supposed he should cut her some slack. After all, her grandmother was injured, and a stranger was rearranging her fridge.

"That doesn't change the fact that you've got a lot of food here," he said.

"And you're trying to organize it?"

"Well, I'm trying to get it all in the fridge."

"What about the freezer?"

"Full."

"What about the freezer in the garage?"

"There's a freezer in the garage?"

"Everyone in Halikarnassus has a freezer in the garage. It's a town of hoarders. Well, hoarders and hunters."

"I guess some of this could go in there." He started pulling out the most precariously situated dishes.

Then Joanna was at his elbow, taking dishes from his hands, flipping over the notes and making various noises that sounded like disapproval.

"You don't like lasagna?" he asked.

"Love it. But Mrs. Johnson's lasagna is terrible." She stepped on the lever to open the garbage can and tossed the whole aluminum pan in.

"Hey! Don't throw it out!"

"You've clearly never had Mrs. Johnson's lasagna."

"How bad can lasagna be?"

"The noodles are so soft they're practically melted, the sauce is mostly onions, and she uses fat-free cheese."

"Okay. Fat-free cheese is a crime. But don't throw out anything else, okay? People brought it over so

Peggy wouldn't have to cook. They're just trying to be nice."

"I can cook."

He tried to picture her in an apron, wielding a wooden spoon. He imagined she'd look fierce and feisty, determined to beat the ingredients into submission. It was an alarmingly appealing image. "Now you don't have to. You can just focus on Peggy."

She snorted. "Like there aren't going to be people traipsing in and out of here all day."

"They love—" He was about to remind Joanna how much everybody loved her grandmother, then thought, what was the point? Joanna was clearly unmoved by their neighborly kindness. No, she wasn't unmoved. She was moved to suspicion.

"It was really nice of you to come back here to help out," he said, trying another tactic.

She just shrugged.

"How long do you think you'll stick around?" He couldn't decide what he wanted her answer to be. Part of him wanted her to stick around so he could get to know her, to see if she was as fascinating as she seemed. Another part of him was intimidated by her coolness and her aloofness and wanted her gone. *Never meet your heroes*, the saying went. Not that she was a hero, but she was a mildly famous person he admired.

Maybe everybody was right. Maybe Joanna Green was nothing but trouble.

"Not sure. I guess until Peggy doesn't need me anymore."

"I think if Peggy had her way, you'd stay forever."

She shuddered. "Forever? In this town? Anyway, we'll get on each other's nerves eventually."

"Well, and you'll probably have to leave to play some shows, right?"

She stilled, her hand on the lid of a container that was labeled "salad" but looked more mayonnaise than vegetable.

"I'm gonna get weird for a second," he said. "I have to tell you, I'm a huge fan of yours."

"You are?" Why was she looking at him with disgust? Was it not cool to tell an accomplished person that you admired their accomplishments?

"Yeah. I mean, when I moved here, I didn't know Peggy's Joanna Green was *the* Joanna Green," he said, covering up his embarrassment with more words. Surely that was the best way to handle the situation. *Oh, she doesn't like what you're saying? Go on, say more.* "I was a huge fan of the Slutty Brontes. I saw you guys in Somerville. And those early Bunny Slippers albums—man. Amazing. You guys were like the Stilettos. Do you know the Stilettos? Debbie Harry's first band? Of course you do, duh. Not that you're not still like the Stilettos. I mean, I don't know. Your last album sort of . . . dropped off my radar. But I heard you guys are really blowing up. Next big thing. That's why I'm so surprised you're here."

He took a deep breath. Surely he would stop talking now, now that he had already used every single word in the English language to simultaneously dork out and insult the granddaughter of his favorite patron—by saying that he used to like her band, but now they kind of sucked.

She didn't say anything. Her face was unreadable.

She just looked at him for a minute, then picked up a tray of unidentified casserole and threw it in the garbage.

Very punk rock. He liked this woman, despite all the signs indicating that he should not, even as she turned on her heel and left him alone in Peggy's kitchen.

Chapter Four

Joanna's fingers itched every time she looked over at her precious '72 Fender Telecaster Deluxe, named Rosetta, after Sister Rosetta Tharpe, who—sorry, boys—invented rock guitar. If she had to choose a best friend in the world, it would be Rosetta, no offense to Trina. Rosetta had been with her through everything, from her first real gig to that last big blowup. Joanna had scrimped and saved from the moment she'd started taking guitar lessons in sixth grade. She mowed every lawn in the neighborhood, walked every dog, weeded every garden. (Although she drew the line at babysitting, not that any of the parents in Halikarnassus would have trusted Joanna with their kids.)

She really, really wanted to play. Not just play, she wanted to rock the fuck out on her best friend in the whole world. She didn't think Granny's painkillers were that strong, though, and the poor woman needed to rest. Maybe if she didn't plug it in.

She picked up Rosetta and ran her fingers down the

fret before settling her body in her lap and strumming her fingers over the strings.

She played the first thing that came to her head, a nonsense melody that was basically anything not by Bunny Slippers. Joanna liked to pretend she wouldn't be able to play Bunny Slippers music again, even if someone pointed a gun to her head. She was pretty sure that wasn't true. No, she was definitely sure. She'd written most of it, a fact that would haunt her until her fingers could no longer play.

Instead she closed her eyes and plucked and strummed whatever she felt like, angry, choppy rhythms that reminded her of the stuff she used to play in high school. Not surprising, since she was surrounded by the vestiges of her former self—ticket stubs taped to the mirror, posters hung crookedly on the wall, CDs spilling over the wobbly nightstand that Trina made in shop class. Acoustic strumming didn't have the same cathartic effect that making a shitload of noise had. Probably because she didn't have an amp. It didn't make sense to try to move it from LA, so she sold it to some creepy Bunny Slippers fanboy who wanted to take pictures of her sitting on it. In her underwear.

She declined.

Besides, even if she did have an amp, she couldn't very well plug it in and rock out, riot-grrl-in-the-suburbs style. Gran was sleeping, and even her drug-induced mandatory rest would probably not stick once Joanna started playing.

Still, the sad, tinny noises coming from Rosetta seemed inadequate to fill her need for noise, and not fair to Rosetta. If she couldn't rock out, Rosetta'd rather not play, Rosetta told her.

And, yes, it was totally normal to have conversations with your guitar, Joanna told herself.

"Sorry, babe," she told her guitar, with whom it was totally normal to have a close, personal relationship. She put Rosetta back in the case, refraining from actually kissing her good night, because that would be weird.

She stood and stretched and tried to decide if she should clean up her room. It had been clean until Joanna lugged her suitcase in and knocked the precarious nightstand where someone—surely Granny—had made a neat pile of the CDs and other junk.

Granny made something tidy; Joanna destroyed it.

Yup, that sounded about right.

She picked up a random CD, the jewel case cracked, the hinge useless. *The Best of Joy Division*, but the wrong CD was inside. She dug around for the case that went with the Yeah Yeah Yeahs, and she found the mix Trina had made her for graduation, of songs by bands that were destroyed by being on the *Twilight* soundtrack.

Man, she missed CDs. In the interest of portability, all of her music was digital now, but she missed being surrounded by the physical manifestation of everything she loved. (Oh, great, another inappropriate emotional attachment to an inanimate object.) Whatever, Granny was the same way about books, so it wasn't Joanna's fault. She'd inherited the tendency.

Her phone dinged, and Joanna climbed out from under her mountain of memories, grateful for the distraction. But also a little apprehensive that it was going to be Mandy again, leaving another angry voice mail about how she'd screwed it up for them all and she was out of the band. Which was fine with Joanna. Totally fine. She would be even more fine if Mandy would quit calling.

This, though, was a text.

Bitch, I gave you 12 hrs. Call me.

It was from Trina, her childhood best friend and lead singer of Halikarnassus High's badassest all-girl punk trio, Delicious Lies. Joanna smiled in spite of herself. She and Trina had gone off in totally different directions—Trina married an insurance agent, had kids, and got much better at making furniture; she was now a sought-after designer of handmade curiosities. Joanna, well, Joanna didn't do any of that. But there was something about the longevity of their friendship that made those differences superficial. They were each other's favorite old sweatshirt, comforting, uncomplicated. It was nice to be reminded that she had actual human friends. Not many—Trina was probably the only one—but Joanna could use a dose of uncomplicated right now.

But then she'd have to explain about her big break and how she'd blown it.

PS Sorry abt Granny. Tell her I'll make brownies.

Joanna read the next text with a hint of jealousy. Trina was the only person from Halikarnassus she still talked to (well, aside from Granny, of course), and she knew that the two of them got together sometimes, and that Granny thought of Trina's kids as her great-grandchildren. But reading the text, that familiarity born of two people who actually spent time together, made Joanna's heart hurt a little. Not that she thought Trina would replace her in Granny's heart, just . . .

Dang, she had issues.

One thing at a time, Joanna, she told herself.

Did you know about this dog??

Ha! The kids love Starr.

She seems like she hates ppl.

She does, esp kids. They love her anyway.

I think she hates me.

Prbly. Come over soon?

Don't want to leave G.

I'll get a sitter. Meet at Chet's. Tell me when.

Okay. Ltr. Checking on G now.

Okay. DON'T IGNORE ME, GREEN.

Joanna smiled and tossed her phone on the bed. She should unpack, but she didn't really feel like uncovering the adolescent nightmares Granny had left for her in her dresser. Instead, she decided she would actually do what she'd told Trina she would and check on Granny. Maybe she'd be hungry, and Joanna could scrounge something up in the kitchen. Then she remembered the towers of casseroles and the cute librarian being all nice and helpful. That guy didn't look like a librarian, let alone a library director. But whatever. It didn't really matter what he looked like, did it?

With a last wave to Rosetta, because she was a weirdo, Joanna went to check on Granny.

Chapter Five

A few days had passed since Liam had driven Peggy home from the hospital, and though all the reports that came across the circ desk had been favorable, he wanted to see for himself. And to visit with Peggy, whose company he enjoyed.

And, fine, to see a little more of Joanna.

The neighborly reports indicated that she was still there and still not being very welcoming despite all the nice things people were doing for Peggy.

He reached for the doorbell, but stopped when he got a good look at the series of notes stuck to the door.

Do NOT ring the doorbell.
SERIOUSLY, DO NOT RING THE DOORBELL. It makes the dog bark and that wakes the patient up and she needs to rest.
KNOCKING ON THE DOOR HAS THE SAME EFFECT AS RINGING THE DOORBELL SO PLEASE DON'T DO IT.

If you are bringing food, just leave it. I will
come out and check hourly. DO NOT KNOCK
WITH SPECIAL INSTRUCTIONS. IF YOU
MAKE THE DOG BARK, I WILL DUMP THE
FOOD OUT AND SIC THE DOG ON YOU.
    Thank you.

He started to leave his offering on top of a pile of
covered casserole dishes. He noticed all of them were
labeled in masking tape, laying out cooking instructions and identifying to whom the dish should be
returned. He wondered if he should look for a pen
to label his contribution, but he wasn't sure if he
really wanted to take the credit for a bag of fast food.
But he knew the ladies of Halikarnassus, and he
knew Peggy and Joanna would be up to their eyeballs
in homemade goodness. He also knew Peggy had a
penchant for chocolate milk shakes and French fries.
Still, his bag looked a little shabby next to the Pyrex
and Tupperware.

He was about to leave, even though he knew if the
fries were cold they'd be worthless—which was why
he ultimately decided not to put his name on
the bag—when the door opened. Joanna looked
resignedly at the pile of food, but she picked up the
fast-food bag first.

"Sorry," he said. "That's my pathetic contribution."

She looked inside the bag. "Bless you. Real food."

"I'm pretty sure everyone else would disagree
with you."

"Normally I would disagree with me, but right now
I'm tired of real, real food. Oh, God, fries." She took

one out of the bag and put it in her mouth. She closed her eyes. She leaned against the doorjamb.

He'd never look at a fry the same way again.

"Thank you," she said, her eyes still closed. "And thank you for not knocking."

"I read the note. Notes."

"You're the only one. I've basically been stalking the front door. Unfortunately, so has the dog."

"She's not barking now."

Joanna looked away briefly. "I may have given her a Benadryl."

"You drugged the dog?"

"It's safe! I looked it up online first. Besides, she kept waking up Granny and then Gran would want to know who was at the door and then she'd want to visit with them, and she's supposed to be resting."

"I don't think Peggy knows how to rest."

"I know, and so did the doctor. That's why he gave her painkillers. But she's trying to stay awake for company, so she won't take them, even though she's in pain."

"But she's resting now?"

Joanna looked away again. "I may have slipped them into a milk shake."

"Wow. You drugged the dog and your grandmother. You really are bad news."

"Five out of five Halikarnassians can't be wrong."

"Well, I guess since she's already had a milk shake, I'll just take this one . . ."

"Nice try. I earned this." She took a sip from the straw. He'd never look at straws the same way again.

He cleared his throat. "Yeah, you've been busy with the drugging."

"Hey, I've had to rearrange the fridge six times

today. I forgot how much people in this town like to feed."

"Got a problem? Put a casserole on it."

"To think, there was a time in my life when I missed casseroles."

"Ha. Halikarnassus will never give you that chance. If you stick around."

"Ugh, no. The house is too quiet."

"Says the woman who drugged her grandmother."

"I know."

"And her grandmother's dog."

"I know! Shut up and help me carry this food inside, will you?"

Joanna went back to make sure Peggy was still comfortable and to make sure Starr was still breathing. The dog let out a silent bark when Joanna leaned in. Clearly, Joanna had made the right decision, medicating the dog like that. So she shouldn't feel guilty, and she shouldn't feel a teensy bit better after confessing her sin to Liam. What was it about him? He struck her as someone who could take just about anything in stride. There was something sort of . . . absorbent about him.

And there went any fears that she would find herself romantically attracted to the librarian. He might be good-looking and compassionate, but she really didn't see herself getting it up for a guy she thought of as "absorbent."

When she got back to the kitchen, Liam was standing in front of the open fridge, assessing.

"I told you," she said to his back. "No room."

He opened the freezer, which was equally stuffed.

"See?" she said. She liked being right. For once.

"I am determined," he told the fridge. He took a deep breath and dove in.

Joanna shook her head, but she was secretly glad she wasn't the most stubborn person in the room. It was a nice change for her. Instead, she just sat on a bar stool, grabbed the fast-food bag, and watched Liam work.

He took everything out. Everything. She should be insulted—after all, she'd told him that she'd already tried to fit stuff in—but she was fascinated.

"There," he said, once everything was back and the doors closed with only a minor push from the outside.

"Not quite," she said, and inched a casserole across the island toward him.

He looked at it, and at her, then back at it. "That's going to be dinner," he said with confidence.

"Not hungry," she said, tilting her head toward the empty fast-food bag.

"That's not my fault, young lady."

"Good God. You really are an old woman in a young man's body."

He flexed at her. "Better believe this is a young man's body."

She rolled her eyes, even though, quite frankly, she appreciated this young man's body. "Thanks for your help."

"No problem. Let's just hope there's not more outside."

"Ugh. Surely everyone who knows Gran has already dropped food off."

"I think you underestimate your grandmother's popularity."

"I don't. Believe me, I don't. I just . . . Didn't anyone think I would be able to feed her? And us?"

"I don't think it's that. I think people just want to be nice. And they feel bad, so it probably helps them to be able to do something."

"So they're drowning us in casseroles to make themselves feel better?"

"That is a completely messed-up and cynical way to look at it, but then so is the idea that people are only being nice to you because they think you're incompetent."

"I'm complicated, man." She balled up her burger wrapper and tossed it at him. She missed.

Chapter Six

Joanna was bored. Like, climbing the walls bored. Why had she thought Halikarnassus was a good idea?

She hadn't. But Granny was a good idea, and Granny needed her.

Sort of.

Granny liked spending time with her, and it was mutual. But Granny did not need her. She was feeling much better and now spent more time out of bed than in it. She had friends dropping by every hour, it seemed, and enough food to feed a whole army of broken-legged grannies. Every time Joanna thought of something Granny might need, a neighbor rang the doorbell, delivering just that thing. Joanna was starting to think she was telepathic.

Or maybe Granny just had some really thoughtful friends.

"What's on your agenda for today?"

Joanna placed a mug of coffee in front of Granny, then curled up in the corner of the sofa with her own. "I thought I was taking care of you."

"Hmm." Granny took a sip of her coffee.

"Why, you think I'm not doing a good job?" That was not her heart plummeting to the soles of her feet, and that was not her hackles hitting the ceiling. Not at all.

Granny reached across the table for Joanna's hand and squeezed. Heart and hackles retreated.

"I love having you here and you know it," Granny said. "I wish you would stay, not that I would ever pressure you into doing something you don't want to do."

"Not at all." Joanna smiled into her mug. At least Granny wasn't passive-aggressive.

"I wish you would stay for the coffee alone," Granny said. She took a sip from her mug and smiled. "I had no idea my coffeemaker could do such a thing."

Joanna decided now was not the time to tell Granny that she had done the reverse Folgers switch, and that, while Joanna was here, she would never again drink off-brand budget coffee. Because the coffee Joanna had bought came in a bag, not a giant bucket, and it cost money. Which wasn't fair because it was Granny's money, but also she knew Granny would enjoy it, which was how she justified the expense. Granny needed a treat. And if Joanna was not forced to drink weak dirt masquerading as ground coffee, well, so be it.

"Do you need me to do something? Is that why you're asking?" Joanna would jump through fire for Granny. But first she would make sure that she really needed to jump through fire.

"That's the thing, sweetheart, there's nothing I can

think of. I have food, I have visitors, I have painkillers. What else does a girl need?"

Joanna thought about that for a minute. Probably nothing. Well, coffee. But Granny had coffee. Sex. But no. Not Granny. At least not in Joanna's imagination.

"I just don't want you to get bored, that's all."

Joanna leaned her head on the back of the couch. Getting bored was the main thing to do in Halikarnassus. *Halikarnassus: Come for the Family, Stay for the Mind-Numbing Boredom.* Joanna really didn't know how she could avoid being bored.

But that was not what Granny meant. Granny meant she didn't want Joanna getting bored so that Joanna took off again.

Besides, after the chaos of the past couple of years, getting bored would be a nice change of pace.

It would be good for her to be bored.

Great.

Bored.

No problem.

Lots of time for self-reflection and stuff.

And Granny.

Self-reflection and Granny.

So fun.

"Oh, there is one thing," Granny said, and Joanna nearly levitated off the living room couch with purpose and action. "I need a book."

Joanna eyed the floor-to-ceiling bookcases covering one of the walls she was about to climb.

"I see that look. I mean I need one specific book. For my book club."

"Okay. Do you want me to order it for you?"

"I do know how to use the Internet, you know. But I would like to start it today. The meeting is next week."

"Ah." Joanna tried to remember where the nearest bookstore was. Or if it was even still there. It had been ten years. Or the e-book. She didn't think Granny was the type to do e-books, but she also didn't think Granny was the type to go all stupid for running shorts.

"Liam reserved it for me at the library. If you could pick it up, that would be a big help."

Speaking of running shorts.

Ugh, the library.

The last time Joanna went to the Halikarnassus Free Public Library, Mrs. Pratt glared at her so hard she had Trina check the back of her head to make sure there wasn't a hole there. So what if, the week before, she had been caught making out in the biographies. Everyone made out with Dan McErlean sooner or later. And wasn't it thrilling that books made her so excited? Besides, Dan didn't last long. That fact was lost on Mrs. Pratt, whose philosophy was "Once a Miscreant, Always a Miscreant." She had a cross stitch sampler saying just that in her office. Or so Joanna had heard.

The idea of going to that musty old building full of crabby old people was not inspiring Joanna to do any great favors for Granny. Maybe she could get her an e-reader.

Or maybe she could suck it up and do one favor for Granny, who had taken care of her through all of her miscreant days and asked for little in return and who was laid up and only wanted a good book to read. Maybe the library wasn't as bad as it used to be.

Except that nothing in Halikarnassus ever changed.

Joanna braced herself, picked up Granny's car keys, and headed for the library.

Chapter Seven

Granny always prided herself on not being a stereotypical old lady. She didn't let her hair go gently gray, but dyed it blonder and blonder every year. She refused to wear pants with an elastic waist unless she was exercising. She read, she traveled, and she refused to talk about millennials like they were going to destroy the moral fabric of society.

So why in the name of pants, Joanna wondered, did she drive such an old-lady car?

To be fair, the car was the same car she'd had for the past dozen years or so, and a dozen years ago, she wasn't such an old lady. Still, maneuvering the giant sedan around Halikarnassus's little streets was something Joanna was not used to.

Also, the car had a cassette player, a technology that had been outdated before Joanna was born.

As she backed out of the driveway looking like a contortionist trying to see behind her, Joanna promised herself that if she ever sold her soul to the corporate rock machine again, she would buy Granny a new car. A much smaller car. Maybe a Mini Cooper.

With a sunroof. Granny would like a sunroof. Anything that wasn't a size that could comfortably house a family of five.

Joanna should have just walked to the library, she thought as she boated down the familiar roads. But she had a list of other errands to run—once Granny got started on things she needed, the floodgates that were trying not to inconvenience Joanna burst.

Well, at least Joanna was useful.

She rolled down the window and rested her elbow on the door, trying to look cool and ironic in Granny's boat car. She fiddled with the radio because the indie rock station she'd grown up with now played nothing but country. Joanna could do a lot of things, but new-school radio country was not one of them. She finally found some music she recognized and mostly liked.

This was living. Mediocre music in an unmaneuverable car in a suburban town she hated.

She turned into the library parking lot, surprised to see it full. She didn't remember the library ever being crowded. Mrs. Pratt seemed to prefer it if people didn't come to the library at all. Maybe that was just Joanna. Maybe now, everyone in Halikarnassus came to ogle Foxy Librarian's legs.

A car was pulling out, so Joanna signaled that she was going to attempt to steer her ship into the spot. The driver waved at her. "Just pull out of the damn spot, please," Joanna muttered. Not that she was in a hurry. But come on.

While she waited, not waving, Joanna half heard the DJ announce the next song. "Coming back from a disastrous first show with the Penny Lickers, when their lead guitarist froze like a bunny in headlights and was kicked out of the band. Oh, folks, it's moments like this that YouTube was meant for. Let's show these poor girls some love, shall we? Here's the latest . . . from Bunny Slippers."

She was halfway into the spot and trying to turn off the damn radio, so she didn't see the kid running toward the parking lot. But she did hear the kid's mom scream.

Snapping her head up, Joanna slammed on the brakes as the mom scooped up a squirming kid from right in front of the car. Joanna's stomach dropped, but she threw on the parking brake and jumped out of the car.

"Oh my God, I didn't see—"

"Are you crazy?" the mom screamed at her. The kid, who had been looking dazed, started wailing. "Watch where you're driving!"

"I didn't see him! He ran out in front of the car!"

"You could have—"

"I'm sorry, I'm sorry!" Joanna hurried onto the sidewalk to . . . she didn't know what. Throw herself at the mercy of the woman whose child she almost ran over?

The woman turned away, shielding her screaming kid from Joanna. She was cooing at the child, trying to calm him down.

"I'm so sorry—"

"Learn how to drive." The woman turned just enough to spit the angry words at Joanna.

They stood there for a moment, staring at each other, as the kid, apparently done crying, squirmed and tried to get down from his mother's arms.

"Oh. My. God. Joanna Green?"

Joanna's eyes widened at the tone in the woman's

voice. It was not a kind tone. She looked at her for a moment, then . . .

"Holy shit. Kristin Walsh?"

"Holy shit!" the kid shouted, clapping his hands.

This was why Joanna didn't want to go out in public in Halikarnassus, to avoid this exact situation. Not the vehicular manslaughter, although her hands were still shaking enough for her to admit that, yes, had she thought of it, she also would have thought to avoid that. Mostly, she wanted to avoid people like Kristin Walsh.

"It's Kristin Klomberg now," Joanna's high school tormentor said, wrapping her left hand protectively around her son's head as he laughed and cursed. Her big ol' diamond glinted in the sun.

"Of course it is," Joanna muttered. Of course Kristin Walsh would marry the guy who practically inherited the mayorship of the town.

"What are you doing here? I thought you were a big fancy rock star?" Kristin sneered. "Oh, that's right. I think I heard something about that." Her tone turned sweet, like honey. Like really bitchy honey. "You screwed that up somehow, didn't you? As usual."

Joanna closed her eyes. She really, really wanted to hit Kristin in her perfect little mouth. But Kristin was holding her child, the child Joanna had almost run over with Granny's giant car, and even though the kid was apparently an uncontrollable speed demon, that didn't change the fact that Joanna should have been paying better attention.

Just what she needed. To be beholden to Kristin Walsh-Klomberg.

"I'm here to take care of my grandmother," Joanna

said through gritted teeth. The other stuff was true, too, but she didn't need to dwell on it.

Kristin's face softened a fraction. "I was so sorry to hear about Peggy. Is she all right? Well, tell her to call me if she needs anything. She has my number."

Granny had Kristin Walsh-Klomberg's number? This small-town garbage was too much.

"I sure will," Joanna said in a voice laced with aspartame—sweet and totally fake. Then she remembered that she had nearly run over the woman's kid. She took a deep breath. "Is he okay?"

Kristin looked surprised, but just for a second. The kid was twisting to get out of her arms, but Kristin wouldn't let go. "Wun! Wun!" the kid screeched while Kristin tightened her grip.

"No running right now, Kale. It's too dangerous," she said with a pointed look at Joanna.

Joanna took another deep, shaky breath. She deserved that. She didn't like it, but she deserved it.

Also, the kid was named Kale?

Kristin turned and moved away from Joanna, holding tight to her squirming toddler as she walked into the parking lot. Joanna heard the beep-beep of her car and watched her strap the kid into a seat in an enormous and very shiny SUV. It took everything in her power not to roll her eyes at the ridiculousness of the car—after all, Joanna was driving a car that was just as gigantic.

Joanna checked her parking job. It wasn't the straightest, but she was mostly inside the lines. The idea of getting back in and trying to straighten it out was not appealing—way too many kids coming out of the library for her to feel comfortable doing that.

She watched Kristin and kid drive off, and turned and walked into the library.

"Sure, Peggy, no problem." Liam put away his grant proposal and headed toward the closet where the book group books were stored. One great thing about being a small-town librarian, he was discovering, was the personal relationships he developed with his patrons, who constantly surprised him with their tastes and experiences. The not-so-great thing was that the personal relationships translated into patrons calling him and interrupting his mind-numbing fight with federal government paperwork to put a book club book at the desk for a granddaughter to pick up.

Of course, he could have gotten someone to pull the book for him. But he still wasn't comfortable delegating. When he had been at his Big City job, he was the peon, and his superiors were always interrupting him to get him to do simple things like pull books right away.

Hmm. Maybe he was still a peon. But if he was, then he was a peon for patrons.

He should probably learn to delegate.

But if he was honest with himself, he would drop anything for Peggy. She was his favorite patron, and she was injured and homebound, two things that could not be easy for her. He hoped she would be able to make it to the book group. He was really looking forward to hearing her thoughts on the book. He was pretty sure they wouldn't be overwhelmingly positive—she'd made it clear that she didn't want to read another really long historical fiction book set in World War II, but she'd been seriously outvoted. What was it with book groups and World War II fiction? And why were all of the books at least five hundred pages?

He tried to get the self-described white-haired old ladies to mix it up, to stretch their reading wings a little bit. And once or twice a year, they did, mostly because of Peggy's persuasion. Liam would take that small victory for now, but he wouldn't give up. He eventually hoped to expand the membership a little bit. Maybe a few men. Or people who didn't qualify for Medicare.

Not that he had a problem with Medicare. Or any health care. Heck, didn't he spend the fall creating programs around the Affordable Care Act?

He just thought the Halikarnassus Free Public Library Book Group could use some fresh blood.

And probably a new name.

HFPLBG. It wasn't even a good acronym. Acronyms were sacred to librarians.

He closed the web browser where he had been about to avoid mind-numbing paperwork by looking at YouTube. Which was a terrible and unprofessional use of his time, but Kristin Klomberg had piqued his curiosity.

He shouldn't listen to Kristin. She had a nasty tendency to gossip, although, to be fair, so did most people in town. But there was something especially cruel about Kristin's gossip, especially when it came to Joanna. That was how he'd learned that she was *the* Joanna Green, when Kristin made a snotty remark about Peggy's granddaughter being in a trashy, un-washed punk band.

Unfortunately for Kristin, that was Liam's favorite kind of music.

But this morning she came in, practically vibrating

with the news that Joanna wasn't back to take care of
Peggy, but because her band had imploded and it
was all Joanna's fault. Liam was surprised. Bunny
Slippers wasn't on his radar anymore, not since their
last album, which had managed to sound both
overproduced and watered down. Joanna was definitely the best part of the band. Why would they kick
her out?

Because she's a screwup, Kristin told him, then launched
into an explanation of the video she'd found that
showed Bunny Slippers opening for the Penny Lickers.
(And Liam tried not to be judgmental, but he just
could not with that band.) Apparently they got onstage
for their first song, and Joanna just froze. She had
some kind of hissy fit and ran off the stage.

Kristin described it like it was hilarious, like someone just played a funny prank. Liam disengaged
from the conversation as quickly as possible, but it
was too late. The seed was planted. And the seed
grew into a mighty oak of curiosity—*not* nosiness, he
assured himself—and before his conscience could
catch up, he was Googling "Bunny Slippers" and
"first concert" and "Joanna Green."

And there it was. The news was old, in Internet
time, but it was there—with videos included! He
shouldn't. But he did.

Then Peggy called and he was reminded that
Joanna's music career (or apparent lack thereof) was
none of his business.

He went out to grab a copy of the book group
book, and when he got to the desk, book in hand, he
had a patron waiting. He quickly looked around for
Dani, who was supposed to be covering the desk

while he fought with paperwork. No Dani. He could hear her voice coming from the children's area. So she was either helping a patron or practicing her lines for her role in the Halikarnassus Community Theater production of *The Crucible*. She wasn't yelling about Satan, so she was probably helping a patron.

He really had to work on his management skills.

"Hi, how can I—" He started talking before he even reached the desk, so when he got there he was surprised by the woman standing there. He shouldn't have been surprised. He knew she was there. That was the whole reason he came out of his office, because there was a person out there.

Joanna Green really flustered his inner monologue.

She wasn't looking at him. He wasn't even sure that she had heard him. He was struck, once again, how she looked . . . cool. It made him feel like an old fart to think that, but it was true. She wore it like an old leather jacket, comfortable and easy. Her dark hair wasn't piled up in a messy topknot, but fell in a blunt straight line to her shoulders. She was wearing a worn-looking tank top with a unicorn crying tears of gold coins on it. She had an armful of bracelets on one wrist and a leather cuff on the other. Her nails were painted black, but—and he didn't know much about manicures—it looked like she had done it herself, and a while ago. And she was scanning the library with a look of wonder that Liam really could not account for. The Halikarnassus Free Public Library was great in a lot of ways, but no one had ever accused it of inspiring wonder.

"How can I help you?" he recovered smoothly,

trying his hardest not to stare, but it was hard. Nobody in Halikarnassus looked like Joanna Green. She was like his teenage dream girl come to life. It was not doing great things for his professionalism.

"*This* is the library?" she muttered. Liam wasn't sure if she was talking to him or not. He cleared his throat.

She swung an annoyed glance at him.

She was definitely Peggy's granddaughter.

Not that Peggy shot him annoyed glances very often, but he'd seen that look directed at others. And he'd seen that look on Joanna's face in the photographs Peggy would occasionally parade out, of her adventurous, talented granddaughter who was a badass rock-and-roller. The picture was from high school and included some other Halikarnassus Badass Rock-and-Rollers who were now grown-ups and patrons. They were recognizable from the photo, if he squinted. This woman. She was spot-on. She hadn't changed a bit.

You find a look and stick to it, he supposed. Then he remembered the unfortunate frosted tips from his high school yearbook and shuddered.

"I'm here to get a book for my grandma." She pushed Peggy's worn library card across the counter to him.

"Sure," he said. "She just called."

Joanna rolled her eyes. "Of course she did."

"Here you go," he said, handing the book over. "Already checked out."

Joanna took it and the library card from him. "So," she said. "I thought you were Mr. Big-Time

Library Director. How come you're checking out books to the lowly patrons?"

He nodded at Mr. Collins, who set a stack of books on the counter. Mr. Collins liked to turn his books in in person so they could get checked in right away. For some reason, he had a thing against the book drop.

"There's no such thing as a lowly patron," Liam said.

She snorted. "God, you are such a Boy Scout."

He was a Boy Scout. Or he had been, back in high school. Then he'd sent his Eagle Scout badge back to national headquarters in solidarity with his gay fellow scouts and rescinded his membership. So, technically, he was not a Boy Scout.

Probably not something Joanna cared about.

Besides, she wasn't even paying attention to him anymore. She was looking around again, taking in, well, he didn't know. It was a great library, but not, like, awe-inspiring.

She'd looked in wonder in a circle so her back was to the circ desk, and she leaned back and rested her elbows on the worn wooden surface.

"Why is it that some things completely change and some things don't change at all?"

"Hmm?" He wasn't sure he'd heard her right. Maybe he should offer her a tour. If she'd been gone for a few years, there were definitely some changes in the building. He'd implemented most of the changes. He was pretty proud of them.

If she thought he was a Boy Scout now, wait until he started talking about user experience data.

"Why'd you change all this?"

He didn't want to be rude. And as a librarian, he'd been asked a lot of pretty stupid questions in his professional life. *What's the name of that one book with the blue cover? Do you have Gandhi's phone number? Does this smell bad?* There *were* stupid questions, and his colleagues deserved some recognition for not just giving out stupid answers in response but for considering each inquiry with equitable seriousness. But this one always killed him. He didn't just change stuff on a whim. He studied patron behavior and usage patterns and ADA requirements. He didn't just move the stacks for fun.

Although it had been kind of fun.

"I like it," she announced.

"Huh?" A very articulate response to what he belatedly recognized as a compliment.

"It's nice. You can actually see the windows."

That had been part of his plan, to maximize the natural light. In the summer, they didn't even have to turn on the lights until late afternoon. Saved on the electric bill.

"It looks like a place people would actually want to come to."

"That was the idea."

Joanna turned back to face him. "What did Mrs. Pratt have to say about it?"

Mrs. Pratt had been one of the people who interviewed him, and she'd showed him around the library for a week before gleefully heading off for a blissful retirement with her wife, Charlie. He liked Mrs. Pratt. But then, he had a penchant for crabby old ladies. They were kind of his jam.

"I think she would have liked it." That probably wasn't true, but that didn't really matter now.

"Hmph. You must not know her very well."

Touché.

She turned the book over in her hands. "Is this good?"

"Uh, I haven't read it yet."

"Oh. So you don't do the book group?"

"No, I do. I just . . . I've been putting it off. I'm kind of tired of World War Two books, you know?"

"Sure," she said, and looked at him funny because of course she didn't know about the glut of WWII-era fiction being marketed to book groups.

Not that he would judge her if she did. He didn't judge people's reading tastes as a matter of professional course.

"So . . . will you be joining us?" he asked, even though he knew she wouldn't. She surely had much better things to do with her time.

Confirming his suspicions, she snorted. "I don't think so." She shoved the book in her bag and he winced for the unprotected paperback cover.

"Well, can I help you pick something out to read? Or a DVD?" Why didn't he just let her go? She clearly was not interested in being here.

"No, thanks. See you later, Foxy Librarian."

He waved. Then he processed what she'd said. What did that mean, Foxy Librarian? He turned to ask her, but she was already gone.

Chapter Eight

Joanna shut the book with a watery sigh. She wasn't crying. Over a book? Ridiculous.

She dropped the book on the floor and stretched her arms over her head, straightening out over the arms of the overstuffed chair until her toes pointed and her fingers twitched. Then she flopped her butt back into the cushion and hung her head back.

She sat there, head pointed to the floor, and let the story wash over her. The fabulosity of 1930s Berlin, the bohemian theater with the mousy costumer, the inevitable swoop of history, hard choices, impossible love . . .

Joanna rubbed her eyes. God, did Granny read a book like this every month? How did she do it? *How do you recover from living inside a world like that, then having it ripped away from you by cruel, cruel reality?* Ugh, she was even starting to think like the overdramatic narrator in the book.

She blamed Liam. What was he doing, having the sweet old ladies of Halikarnassus read a book that made everyone cry? *Everyone but me*, she thought, wiping her eyes. (She couldn't stop thinking about that last scene! With the love and the guy and the— ergh!) Stupid, handsome librarian, with his stupid Clark Kent glasses and floppy hair. Who did he think he was, making her feel feelings and stuff?

"You're going to get a headache." Granny, who had been snoring just minutes before, was watching her from the sofa. The sofa was progress, Joanna reminded herself as she attempted to roll her eyes with her head facing the floor. Just yesterday, Joanna had helped her wash and dress, and then the two of them hobbled her onto the overstuffed couch in the living room, where she could receive visitors with a bra on, as Granny said. It gave Granny an excuse to practice on her crutches, which she hated, and to be at the center of all the action that was now her house.

It was a real bonding experience.

But it was that or watch Granny continue to spiral into depression cooped up in her bedroom. Literally watch Granny, because when Granny was bored, she had a bad habit of pretending her leg wasn't broken and she could do things like straighten up around the house or prepare her own lunch. Apparently, breaking her leg a second time was not enough of a threat to keep her resting. Nor were painkillers.

They were getting on each other's nerves a lot less than Joanna had imagined they would. And after a painkiller wrangled a confession out of her, a lot less than Granny had imagined also.

Despite endless rounds of gin rummy, though, they were both bored. Granny, ever resourceful, suggested that Joanna read the library book club book aloud to her so they could both enjoy it. This lasted for about half an hour, then Granny was snoring away and Joanna was too caught up in the story to stop reading and now here they were, four hours later, Granny well-rested and Joanna totally not crying over a book.

"Did you have a nice nap?" Joanna said, pulling herself up to a seated position on the chair. She blinked as the blood rushed out of her head.

Granny yawned and stretched and muttered "yup."

"How was the book?"

Joanna looked at the book, discarded on the floor, spine askew.

"I haven't finished it yet." Which was true. The epilogue was still unread. She wasn't ready to find out what happened to the heroine after the war. It couldn't be as bad as what she had gone through during the war, surely. But could Joanna really expect a happy ending? After the author had put her through all that stuff?

Plus, if she read the epilogue, the book would be over.

Instead, it was just open-faced on the floor.

She picked it up. Mrs. Pratt would have a fit if she saw a library book treated like that.

Good thing Mrs. Pratt was retired.

What would Clark Kent say about the careless treatment of public property?

Maybe he'd spank her.

Whoa. Where did that come from? Too much time cooped up in the house, probably. It was making her brain crazy. There was no other possible explanation for her brain reaching for such an unlikely imaginary scenario.

"Tell me about it."

Joanna looked at Granny with alarm. It was one thing to know that she and her grandmother apparently had a crush on the same man. It was a different thing entirely to acknowledge it out loud, with words and fantasies that should have grossed her out way more than they did.

"The book?" Granny prompted, and Joanna gave herself a mental head slap. Of course. The book.

She leaned down to retrieve the public property of which she was being a bad steward. Starr came over to sit on her lap, which was her new favorite spot now that Granny's lap, which was too close to her injured leg, was off-limits. Joanna flipped through the pages, trying to decide where to begin. "So, it's World War Two, right?" She explained the dressmaker heroine and the Nazi's mistress who secretly had a Jewish grandfather and the gay neighbor who sacrificed himself to save the dressmaker, which Joanna thought was a little cheap, having a gay martyr and all. And how the dressmaker sort of befriends the mistress, who brings her around the Nazi parties and stuff, and soon this Nazi officer falls in love with her and the dressmaker is all, you're cute but you're a Nazi. And even as she starts to develop feelings for him, she has to remind herself that he's a Nazi and that is bad news, morally speaking. Then the mistress gets jealous and somehow switches up some stuff so it looks like the dressmaker is the one with the Jewish grandfather and so she ends up at a concentration camp, but she escapes to Paris, where she falls in with the Resistance and there's this guy, Pierre, who smokes a lot of cigarettes and is real broody, and he falls in love with her. But then she meets this American pilot guy and he's all dashing and charming and on dangerous missions . . . anyway, then the Nazi shows up and is like, you're a criminal! But I love you! And she's all, I just want to make beautiful clothes and the American is like, come to America, we have lots of fabric." Joanna cleared her throat. The memory of that heart-wrenching scene, where the American lets down all his defenses . . . and she didn't even get to the part where her gay best friend risks his life and . . . "I'm not doing a very good job explaining it."

"Sounds like quite a book."

"Yeah. It's messed up."

"And you read the whole thing?"

"Not the epilogue."

"Aren't you dying to find out what happened to her?"

"Yes, but then you woke up and won't stop talking."

"And you had to wait for your tears to dry."

"Hmph," Joanna said, not admitting anything.

"Sounds like there's a lot to talk about."

"Yeah. Like why was the dressmaker such an idiot?"

"Well, I imagine she was just trying to survive. But I don't know. I haven't read the book."

"When's the meeting?"

"The third Thursday of the month."

Time had been passing strangely since she'd been back, so Joanna had to think about that for a second. "So . . . two days?"

"Is it?"

"You better get to reading, young lady."

"You're supposed to be reading to me. You're the one falling down on your duty."

"Typical Joanna Green," she said with a grin. She'd overheard Mrs. Doris saying that about her once, and it had been her favorite thing to lob out at Granny when she was a mouthy teenager. Apparently it still worked as a mouthy adult.

"Oh, you stop that."

"Are you up to making it to book group, anyway?" Joanna tried to imagine the effort it had taken them to get Granny to the couch and multiplied it by a car ride and getting into the non-couched library. Of course, they wouldn't be tripping over Starr at the library.

Of course, they might trip over Kristin Walsh.

Wait, no. Kristin Klomberg.

Either way, Joanna shuddered.

"I'd like to. Doris has a van she can take me in. We'll see how I feel tomorrow." Granny yawned and leaned her head on the back of the couch.

Liam put the book down and wiped his eyes. Dang, that was intense. He wondered if his book group ladies were having the same reaction to the epilogue. Then he wondered if that was a good thing. The last book they'd read almost caused a riot. But how was he supposed to know the dog died at the end? All of the reviews said it was a great, uplifting book club pick and there was lots to talk about. Instead, he'd spent the whole meeting fending off accusations of cruelty and heartlessness, as if he was the one who made them care about the adorable, troublesome mutt who saved the owner's life and then ripped their hearts out when he died in a senseless boating accident. And come on. A boating accident? The only way to assuage the group's ire was to pen a collective letter to the author, telling her what a jerk she was.

The letter was still sitting on his desk. He hadn't sent it, and he was pretty sure he wasn't going to. It did not reflect very well on the character of the people of Halikarnassus.

Although it was an educational experience, in that he learned lots of clever new ways of telling someone you thought they were not a nice person.

"Pernicious gasbag" was his favorite. "Defiler of horses" was still the most alarming.

He stood up from the couch and stretched, his fingertips touching the edge of the ceiling fan. As a guy who hit his growth spurt late, he still liked to do that. He still liked to prove that he was no longer the little guy, available to be messed with. Although he was still a bit of a dork.

He looked out the sliding glass doors that led to his backyard. He should really mow the lawn. It might burn off some of this nervous energy, too. He was surprised that he'd been able to focus on reading for so long. And really, he shouldn't have been reading for that long, even though it was technically for work.

He had a town council meeting to prepare for.

He'd done many things to prepare himself for the role of library director. It was a big change, going from an assistant branch manager for the Boston

Public Library to running a library himself. Of course, the Halikarnassus Free Public Library was less than half the size of his old branch and served a much smaller population. And he didn't actually run the library himself. Toni ran the children's section so smoothly he never felt the need to interfere, his clerks and pages were all well-trained and whip-smart, and one of them, Shirley, had been there longer than he had been alive. Really, they all ran the library. He just ran the book group.

Well, the self-proclaimed White-Haired Old Ladies ran the book group. But he ordered the books.

Unless they were donated, which they frequently were. Or he was able to borrow a set from another library in the county.

Basically, he didn't do anything.

So why was he the one who had to stand in front of the town council and defend the existence of the library?

Heavy is the head that wears the crown, as Shirley was fond of telling him.

And there would be no Peggy at this meeting to back him up.

It was true, the town budget was a mess. And it was also true that the library was not a revenue stream, not with their five cent overdue fines (which Liam refused to raise when the issue was brought up). But people loved the library, dammit!

Shirley and Toni had banned him from working too late the nights before town council meetings— they said he got overtired and antsy and he got on people's nerves. He could work from home or from a bar or wherever—they didn't care, as long as he wasn't at the library.

He looked at his book, which had slid off the couch and was now spine up on the floor. He picked it up quickly, lest anyone from the town council see him disrespecting public property, and went into his home office to justify the existence of the library.

Chapter Nine

Liam missed Peggy.

He kept meaning to drop in on her, but then he was running late for work or it was late in the evening and he didn't want to bother her, especially not when half of Halikarnassus seemed to come into the library to tell him that they had just stopped by Peggy's and that she was doing okay, her spirits were up, that was what was important. This was usually followed by a mention of The Granddaughter, and how they had no idea how long Joanna would be sticking around and wasn't it too bad that Peggy had no one else to take care of her?

Except for the entire town of Halikarnassus, apparently.

Anyway, he knew better than to take the town's Greek chorus at its word.

He missed Peggy's laugh and wisdom and the way she acted all no-nonsense but really offered him unwavering support. He missed seeing her pop up at the library or running into her at the grocery store.

She always seemed to show up when she was least expected, but when he most needed to talk to her.

If she had wings, he would have sworn she was his fairy godmother.

Like that time when Mr. McElroy came in drunk and Liam really didn't want to call the police. The man was harmless and Liam didn't want to be responsible for adding to his troubles. But Mr. McElroy was starting to sing some pretty salty sea shanties, so he wasn't sure he had a choice. Then Peggy stopped by, called Craig, who owned the deli, and asked him to come bring Mr. McElroy a sandwich. Which he did. Or the time when Toni was out sick and two moms were fighting over whose kid was going to check out the last Elephant and Piggie book, and Peggy happened to be perusing the new paperbacks and came to see what the fuss was about, and she told them, Solomon-like, that Liam would rip the book and let each of them take half. This made the kids cry (and Liam a little bit, too, on the inside), and the mothers left in a huff with a stack of non-Willems easy readers for their kids.

It wasn't that Liam couldn't handle bad stuff that happened at the library. It was just that he was very grateful when Peggy was there to lend a hand.

He should think about putting her on the payroll.

If he still had a payroll. This, unfortunately, was not something guaranteed to be in the next budget year.

He would so rather be alphabetizing his record collection.

Which was already alphabetized.

So he tried not to be too hard on himself for the faux-casual laser focus he kept on the door to the town council chambers. True, Peggy had never missed a meeting since he had been in town—and it sounded as if she barely missed one before that. The old mayor used to joke that she was the conscience of the council, even though she never ran. She had no time for politics, she always said. Except when it came to the town council. And the occasional phone bank for a Democratic senator. And periodically hosting meetings about bond initiative campaigns in her living room. And the League of Women Voters voter registration drive.

Still, it was too much to expect that the Council's Conscience would become miraculously mobile enough to attend the meeting. Especially since she had called Liam earlier that afternoon telling him that she was not. He thought she might have been crying. Then Joanna got on the phone and accused him of making Peggy cry. Even though he hadn't said anything! He just listened to her saying she wasn't going to be able to make it to the meeting and assured her that it was okay, that he would be fine and that he would let her know tomorrow how it all went. He had tomorrow off, he told her. He could bring some lunch and they could complain about the new mayor. He'd take notes and everything.

But now, as he sat here nervously manhandling his notes, he felt sure that a breakdown tomorrow wouldn't be enough. He needed Peggy there, Peggy and her friends who knit through the whole meeting. The knitters were here, but without Peggy paying rapt attention, it didn't have the same effect. Kind of creepy, actually. Like a jury of Madame Defarges, knitting in code all of the ways the new mayor had failed to live up to the expectations set by his father.

Hal Klomberg Jr. wasn't such a bad guy. Well, he wasn't a great guy, Liam thought, but he hadn't voted for him. The election was well before Liam moved to Halikarnassus, and anyway, Hal ran unopposed, like his father before him. The way the residents of Halikarnassus talked about Hal Jr., you'd think someone would have stepped up to try to defeat him. Entitled, they said. A bully, they said. Didn't have any of his father's integrity or common sense. Never mind that Liam's library housed the archive for the *Halikarnassus Herald*, and he had read a few of the letters to the editor. Hal Sr. was not so beloved in his time. But, well, greener grass and all that. People always had a tendency to look at the past with rose-colored glasses. And nostalgia was a powerful drug. The other day one of his teen volunteers came in wearing a Nirvana T-shirt with a beat-up flannel over it. Swap out the skinny jeans (Liam could not get behind skinny jeans) and the kid could have been teenage Liam. It was alarming. Nobody needed to be teenage Liam, that gawky, gangly mess of hormones.

But apparently gawky and gangly was cool now. Thoughts like this made Liam feel very old, and he wasn't even thirty. They also made him misremember how hellish his high school life was, being a gawky, gangly kid with glasses who was into music and books and feelings. Seeing that kid dressed as Young Liam made him think that, yeah, it was cool back then. He had no problems, no worries. No desk schedules to fight with, no bills due, no town council meetings to deal with.

Nostalgia, man.

It made Liam feel a little bad for Hal Jr. Just the fact that he went by Hal Jr. meant there was no escaping

his father's legacy. But what could the guy do? That
was his name. Liam would really feel bad for the guy
if he wasn't trying to cut the library's budget.

No, not cut it. Adjust it, was how Hal Jr. described
it. Because the roof had sprung a leak during the
very snowy winter, and so thousands of dollars were
spent replacing said roof in the spring. Which was
now done, and Liam had submitted a very detailed
and specific list of all the materials that were damaged
in the leak—the specific books, the exact model of
public printer, and the very expensive microfilm
machine. The insurance company cut the check and
Liam placed the order and they had a shiny, almost-
new microfilm machine and a new printer that also
scanned, and the holes in the collection were filled
with shiny new books.

Fixing the damage wrought by the leak, Liam was
prepared to argue, didn't actually cost the town anything beyond Liam's time to assess the damage and
order replacements. And the insurance money did
exactly that—replaced things that were lost. So
Hal Jr.'s argument that the library had already
bought a bunch of new stuff this year and so did not
need the line item earmarked for new books was . . .
flawed.

The problem was, Hal Jr. knew it was flawed. He
just didn't care. He wanted the money for his pet
projects, mostly the Halikarnassus High School football team, which killed Liam because of the stereotypes. Couldn't he want the money for the theater
club? Or girls' sports, for the love of Pete? But no.
Football.

Liam liked football. And he enjoyed going to the
HHS games, even though the team was absolutely

terrible. Putting in lights on the football field was not going to fix that. But try telling that to Hal Jr.

Which was what Liam was at the town council meeting to do.

Man, he missed Peggy.

The gavel banged for order, the flag was pledged to, and Liam sat, using all of his active listening skills to not fall asleep while reports were given about the status of public works projects and yet another proposal to name the community center after Derek Jeter, which was a badly concealed attempt to get Derek Jeter to come to Halikarnassus.

"And now it looks like we have the library here to ask for a budget increase?"

That wasn't at all what Liam was asking for, as Hal knew, but he stood and approached the podium, bracing himself for what was coming.

"All right, Big, what've you got for us?"

Ha ha ha, yes, great, every time. Big as in Big Bird, because Liam's last name was Byrd and he had to smile because Hal was trying to cut the library's budget midyear and Liam couldn't make an enemy of him by not finding his jokes funny.

He did not go to library school for this.

"Yes, hi," Liam said into the mic.

"Hold on, before you start." Hal leaned forward like he was ready to dig into a long, hilarious comment.

"Now you wait a minute, Hal, he has the right to speak," said Councilman Maguire on Hal's left.

"I'm going to let him—"

"Let's follow the protocol, shall we?"

"Your father always followed the protocol."

Great. Just what Liam needed. That kind of comment always got Hal to shut up, but it also got him crabby and pouting, and that made him vote like a petulant child instead of the forward-thinking, open-minded mayor he claimed to be.

"Go on, son," said Councilwoman Hopson to Liam.

Liam took a deep breath. "As you know," he started, which was maybe too challenging but he did it anyway because they did know what he was about to say—that they had budgeted this bunch of money for the library and it was approved and the money to replace the roof came from the town's improvement fund while the money to replace the damaged materials came from insurance and so, while expensive, the roof actually didn't spend any of the library's budget and was fully covered by these other funds so he was really just calling to keep the library budget intact. Which he said in a rush into the mic, looking at all of the council members but Hal, whose fuzzy logic was the whole reason he had to stand up and say this dumb stuff in the first place.

"Gentlemen?" asked Councilwoman Hopson. "Comments?"

"First of all, I want to say what a great job you've done with the library, Liam. You've really opened it up and made it fun. At first a lot of us were concerned that you were undoing all of Mrs. Pratt's hard work, but it looks like that was just a strong foundation that you built on. I understand that kids and teens are using the library now, which makes it less quiet"—some grumbles from the council—"but also keeps them off the streets, which I'm sure Chief Savage appreciates."

A bewildered nod from the police chief, who knew as well as everyone on the dais that if kids were going to get in trouble, there was much more fun trouble to be had in neighboring towns. Halikarnassus was too boring even for trouble.

All rumors about Joanna Green notwithstanding.

"So this is what I need you to help me understand, Big. If you bought all these new books a few months ago, why do you need more new books?"

The dumbness of Hal's statement was so powerful that it radiated stupidity and struck Liam momentarily mute. "Uh," he started. Then he recovered. "New books are constantly being published, and the library's collection needs to—"

"Yes, but you already bought new books."

"Well, not all of those books were new."

"You're saying you bought old books?"

"We bought new copies of older books, yes, to replace the titles that were damaged in the roof leak."

"So you wasted your money on old books?"

"No, we used our insurance money to replace the important volumes that were destroyed."

"But you could have used it to buy new books."

"The terms of the settlement—"

"I remember the terms, and you didn't have to buy exact copies of what was lost because, as you pointed out, some were out of print or not worth replacing. So why did you replace them?"

"In those cases, I replaced them with newer editions or similar books that had updated information—"

"But not new books."

"Some new books, yes."

"So you've already had your fair share of new

books, don't you think? There are other places that can use that money."

Liam looked at the other members of the council, who were all studiously taking notes instead of meeting his eye. He knew what was happening. Some of those guys supported the library, but they were all dazzled by Hal's vision of a new revenue-generating football stadium, and they were convinced the only way to pay for the lights was to take away the library's money.

"Let me try an analogy," Liam started. "Let's say you have a football team. And that football team needs equipment and uniforms to be competitive. So the town approves the funds to buy some."

"Great. Smart town." Some laughs from the audience.

"Now let's say it's six months later, and Nike comes up with this new kind of shoulder pad that is less bulky but just as strong as the other kind of shoulder pad."

"Bob, do you know anything about this shoulder pad?" Hal asked Coach Simonetti, who liked to come to council meetings to show support for Hal's lighting project, even though his time could be better spent actually trying to make his team, you know, good.

"No," Liam interrupted Hal's interruption. "I just made it up. It's for the analogy."

"Well, it sounds like a great idea. Maybe you could work on it and use your millions to buy however many books you want for the library."

Liam gritted his teeth, but continued. "These shoulder pads are great, but you already have shoulder pads for your team. But you would still want to get these new ones, right? Because they're so great?"

"Hell yes, Big, I would want to get them."

"But you already have shoulder pads."

"Are you saying our kids don't deserve the best?"

"No, I'm saying they do, and so you should get the new shoulder pads."

"Great. Go out and invent them and I'll be your first customer."

More laughs from the audience.

"Well, as I mentioned, that was just an analogy. So now imagine the shoulder pads were books."

"I can't imagine books would do a very good job of keeping our boys safe."

"Ha ha." Then Liam looked at Hal and realized he wasn't joking. Oh boy. "No, the shoulder pads were just a metaphor for the books. We have other books that are great, but we also need the new books, not only so we can stay competitive, but so we can continue to provide great service to the community."

"Yes, but new shoulder pads would protect our children. New books won't actually do anything for kids, would they?"

"Are you fucking kidding me?"

Liam suddenly felt the crush of the silent shock and disapproval of the entire council and everyone in the audience.

I guess I said that out loud, he thought. Oops.

He looked at Hal's face, a mixture of cold fury and righteous victory. For a dumb guy, he had a very complicated face.

"I think that's enough from our esteemed librarian," he said. "We'll take it into consideration. I don't think we need to vote on it tonight. What do you say, fellas?"

The other members of the council gave Liam disgusted looks and nodded. Well, there went all of the support for the library.

Shaking with fury at himself and at Hal, Liam sat down and listened, numb, as the council went through the rest of the agenda.

He'd really screwed that up.

He needed Peggy.

Also, he needed a drink.

Joanna's Doc Martens squished in the damp grass as she crossed the baseball field. She couldn't believe she was wearing them, but as soon as she dug them out of her closet and put them on, it was like her feet were reunited with an old friend. Because all of her friends were inanimate objects. Except for Trina, who was human, and who was meeting her at Chet's to check out whatever band was passing through town. Besides, Trina would laugh her ass off to see she still had them.

She emerged from the six-foot patch of woods and onto the gravel lot of Chet's. She was reaching for the iron door handle—God, even that twisty iron handle brought back memories—when her phone beeped.

Sick kids. No beer for me. :(((

Great. Joanna did literally nothing all day, but every time Trina wasn't shuttling kids or furniture around, Joanna was taking Granny to the doctor. She was starting to think that Trina was avoiding her.

Joanna had a choice. She could either go into Chet's alone, drink at the bar alone, watch the band alone, or she could just go home. Alone.

Don't chicken out. These guys are supposed to be great.

This whole night out at Chet's had been Trina's idea. She thought it would be fun to visit their old stomping grounds, and this time with an actual, legal ID. And Trina was convinced the band would be worth the five-dollar cover. Which, frankly, wasn't saying much.

Growing up, Joanna and Trina had seen every Fall Out Boy-emo-punk band to come through town. There were a surprising number of them. Halikarnassus was a convenient stopping point between Brooklyn and Buffalo, and Chet's was uncool enough to be very cool. It was sort of a rite of passage for bands from the New York suburbs. You might get a fancy record deal and open a stadium show for the actual Fall Out Boy, but nothing compared to the unpretentious good time of pitchers and bad PAs at Chet's.

Chet had never looked too closely at Joanna and Trina's IDs back then, but looking back, Joanna did find it suspicious that he never served them at the bar. Oh, sure, the visiting rock dudes would buy them beer. And then when he finally let Delicious Lies play, drinking was the last thing on her mind. She was drunk on rock and roll, man.

Standing under the lights outside of Chet's now, she had a decision to make. She could go in, listen to some rock music, drink a beer, and walk home. It wasn't like she'd never been to a bar alone before. And she was there for the music. Sure, she was wearing fifteen-year-old shoes as a nostalgic joke for a person who wasn't even there, but it wouldn't be the dumbest she'd ever looked at Chet's. It wasn't as bad as the Halloween show when she tried to play a gig dressed as a sexy chicken. She didn't think Rosetta would ever forgive her for those prematurely molting feathers.

Just as she was reaching for the door, it opened with force, jamming into her fingers.

"Ouch!" She backed off the concrete step into the gravel, shaking off the pain.

"Oh, shit, I'm sorry!" Chet, the man himself, let the door slam closed behind him and shook a cigarette out of his pack. "You okay?"

The man hadn't changed a bit. His hair was still gray and slicked back, his face was still tanned and wrinkled. His rough hands still bore the tattoo of a wedding band, and he still flipped that Zippo with the American flag on it.

"Yeah, Chet, I'm fine." She watched him suck the smoke in, blow it out over his shoulder, away from her.

He looked at her, like he was trying to place her. He shook his cigarette in her general direction. "I know . . . holy shit, Jo Jo?"

And again with the Jo Jo. Usually kids she didn't like at school called her that. But even when a guy she liked and respected and admired called her "Jo Jo," she still couldn't stand it.

"I know that scowl," Chet said, his smile splitting

the crags of his face. "Joanna Green, what the hell are you doing here?"

Before she could answer, she was enveloped in a smoky hug. She grunted as her feet left the ground, and when Chet put her down, he held her at arm's length. "Look at you, girl. All growed up."

"Old enough for a beer now."

He raised his hands up. "I don't know what you're talking about. Go on in and spend some money. You owe me, kid."

She laughed and ducked under his arm through the open door.

Chet's was exactly as she remembered it: dark and divey. She had never found another bar quite like it, where hipsters with beards mingled with men who wore their beards without irony. Where you could walk in with as many pretensions as you want, but nobody was going to pay them any attention, so you might as well leave them at the door. Where there was only Bob Seger on the jukebox, and if you wanted to listen to something different, you better just stick around until the band started.

It was pretty crowded for a weeknight, but Joanna found a place at the far end of the bar. The bartender made his way over and when he got to her, his craggy face split into a grin. "Jo Jo?"

Gus was a legend, as much a part of Chet's as the cheap beer and the plywood floor. He knew everything about music, could go toe-to-toe with any music head on everything from Mozart to Mingus. But all he really cared about was the soulful tone of Bob Seger, and since he had been at the bar longer than most of the patrons had been alive, they let the jukebox be Gus's. That was how you knew Gus liked you, if he started talking about the time Bob Seger had come through town and played a set, unannounced. Gus still had his whiskey glass in a place of honor above the bar. But he was also a great bartender, heavy-handed with the booze early in the night, knowing just when and how to cut someone off. He could break up a fight with his army voice, and he could soothe the most heartbroken girl better than whiskey. He did not make margaritas.

Gus had always told her and Trina that he never forgot a face, and, given the dozen or so years Joanna had put on hers, he wasn't kidding.

Although he did forget that she hated that nickname.

Or maybe he didn't forget. Maybe he just remembered that he was the only one who could get away with it.

Well, him and Chet.

Man, she was getting soft in her old age.

"I heard you were back in town! Wonderin' when you'd make it in to see your old friends. Or you too big for us little folks now?"

Coming from most people, Joanna would have considered that a dig. She knew the word was around town that Joanna was no longer with Bunny Slippers. She knew that the good people of Halikarnassus saw her as a failure. She preferred to think that she'd given up fame and fortune for artistic integrity.

But Gus was incapable of passive aggression, and insincerity was not something he practiced. This could result in stony silence or a lifelong bond—regardless, Gus didn't bullshit you.

And he didn't make margaritas.

She waved off his proud papa grin—obviously Gus hadn't heard the good news. "Just came in for a beer and some music."

"That's my girl. How's Peggy?"

Geez. Small towns. Peggy, as far as Joanna knew, had never even been to Chet's.

As far as Joanna knew. Granny seemed to have some hidden depths.

Joanna gave Gus a thumbs-up. "She's doing great."

"Great. She's a tough old broad, your grandmother."

Now Joanna was confused. "How do you know—?"

"The usual?" Gus cut her off. Was he blushing?

Good Lord, did Granny and Gus have a thing?

She needed a beer.

She nodded for the usual, then scanned the crowd for a better place to hover while she waited for the music to start. Preferably a quiet corner where she could avoid the curious looks from locals and the overenthusiastic bouncing of the SUNY kids. Didn't they know you weren't supposed to bounce at rock shows anymore? Just stand there and appreciate it, dammit. That's what the cool kids did now.

She headed toward her ideal corner of the bar, but when she got there, she saw that it was occupied. And that it was occupied by Liam the Librarian. Liam the Librarian, who was wearing a tie, loosened at the neck, and a dress shirt rolled up to his elbows.

Do not notice the forearms, she told herself. *And do not, instead, focus on the shoulders. Or the neck.* Who even had a sexy neck? This guy was ridiculous.

Before she had a chance to wipe the scowl of disapproval off her face (really, it was unnatural for someone that dorky to be that sexy), he looked up and caught her eye. He gave her a confused look—apparently he was unaware of how wrong his sexiness was. She thought about sticking her tongue out and finding a new corner. But she was a grown-up now. She didn't need to hide her mistakes with aggressive posturing.

So she smiled.

Now he looked frightened.

Great, Joanna. You can't even flirt with the sexy librarian.

He seemed to shake off whatever it was about her that was frightening him (her personality, she realized) and he gave her the same smile as when she'd seen him in the library. The How Can I Help You Smile.

Great. She could either spend the night trading confusing glances with Liam the Sexy Librarian, or she could get trampled by the SUNY students pouring in to see the band.

"Hey, Joanna."

The librarian spoke! And now his customer service smile was replaced with a look of mild curiosity.

She was getting really good at reading this guy's face.

"Yeah, hi. I almost didn't recognize you without your head in my grandmother's fridge." Hey, that sounded nice and weird.

"Are you here to see the band?" She recovered smoothly, because of course he was, wearing a tie. Totally the kind of thing one wears to a post-punk hipster band show.

He nodded, which surprised her. So he had good taste in music (Bunny Slippers aside), bad instincts for fashion. "I've been hearing good stuff about these guys," he said, pointing his beer toward the stage where a bunch of guys—in suits!—were starting the sound check. "It was supposed to be my reward for surviving the town council meeting."

She took in his rumpled-up sleeves and his tie, askew. "How'd it go?"

He raised his glass.

She took that to mean not well.

"So that's why you're wearing a suit in a dive bar?"

"Yup."

"I thought you were auditioning for *Death of a Salesman*."

He laughed. "I didn't think—"

"What, you didn't think I could make literary references? I took freshman English, same as everyone else."

He held up his hands. "Okay! You're right. That was an unfair assumption."

She took a drink of her beer. It was delicious and cold and tasted like the best and worst times of her misspent youth. Mmm . . . beer. Too bad the company was leaving a bitter taste in her mouth.

Don't look at the sexy librarian's mouth.

"Do I look ridiculous?"

She looked at the sexy librarian's mouth. But only because that's where the words were coming from.

"Huh?" she asked, because she took freshman English.

He waved his hand up and down, indicating his body. No, she corrected herself, indicating his clothes. His body was ridiculous, librarian-wise.

She shrugged. "You'd look more ridiculous in skinny jeans."

He looked pained. "I do not understand skinny jeans. How can they be comfortable?"

"Hey, it's about time men learned to suffer for fashion."

"Yes, but that just seems so . . ."

Whatever it seemed was cut off by the band.

And Joanna had a major flashback. The sound pouring through the speakers went straight to her heart. Part of her wanted to jump up on the stage and steal the skinny suit–wearing lead guitar, and part of her wanted to curl up in a corner and cry. That could have been her up on that stage. Up on any stage in the world. She just had to play crappy radio music.

"They're not that bad." Liam nudged her with his elbow.

She gave him a weak smile and a thumbs-up.

"They got nothing on you, kid," Gus said, sidling up to them.

"I'd love to hear you play live," Liam said, his eyes lighting up with interest.

Joanna hmphed noncommittally. She'd love to play live. Her fingers were itching to do it. But in this shitty town? And who with?

"She was the heart and soul of Delicious Lies," Gus said like a proud papa.

Liam raised an eyebrow at her.

"High school band," she explained, hoping the band onstage would continue their excessively rowdy guitar riffs. It didn't make for a great balance of sound, but it did the trick when she was avoiding talking about things Gus was not getting the hint about.

"Great name," Liam said.

It was a great name. It perfectly captured how she and her angry high school girlfriends felt about society, man. She was glad she hadn't taken it with her to LA. LA would have beaten Delicious Lies into sexy-boring rock submission.

"Too bad that other gig didn't work out." The look on Gus's face was getting awfully close to pity, which was alarming enough. Coupled with the fact that she did not want to talk about bands not working out, it made Joanna suddenly decide she'd had enough rock music for one night.

She put her empty beer bottle on the bar. "See you, Gus."

"'Night, kid."

"You're leaving?" Liam the Librarian actually looked a little sad about that.

"Not my scene."

"I thought you came here for the music."

Which was true, and which had just started.

"It's the company," she said, bitterly.

His face told her that he got the hint, but the rest of him clearly did not.

"Hold on, I'll walk you to your car." He reached for his wallet.

"No, it's fine. I walked."

"Well then, let me walk you home. It's late."

She raised an eyebrow. "It's Halikarnassus. Besides, I know self-defense."

She watched the thoughts pass over his face—he

wanted to be a gentleman, but he wanted to finish his drink. This guy should definitely never play poker.

She put him out of his misery and made it easier for him. "Your nice-guy bullshit? Don't bother." She didn't wait for his response, just waved and was out the door.

Chapter Ten

Walking across the parking lot and the woods and the field, Joanna wished she had a cigarette. She hadn't smoked since she'd graduated from high school, and since the only place to buy cigarettes at this hour was Chet's, she wasn't going to have one. She needed something to distract her from the assault on her feelings.

The band sucked. There was no doubt about that. That was the only possible explanation for her heart-pounding desire to get onstage and play with them. She just wanted to fix their bad songs, that was all. She was done with music. Even if she thought she could get away with playing without selling her soul (or selling out), Rosetta was all, nope. You're done with that.

She tried her best not to think about what she'd said to Liam. It wasn't his fault that she couldn't handle her feelings. And it hadn't felt particularly good to take it out on him. But it was over now. She couldn't worry about the delicate feelings of the town librarian.

"Hey!"

Joanna turned, her fists ready for a fight.

But this was Halikarnassus, where nothing happened, good or bad, so she shouldn't have worried. It was just Liam the Librarian, suit jacket in hand, striding across the field toward her.

"Do you have some kind of problem with me?" he asked, getting up in her face.

She inhaled. He smelled like beer and breath mints. She saw his eyes flick to her lips. His Adam's apple bobbed. He licked his lips. She leaned in. His neck smelled like oranges. She loved oranges.

She licked the pulse point in his neck. He might have shivered, he might have groaned, she didn't know and she didn't have time to find out before his mouth was on hers, hard and rough and desperate, and she grabbed a handful of his hair and pulled him closer, battling with his tongue, stretching tall so her whole body was flush with his. His hands were rough on her hips, insistent, and he walked her backward so they were under the old covered bleachers. Her calves hit the ancient wood and she fell back but she took him with her, and his hands were crazy, grabbing, squeezing, driving her wild. She was wild. She was a sex-starved rock beast and she was being ravished by a librarian on public bleachers.

She reached for his shirt and pulled, buttons flying as she revealed his chest, taut and glistening. She ran her hands greedily over his muscles while he lifted her hips and—

Joanna woke with a gasp, her sheets a tangled,

sweaty mess around her legs. Her T-shirt was bunched around her armpits, and if she'd had underwear on before she went to bed, it was gone now.

Holy hell. She ran a shaky hand through her hair, trying to catch her breath.

Then she noticed Starr sitting in the open doorway, watching her.

"Don't judge me, dog." Joanna pulled her shirt down and stalked over to the door. "He's a lot hotter than he seems." She shut the door in the dog's face and went back to bed, praying that in the morning, she would forget about the whole sordid dream.

Chapter Eleven

The third Thursday of the month at 2:30 in the afternoon was simultaneously Liam's favorite and least favorite time of the month. Favorite because on top of the usual afternoon craziness, the library was bustling with kids getting out of Toni's afternoon storytime and his White-Haired Old Ladies coming in early for book group to scour the new releases. Least favorite because, gah, so many people.

"What do you know about this one?" Phyllis Parker asked him, holding up the second-latest thriller with the word "Girl" in the title. (The latest was checked out and had a holds queue a mile long.)

"Eh, probably not for you," he told her. Not because it was too violent, although it was, but because Phyllis hated to read about a stupid heroine. This heroine, this girl, she didn't make the best choices. "What about this one?" He picked up a mystery set in the 1920s with a ferocious lady detective.

"Read it. Loved it. You need some more new books in here."

Tell me about it, he thought, but did not say. If he said it, Phyllis would launch into a long rant about Hal Jr.'s asshattery (her word), and as much as Liam appreciated her passion, parents tended to stare when Phyllis went off like that. Then they would write him angry e-mails about inappropriate language, then he'd have to talk to Phyllis about her language, or at least her volume, then she'd tell him she'd say whatever the hell she wanted but for his sake, she'd keep it down. He tried to keep these conversations down to once a quarter, and she'd already met her quota for Q2.

They just needed some more books.

"Hi, Mr. Liam!"

Liam looked down to see Max and Hazel Flunderman at his hip, their mouths ringed in what looked like the remnants of red juice. Which was amazing, because Toni would never serve red juice at storytime. But then, if there was something to be gotten into, Max and Hazel Flunderman would get into it.

"Hey, guys," he said, squatting down to their level. "Did you have a good storytime?"

"It was okay," Hazel said with a serious sigh. "I wanted Miss Toni to read the snow time story again."

Her devotion to the classic *The Snowy Day* was adorable. And obsessive.

"Well, I think Miss Toni was reading summertime books since it's almost summer."

"I hate summer! It's not fair! It doesn't snow at all!"

"But the pool is open in the summer," Max told his sister with deadly seriousness. "You can't even swim in the winter."

Hazel sighed again. It was hard, dealing with the seasons.

"Guys, quit bothering Mr. Liam." Their mom, Trina, came out from the children's area, her arms overloaded. "Help me carry some of these books, would you?"

"But my arms are noodles!" Max said, flopping his arms at his sides to prove that, indeed, his arms were noodles.

Trina rolled her eyes. "Jesus. The old noodle-arm trick."

Liam stood and took the most precariously placed books from the pile. "Ready to check out?"

"Yes, I think we've managed to find the forty thousand books they need to tide them over until we come to the library again in like three days."

"And *The Snowy Day*?" Hazel asked.

"You know, you have a copy of that book at home."

"But I like the library one! It smells like a library."

"Yes, we have the library-smelling *Snowy Day*."

Hazel jumped up and down and clapped her hands, and her twin brother followed.

"You know, you're supposed to be quiet in here," Phyllis said with a smile. "Hey, Mr. Liam, how come they can shout but I can't?"

"Because your shouts are not rated G." Trina laughed.

"Miss Phyllis, when can we come over and play with Baby Louise?"

"Oh, soon, I'm sure. Or maybe your mom will get you your own kitten."

"Thanks, Phyllis," Trina said.

"We can't because Daddy's allergikt," Hazel said

as if she was imparting the sad news that Daddy had betrayed them all and was a severe disappointment.

"Is he now?" Phyllis asked.

"Yes, very allergikt," Trina said.

"Hmm, that must be a new allergy."

"Yes, I think he developed it around the time they started visiting Baby Louise."

"Curious."

"Isn't it? Well, we've got to check these out so we can go home for n-a-p-s."

Max rolled his eyes. "Mommy, we know that means naps."

"I'm too big for a nap," Hazel announced.

"I know, but Mommy isn't."

"Mommy, you're weird."

Trina didn't say anything, just led her kids over to the checkout. Liam followed. "See you in a minute," he told Phyllis. She waved him off with a smile and went back to judging the stupidity of the new books' heroines.

"Sorry to drag you away," Trina said.

"That's okay, I'll talk to Phyllis plenty in book group."

"Oh, that's right, that's today. We were going to stop by to see Peggy on our way home, but maybe if she's coming here . . ."

"I'm not sure. Her granddaughter came to pick up the book for her, though, so maybe."

"Oh my God, you've seen Joanna?"

"Who's Joanna?" Max asked.

"Joanna is Mommy's best friend who is dead meat because she's been to the library but not to visit us yet."

"Dead meat!" Hazel said, in wonder.

"Sorry," Liam said, as if it was his fault that Joanna

had time to go to the library and to rock shows but
not to visit her best friend. It did seem kind of shady,
though.

"I was supposed to meet her last night at Chet's,
but someone got sick."

"I threwed up," Max said, proudly.

"I didn't," Hazel said, just as proudly.

"I'm all better now, though, so I don't throw up
anymore."

"Great," Liam said. Because, well, it was great.

"Hey, guys." Kristin Klomberg came up behind
Trina's brood, Kale in her arms, his mouth full of
board book. Liam winced, more for the health hazards of Kale putting a book that had been in the
mouth of half of the toddlers of Halikarnassus in his
mouth than out of concern for public property.

"Baby Kale!" Hazel squealed and proceeded to
tickle Kale's chubby little legs. Kale started giggling
and squirming, so Kristin let him down.

"Now you hold Hazel's hand and be good, okay,
Kalie?"

"Hay-thuh!" Kale proclaimed, dropping the board
book and trading it for Hazel's hand.

"Do you want to read *The Snowy Day*?" she asked.
Without waiting for an answer, she took the book
from the pile and sat down in front of the desk.
Kale climbed into her lap and listened as Hazel
recited the book from memory.

"She's the only one he'll sit still for," Kristin said,
in wonder. "What is her secret?"

"She inherited her mama's charm," Trina said.
"And he listens to her because she's not his mom."

"Hmm. I can't imagine a Klomberg man being stubborn. What are you guys up to now?"

"Well, we were going to see Peggy, but Liam thinks she might be coming to book group," Trina said.

"Oh, is she out and about?"

"I don't know," said Liam. "I'm just hoping."

"Trust me, we would have heard if she was," Trina said.

"Well, if Joanna's her nurse, I wouldn't hold out hope for a quick recovery," Kristin said with a sneer.

"Oh, God. Will you let that high school crap go?"

"I'm just saying, she's not very maternal. Did I tell you she almost ran over Kale in the parking lot?"

"Holy shit. What?"

Liam was alarmed on many levels. One, that a child was almost run over. And two, that it was on property he was responsible for. And three, that he was only now just hearing about it.

"Mr. Liam said 'shit,'" Max helpfully told his mother.

"I know. He'll get a spanking later, I'm sure."

Liam blushed. Trina's outrageous sense of humor still caught him off guard sometimes. Also, he had a little bit of a guilty conscience vis-à-vis adults spanking each other, what with him fantasizing about Joanna and all.

Oy. What a mess.

"Is Kalie okay?" Trina asked, peeking down at the kids absorbed in the book.

"Yes, no thanks to her. She was pretty rude about it."

"Kristin," Trina said. "You're not suggesting she did it on purpose, are you?"

Kristin looked like she was about to argue that, yes, another human being tried to run over her child because of some long-held high school grudge. She must have talked herself out of it, though, because she rolled her eyes. "No. She was driving Peggy's boat of a car. And once I had Kale corralled, I could see that she looked pretty terrified. Before she recognized me, at least."

"Have you ever thought about getting a leash for that kid?" Trina asked. "For reals. He's a runner."

"I know. Hal thinks he'll make a great running back."

Good ol' Hal and his football, Liam thought. So much more fun than reading.

"Whoa. Don't talk about Hal in front of Liam. I think we might actually provoke a reaction out of him." Trina was always teasing him for his professionalism, even in the face of the frequently ridiculous situations public librarians found themselves in. She was right, Hal provoked a reaction. Still, it wasn't a great idea to give in to that urge. Not when Hal was the mayor. And not when his wife was standing right there.

"I have no problem with Hal," he said, diplomatically. On a personal level, Liam was sure that Hal was perfectly delightful. Actually, he wasn't sure of that at all, but he was willing to pretend he was.

"He's being ridiculous with this whole football lights thing," Trina said. "You should have a problem with him."

Liam shot a quick look at Kristin.

"Don't worry about me, Liam. You know if I had my way, he'd drop this whole stupid idea. Even if I hated the library—which you know I don't—you think I want my kid growing up to play concussion ball?"

"A controversial position, Mrs. Klomberg," Trina teased.

"Don't even get me started," Kristin said, and then she took a deep breath and looked like she was going to launch into, well, starting. But she was interrupted by little Kale proclaiming proudly that his diaper was full, so she whisked him off to the changing table in the restroom. Trina took that opportunity to gather her children—each carrying their own stack of books— and headed out, presumably for n-a-p-s. Liam waved them off and took a moment to enjoy that little glow he got from realizing he'd made friends in Halikarnassus, and he really, really liked it here. Then Phyllis reminded him that book group was going to start soon and if he didn't stop mooning around, he wouldn't have time to set up the tables for their cookies. So Liam dutifully followed her into the meeting room and started setting up for book group, under the watchful eyes of the White-Haired Old Ladies.

For the entire twenty-minute walk to the library, Joanna changed her mind.

She was glad she'd decided to walk. It would be hard for her to almost run over toddlers on foot. And even if Kristin Walsh—no, Kristin Klomberg— was her archnemesis, Joanna was not a total monster.

Then she thought that if she was going to the library, she should probably pick up a book or two for Granny, who was feeling better (broken ankle aside) and would appreciate some new reading material. Then Joanna realized that the library was not far from the grocery store, and she needed to pick up a few things so she could show Granny that a meal without a casserole was worth the effort, but then she'd have to walk home with library books and groceries and ugh.

Her life was hard.

Then she thought she might just skip book group altogether. She didn't know these women. Well, she probably did know all of them, but they weren't friends or anything. And most of them had certainly been by to see Granny this week, and if at least one of them had, all of them would have heard the news, so there was no need for Joanna to give an update on Granny's health.

Plus, she'd probably see Liam at the book group, and she didn't know if she could face him, knowing that in her dream, she had done severe damage to his perfectly innocent shirt.

But she did want to talk about the book. She couldn't decide how she felt about it. That epilogue, man. That threw her for a loop. She wanted to talk about that loop.

But with a bunch of Granny's friends who all thought Joanna did not deserve such a wonderful, kind grandmother? And a man whom her subconscious had decided was the world's greatest lover?

By the time she'd decided that, no, she wouldn't go to book group, she'd just go to the store, she was at the library and it seemed a little silly to turn around. So she went in, followed the signs to the meeting room, and walked into the book group.

Joanna was the youngest person in the room by at least twenty years.

Well, except for Liam, and Liam acted like an old man, so he didn't count. She wondered how old he really was. He didn't look like he was even thirty, but he must be. He was the director. Only old people could be library directors.

Unless Joanna was old now, too.

Oh, God. Old people were her.

She wasn't old. She was barely twenty-five. No, wait. She'd turned twenty-seven a few months ago. Still, a kid! Compared to all these other book clubbers, she was a kid. And if Liam had a grown-up job like library director, he must not be a kid. God, she hoped not. What did she have to show for her twenty-seven years on the planet? One album of music so terrible she couldn't stand to listen to it, no discernible plans for the future, and oh yeah, now she was living in her childhood bedroom and attending an old-lady book group by proxy for Gran. And having unspeakably naughty dreams about a librarian.

Liam better be older than her. Otherwise she was going to have to feel really bad about not having her shit together. Well, she already felt bad about it. She was going to have to feel really worse.

She wasn't sure she could handle feeling any worse.

Besides, who could feel bad sitting around a library table with an elaborate tea set up and many different kinds of cookies while white-haired old ladies alternated between cooing all over Liam and yelling at each other over which guy the heroine should have chosen?

Oh, wait. *She* felt bad.

Her life sucked.

At least the cookies were good.

"Are you seriously telling me that she should have chosen Pierre? He was a terrorist!"

"The French Resistance! Not a terrorist."

"He bombed that café!"

"Because it was a Nazi hangout!"

"But there were regular people there, too."

"As if Robbie was much better? That cocky American fighter pilot?"

"He was ruggedly handsome!"

"So was Pierre! But Pierre didn't try to buy her love with chocolate and panty hose."

"Because Pierre couldn't afford chocolate and panty hose. Besides, Pierre would always choose his country first. She deserved better than that."

"But not in the context of this book. Listen to this." Betty Anne flipped through the Post-its in her book until she found the passage she was looking for. She perched her glasses on her nose and bent the spine of the book so hard it cracked. As she read the passage that proved Rolf was working to undermine the Nazis from within, Joanna watched Liam wince. She laughed at him, but she couldn't blame him. It was a library book, after all.

"But I thought she didn't end up with either of them," Joanna said. She'd read the book. She was pretty sure it ended with Mariah walking off into the sunset alone. Joanna liked that ending.

"No, but she should have gone off with Pierre."

"Robbie was the only one who really understood her."

"Robbie wanted to take her back to America and turn her into a housewife."

"What's wrong with being a housewife?"

"Okay! Okay, wow. That's . . . you guys have really thought about this, huh?" Liam, apparently sensing the impending danger, finally stepped in. "Joanna has a point. Mariah didn't go off with either of the men."

"But she should have—"

"Why do you think the author had her end up alone?" he asked.

"You say that like it's terrible," Joanna said. "Alone. She wasn't alone, she just wasn't beholden to any of those jerks who wanted her to be something she was not."

"You young people and your independence."

"I think she's right. Why should a man tell Mariah how to live her life?"

"But how would she support herself?"

"Bonnie, you lived in the city when you were Mariah's age, and you worked."

"Yeah, and I lived in a shitty boardinghouse and barely made enough to go out dancing once a week."

Whoa. The thing that Joanna remembered most about Bonnie Gunderson was that she ran a petition every Fourth of July to cancel the fireworks because they upset her schnauzers. Apparently Bonnie used to be cool. Partying it up in New York City when she was younger? That was rad.

Then she got married and moved to Halikarnassus and spent all her time worrying about schnauzers.

This town really did things to people. Joanna took comfort that she was not the only one. Well, small comfort. Just because Halikarnassus had sucked the life out of Bonnie didn't make Joanna feel any better about its sucking her life away as well.

"Why do you think Mariah would prefer that kind

of life to whatever Robbie or Pierre could have given her?" Liam asked.

"Because she was an idiot," Bonnie said.

"Because she was tired of living her life for other people," Joanna said. "She'd been taking care of her family, then Pierre, then Robbie. All she did was nurse people back to health, and then they left her. If I were her, I would have said 'screw it' after the first guy left me."

"Do you think she had the same choices that we have now? Or that women have now?"

"What, like she chose to have crappy people in her life? Or that she chose not to be good enough for them?"

Joanna realized her voice was raised. And that all of the book clubbers were staring at her.

Liam cleared his throat. "Well, sort of. I mean, if her situation was different, might she have chosen to surround herself with better people?"

Right. This was a book group. Not a therapy session.

"You mean people who weren't Nazis?" Bonnie asked, with an arch of her eyebrow. "I'm pretty sure she would have chosen to not be sent to a concentration camp."

"Yes. Yes, of course." Liam looked embarrassed. "I think we all would have chosen that."

"I think maybe the question is not why did she end up alone, but why do we feel like her ending up alone is the worst thing to happen to her?" That was Mildred Pearson, a quiet widow who hadn't spoken all meeting. Even now, her voice was soft and she spoke mostly into her copy of the book. "I think what Joanna was saying is that Mariah thought she had to choose between a Nazi and a Resistance fighter and a pilot, but by the end, she realized that she didn't. She was finally able to choose her own happiness. But it came too late, and walking into the sunset represented her death. But her life is meant to be a lesson to us to love ourselves before we lose ourselves in loving someone else."

Everyone was quiet, looking at Mildred and taking in what she'd said.

"I don't want to put words in your mouth, Joanna," she muttered.

"No, please. Those words were much better than my words."

"Mildred, that's a really wonderful insight," Liam said. "I didn't read the epilogue as her death, but now that you say that . . . it changes the book a little, doesn't it?"

"It makes it bittersweet," Bonnie said.

"I think I like it even more," said Phyllis.

"Huh," said Joanna. Because it really made her think. A bittersweet ending.

"I still think she should have chosen Robbie," said Fiona. "But I just have a thing for pilots."

Liam was glad to see everybody laughing, finally. He'd only led one book group before coming to Halikarnassus, and when he found out he'd be taking over this one, it quickly became the most intimidating part of his job. More intimidating than town council meetings.

Not that the Ladies weren't nice. They were delightful. And thoughtful, and they made really good cookies. They were just so . . . opinionated. Which was a good thing for a book group to be, it was just . . . sometimes it was a little hard to control.

"On that note," he said, taking advantage of everyone's good mood, "here's what we're reading for next time." He passed around a stack of books and the sign-out sheet.

"Aren't you taking one, dear?" Mildred asked Joanna, who let the stack pass her by.

"Oh, uh. No, I'm not sure if I'm going to be here next month."

What was that in Liam's gut? Was it disappointment?

"That doesn't mean you can't read the book. Just turn it in when you're done," said Phyllis.

"Um, I'm pretty sure my library card isn't good anymore."

"Oh, those things are good forever, aren't they, Liam?"

"Well, I wouldn't say forever . . ."

"What, do you owe money or something?"

"Maybe," Joanna hedged. "Probably."

"Liam will take care of that, won't you, Liam?"

The Ladies had quickly discovered that, unlike Mrs. Pratt, he was pretty free with waiving the overdue fines. He didn't really think a nickel a day was motivating anyone to bring their materials back on time. And to his delight, he found that if he waived fines, folks would give a few dollars' donation, which was usually way more than their overdue fines.

If he kept waiving fines, he might even be able to buy from the fall catalogs.

Hey, that was depressing.

"Okay, sure," Joanna said. "I mean, I'll just take it for Gran."

"Oh no, take Peggy her own copy. Then you two can talk about it when you're done."

"Great," she muttered, seeming annoyed. But she took two copies of the book anyway.

Everyone said their good-byes and left, and Liam was alone in the meeting room with leftover cookies and a bunch of chairs that needed to be stacked.

"Do you want help?"

He turned, leftover cookie halfway to his mouth, to find Joanna standing awkwardly in the doorway.

"No, that's okay. I've done this a million times."

She ignored him and picked up a chair.

Okay then.

They cleaned up in silence, and she was still standing there when he closed the door to the storage closet.

"Do you need something else?" he asked, because he had a way with the ladies.

"Oh, uh. Can you check and see if I still have a library card?"

"Oh! Sure, no problem. Let me just drop these in the break room," he said, indicating the plate of cookies. "There'll be a riot if I don't share the leftovers."

"Sure. I'll just, uh, see you over there?" she said, pointing to the desk.

"Okay."

He dropped off the cookies—and good thing because his Thursday shelver, Marcus, was there waiting for them—and headed back to the circ desk.

"So, did you enjoy your first book group?" he asked, taking the books from her.

"Mm-hmm," she said in a voice that did not sound like the voice of a woman who had just enjoyed herself.

"Let's see here," he said, looking her up in the computer system. "You have the same last name as Peggy, right?"

"Yup."

He wondered where her parents were, that she was raised by her grandmother. He wondered if they were even still alive.

Probably not a great conversation to get into over the circulation desk.

"Ah, here you are. Joanna H. Green. What's the 'H' for?"

She blushed. "My middle name."

"Ooookay."

"It's Hortense."

He snorted.

He shouldn't have snorted. It was not very nice to make fun of patrons' private information, especially not to their faces. But there was nothing about Joanna Green that seemed even vaguely like a "Hortense."

"Is that a family name?" he asked, to cover the fact that he was, in fact, an incredibly rude person.

"No. My parents were just weird."

Were. Okay, definitely not a circulation desk conversation.

"Well, you still have a card." He looked at her record, a little alarmed at what he saw.

"What? Do I owe you guys some money?"

"Um."

She reached into her bag and pulled out her wallet. "How much?"

"Eight hundred thirty-two dollars."

"What the—"

He gave her credit for not cursing out loud. If he'd just found out that he owed the library nearly a thousand dollars, he would have definitely cursed.

"It looks like you didn't return a whole mess of CDs. Is there any chance you still have them?"

"What are they?" He tilted the monitor toward her as much as it could go, which was not much. She leaned over the desk and he noticed that she smelled like strawberries.

Huh. Joanna Green smells like strawberries.

"Oh. I mean, those sound vaguely familiar," she said to the monitor and the list of rock CDs from the 70s and 80s listed thereupon.

"Do you think they're still at Peggy's? If you can find them, you won't have to pay for them."

"Jesus, I hope so. God, that's embarrassing."

"A lot of people forget to return things. It's okay."

"I know, but Creedence Clearwater Revival?"

He looked at her. She was wearing a torn shirt with the famous image of Johnny Cash defiantly giving the world the middle finger. "It does seem a little out of character."

"Well, you guys have a pretty crappy CD collection."

"Hey now, I've added a lot to it." Mostly by donating stuff from his personal collection and soliciting donations from his favorite bands, but they didn't need to get into that now. "Hey, we just got the new Bunny Slippers."

"Like I said, crappy CD collection. So, uh, I'll have to look for those CDs."

"Sure, I'll print you a list. Oh, do you not want to check that book out?"

"I owe you eight hundred dollars. You're really going to let me check something else out?"

It was eight hundred and thirty-two dollars, but that clarification didn't seem helpful. And, no, he probably shouldn't let her check anything else out, her track record being what it was.

"Can you put this one on Peggy's card?" she asked, holding up one copy of the book. "She's much more vigilant than I am."

"Sure." He started to look up Peggy's account. "So, I'm glad to see you didn't get murdered last night."

And that is called flirting, folks.

"What?" she asked, clearly not affected by his charm.

"After Chet's. When you said you were going to walk home and I offered to walk with you but you said you could handle yourself."

"Right. Nope. Didn't die. I did have to fight off a trail of assassins, though."

"Really? And they didn't leave a mark on you."

"Nope. Although I did have to sell my soul to a crime syndicate."

"Too bad."

"Yeah. Say, do you have any books on putting drugs up your butt?"

There was a shocked *humph* behind him, and a mother he didn't recognize walked by, her hands firmly over her daughter's ears.

Great, another angry parental e-mail.

"Oops. Sorry about that."

"If I had a nickel for every time a patron asked me about stuff like that . . ."

"You're right. I should just Google it."

"You wound me, Joanna Green."

"Sorry, man," she said, but she smiled at him when she said it.

Maybe he was good at flirting. All he had to do was talk about murder and drugs. Much more pleasant than last night, when they talked about music. Something to remember for the future.

"Oh, Trina Flunderman was in earlier. She said you're in big trouble for coming to the library before you went to see her."

"Ugh, yes. I keep forgetting to call her."

"It's hard being popular."

"Wouldn't you know it, Mr. Handsome Librarian."

"Ha," he said. Then he thought, *Handsome*?

"Well, I gotta go run some errands and get back to Peggy. Thanks for book group."

"Hey, thanks for coming. You livened it up. I hope you'll be back next time."

"Mmm . . . doubt it. No offense. It's this town, you know? Bums me out."

Huh.

He loved this town.

Oh, well.

And just when he had gotten so good at flirting.

Chapter Twelve

Trina handed Joanna a beer, then sat in the fluffy chair opposite her. They clinked bottles. Max and Hazel circled them like Tasmanian devils, leaving a trail of discarded toys in their wake.

"Stay out of Daddy's office!" Trina called after the dervishes as they ran out of the playroom and into parts of the house unknown.

"Sorry," Trina apologized to Joanna. "I would blame it on the rain, that they've been cooped up all day and that's why they're being crazy. But the truth is, they are always like this."

"Always?"

"Always. Except at bedtime. They are surprisingly good at going to bed."

"They're exhausted. I'm exhausted just watching them."

"You get used to it." Trina shrugged, taking a sip of beer. "Oh, hey, I just lied to you."

Joanna laughed. "They were easier when they were babies?"

"Well, they didn't run around. But they also didn't

go to school. For nine months out of the year, they're the teachers' problem. God bless 'em."

"Poor teachers."

"Oh, they listen to the teachers. Sometimes I think they save all of their energy up until they get home."

Joanna shook her head. "I still can't believe it."

"What? My transformation into Betty Draper?"

Joanna took in her friend's skinny jeans and over-sized Replacements shirt. Betty Draper would never put black streaks in her blond hair. Trina was always more of a Debbie Harry. Except now she had a Pinterest board.

"You're totally a cool mom."

"Thank you. Please tell my children that."

"Tell us what?" Hazel was suddenly hanging on the arm of Trina's chair, her mouth lined with something blue.

"Are you in my makeup again?"

"Just the play stuff!" Before Trina could respond, Hazel and her curls were bouncing down the hallway.

"Play stuff?"

"Max is obsessed with makeup. And I love my children very dearly, but the first time they destroyed my MAC Ruby Woo . . ."

"Ouch."

"Yeah, ouch. So I bought them some cheap stuff and told them if they ever touched Mommy's Very Expensive Makeup again, I would trade them in for a litter of kittens."

"Mean Mommy."

"I know. The idea of kittens living in this house without them was very upsetting."

When they were in high school, Trina was a good girl. At least when adults were around. The truth was,

Trina could outdrink and outsmoke even Joanna. And even though she was determined to stay a virgin (she was saving herself for love, and because she liked a challenge), she still managed to get plenty of action. She just somehow never got the reputation that came with it.

If Joanna didn't like her so much, she would hate her.

Sometimes she did hate her. But that wasn't Trina's fault. It was this town, this small place that arbitrarily picked one girl and called her a slut and picked another and called her a flirt. The Carringtons were a rich, nuclear family, and Joanna had been abandoned by her parents. There was no contest who was going to get picked on.

Trina always stood up for her. She gave out her share of black eyes to guys (and on one memorable occasion, a girl) who thought they could say whatever they wanted about Joanna as if she wasn't right there. Trina was her staunchest defender.

Sometimes Joanna wondered if she wasn't so perfectly imperfect, if she would have resented Trina less.

She certainly didn't want her life now.

"Are you really happy here?" Joanna asked.

"I can't imagine why you would ask that," Trina said, miming downing her beer.

"No, really. I mean, you have a minivan."

"The minivan is Rick's. I drive a badass truck."

"Remember your Bug?"

"Oh, God, that old thing? Damn, I loved that car."

"Mommy said a bad word!" came a shout from down the hall.

"Grown-ups are allowed to say bad words!" she

shouted back. "How many times did we hotbox in that thing?"

"Before every football game?"

"How else were we supposed to get through a football game?"

"And now you're *married* to a football player," Joanna said, swishing her beer bottle toward the family photos on the wall.

"Ex-football player. But yes, I married the enemy."

"With a house in the suburbs."

Trina shrugged. "What can I say? The heart wants what it wants. Anyway, you've never seen Rick without his shirt on."

Joanna dropped her head in her hand. "Trina." She laughed.

"What? My husband's hot. But he's also sweet and tough and he has great taste in music. And he knows how to be happy, you know? He knows what he loves, and he does it."

"Selling insurance is what he loves," Joanna asked, dubious.

"I meant me, dummy."

"Romantic."

"It is. He does his nine-to-five, the kids are psyched when he's home, and he goes crazy when he sees me with power tools."

"Don't you ever feel, I don't know, stifled?"

"Not really. But I never had the same relationship with this place that you did."

"You mean you didn't hate it with an undying fervor and literally count the days until you could leave?"

"I hated that calendar of yours. I wanted you to stick around so badly."

"You could have come with me."

"I had to go to college."

"What, so you could stay at home with your kids?"
Trina narrowed her eyes at Joanna. "You're doing it."

"Doing what?"

"Something is bothering you, so you're picking a
fight with me."

"I'm not—" She totally was.

Damn best friends, all knowing you and stuff.

Rick walked in, loosening his tie and saving Joanna
from too much self-reflection.

"Hey, babe," he said, and kissed Trina on the top
of her head.

"Hey." She turned her head up and waited for a
real kiss. He obliged, then reached around her for
her beer.

"Hey! Get your own!"

"Daddy!" A stampede careened down the hallway
and into Rick's gut. Trina took the opportunity to
stand up and reclaim her beer.

"Children!" he said, swinging each one up in turn.
Swinging needs met, they ran back down the hall.

"That's a new shade for Max."

Trina shrugged, then smiled as Rick put his arm
around her. She smiled a little less when he took her
beer bottle and took a healthy swig, but she was still
smiling.

"Hi, Joanna. Nice to see you again."

"You, too." She raised her bottle from the comfort
of her easy chair. "Been a while."

"Too long. Remember that wild week in LA?"

"That was before we had kids."

"Babe, I think that was when we made the kids."

"Don't traumatize Joanna with your fertility."

Joanna had always liked Rick, even if he was a football-playing meathead. Ex-football-playing meathead.

"Do you know how happy this woman is that you're back?" Rick asked her.

Trina ducked her head. "She knows."

"Just for a little while," Joanna added. "But I'm glad, too." Mostly glad. Afternoons like this, definitely glad.

"So what'd you gals talk about? You getting the band back together?"

"Hardly," snorted Joanna.

"Why not? I heard you guys used to rock." He held up his hand in devil horns and stuck his tongue out.

"Don't make fun," said Trina. "We totally rocked."

"And I bet you'd look great in those leather pants."

Now Trina snorted. "After two kids I think they take away your right to leather pants."

"What are you talking about," Rick mumbled into Trina's ear, then kept mumbling into her neck as his free hand reached around to her ass.

"Gross!" came the shout from down the hall.

Rick stepped back. "How do they do that?"

"Don't look at me." Joanna shrugged. "You made them."

"Hey, progeny! Go get Daddy one of his special juices!" The other room was suspiciously silent. "Fine, I'll get my own beer. What did we have kids for, anyway?"

"Bombastic egotism?" Joanna suggested.

Rick shook his head. "Great to see you again, Joanna. But for reals, you should do it."

"Honey, Joanna does not want to talk about music." Trina shot her husband a look that said *we talked*

about this when we had private couple time and were
talking about Joanna behind her back.

"Hey! I'm going to get a beer!" Rick practically ran out of the room.

"Sorry about that," Trina said.

Joanna took another swig of beer.

"But now that it's out . . . Are we gonna talk about it?"

"What?"

"I don't know if you know about this thing, it's called the Internet? And it means that public figures don't have a private life anymore?"

"I'm not a public figure."

"Joanna."

"Fine! It was nothing, okay?"

"Didn't look like nothing. Looked like you abandoned your bandmates onstage and now you're here. And if you try to tell me you came here for Peggy, I'll make you babysit."

"I didn't abandon them."

Trina waited.

"It just . . . it wasn't right. It wasn't what I set out to do, you know?"

Trina watched her, waiting for the rest of the story. Joanna fidgeted. The label on her beer bottle was suddenly very interesting.

Trina sighed. "Fine, we won't talk about it."

"Thank you."

"So, are you done with music now, or what?"

"I don't know. I'm not really qualified to do anything else."

"Maybe we should do it."

"Do what?"

"Delicious Lies."

"I don't know—"

"Just while you're home. My drums are in the barn. It'll be fun. Come on, just until you figure out your life."

"No big deal."

"You always land on your feet. Anyway, Bunny Slippers suck. You're so much better than that."

Joanna smiled. "Thanks."

"And walking off the stage like that? Totally punk rock."

"Totally."

"So you'll do it? Delicious Lies?"

"Yes, okay, fine!" Joanna wasn't sure why she was pretending to be annoyed. This was the first good idea she'd encountered since she'd moved home.

"Yes!" Trina jumped up in triumph. "Did you hear that, hon? We're getting the band back together!"

Chapter Thirteen

It was way too early in the morning for Joanna to be awake.

Starr did not care.

She was happily sniffing the sidewalk, stopping wherever any other dog had ever been in the history of Halikarnassus and making sure that past dog understood that this was her town now.

It was not very conducive to getting exercise.

Which was just as well, because it was also way too early for Joanna to be exercising.

She needed to find a way to burn off some of this energy, that was all. She'd felt guilty about last week, abandoning Granny for book group (although Granny insisted that she go as her proxy) and for Trina (although Granny also insisted that Joanna visit her friend). And as the urgency of Granny's injury passed, so did a lot of the visitors, although Doris still managed to stop by to help herself to the contents of the freezer.

Which, actually, was a good thing. Joanna was getting really tired of food reheated from a pan.

But Granny didn't want to insult any of her friends by not eating the food they'd so generously delivered. Good thing Granny didn't know about the garage freezer, which Joanna had emptied and delivered to the soup kitchen.

Still, Joanna was trying to spend more time at home. She hadn't been lying when she said she missed Granny. Talking on the phone was okay, but there was nothing quite like just being with her. It was the only good thing about Halikarnassus. Well, Granny and Trina. And she liked Chet's a lot. And Liam.

She stopped walking, and Starr gave her an annoyed look. "What, like you haven't been stopping every three feet to mark your territory?"

Because now, in addition to crushing on Clark Kent, she was also talking to the dog. In public.

"Hey."

Joanna yelped.

"Sorry. I thought you heard me running up," said Liam, all sweaty and breathing hard.

"No, I didn't hear you." She shouldn't sound so annoyed. But she was annoyed, dammit. *First he erotically invades my subconscious, then he gives me a damn heart attack in the middle of the road.* And he was wearing shorts.

Damn, Granny was right.

Oh, God, she thought. *This is it. This is where the cool police come and take away all your cool points and make you take up needlepoint.*

"How're you doing?" he asked, still running in place.

The nerve of him! To destroy her life, then be *nice* to her?

"I gotta go," she said and turned and walked away, pulling Starr behind her.

When she turned around, Liam was running in the other direction.

Good.

Good.

That was what she wanted.

Chapter Fourteen

Liam heard the barking even before he answered the doorbell. He opened the door to find Starr trying to bust a hole in his screen door with her little paws. Starr was attached to a giant bag of groceries, which was attached to Joanna.

This was a lot to take in. So he stood there, taking it in, while Starr continued to bust.

"Hi," Joanna said after a while, and Liam realized he had been staring at her. He didn't want to be rude; he just wasn't sure she was real. But she'd just spoken, so she had to be real, right?

"Hi," he said back. *Man, I hope she's real,* he thought.

"Um . . . I don't suppose you made other plans for dinner?"

Dinner. Oh, dinner. He knew about dinner. That was the meal he was going to start eating now. Well, as soon as he opened the box of mac and cheese.

"No . . ." He realized that he sounded skeptical. But, well. What was she doing here? Every time he saw Joanna, she acted like he'd done something to piss her off. Except for the times when she didn't, and they chatted and laughed like two people who were interested in getting to know each other. But the rest of the time . . .

"I just thought—Starr! Knock it off!" Starr did not knock it off.

"Come in, come in," Liam said. "Before Starr breaks down the door."

As soon as the door was open wide enough, Starr shot into the living room. Joanna dropped the leash with a curse, and the bag wasn't far behind. Liam threw the door the rest of the way open and reached for the grocery bag.

And ended up with a handful of Joanna's chest.

Well, this is awkward.

"Um," she said.

"Right," he said, whipping his hands away from her breasts and onto the grocery bag. "Let me help you with that."

She gave up the bag and, if he wasn't mistaken, gave a snort. He couldn't tell because he was headed into the house, where Starr sat on the back of the couch, panting happily. "Make yourself comfortable," he said.

"Wait, I'm supposed to—" She took the bag back from him. "I'm going to make you dinner."

"You are?"

"Why did you think I came over with a bag of groceries?" She raised an eyebrow. She was making fun of him.

"I thought you wanted me to do you a favor and mind my own business." He matched her, raised eyebrow to raised eyebrow.

"Yes, well. I may have been a little . . . listen, you shouldn't just run up to people in the street like that."

"Why not?"

"It's just . . . it's rude, that's all. It's rude to make conversation that early in the morning."

"And that night at Chet's?"

She blushed. He wasn't sure why, but she was definitely blushing.

"It's also rude to . . . Ugh." She hung her head, and he thought the grocery bag was done for. "I'm doing this wrong. Hold on."

She turned on her heel and went out the front door. Starr lifted her head from the couch but otherwise was not bothered by the fact that the person who had brought her over was now leaving.

Liam was bothered by it. Sure, Joanna had bitten his head off, but he still liked her. He was attracted to her and he was curious about her and she did things like tell him to mind his own business, then show up on his doorstep with a bag of groceries.

And her grandmother's dog.

The doorbell rang.

Starr gave a halfhearted bark.

"Some guard dog." Liam opened the front door, and there was Joanna. With her bag of groceries.

"Hi," she said brightly.

"Hi. Uh. This is a surprise?"

"I messed up the last time. I'm starting over. Okay, here we go." She threw her shoulders back. "Hi, Liam. Sorry I was such a bitch this morning—you kind of caught me off guard. Instead of running away like a weirdo, what I meant to say was, hi, you seem nice, I would very much enjoy having dinner with you this evening."

"Okay." He stepped back as she walked through the door.

"I thought, since I owe you a grovel, that I would cook for you."

"Okay, wow. Great." Then he saw her headed for his kitchen, which . . .

"Oh."

Yes. When Liam couldn't sleep, he watched home improvement shows. He couldn't sleep last night because of the town council and, okay, fine, Joanna, and then he was inspired to change his kitchen cabinets. And this afternoon, after Joanna brushed him off so coldly, he needed to burn off some frustrated energy, so he'd started.

He hadn't gotten much further than taking the doors off their hinges when he realized that this was a ridiculous idea because he barely used the kitchen, so what did it matter what it looked like? But when he tried to put the doors back on, they would not go. Somehow, in between his taking them down, grabbing a burger for lunch, and coming back home and to his senses, the hinges had shrunk. Or moved. Or done something.

So now he had no cabinet doors. Well, he had cabinet doors, they were just on the counters. And he had pretty crappy counter space to begin with.

Also, his dirty socks were on the floor. In his defense, they were very close to his washing machine. Still.

One of the things that didn't help was the sheer number of Hostess cake wrappers he had on the counter. In his defense, it was his favorite post-running snack. He just . . . he just liked them, that was all. A lot.

"Cute." Too late. She was already in there, putting the bag on the only spot on his already small countertop that was not covered in cabinet doors or junk food wrappers. She stuck her purse next to it.

"I was in the middle of cleaning," he lied, but made a beeline for the dishwasher anyway and started to put clean dishes away.

"I meant the pink."

Right. The pink. The primary reason for his nocturnal renovations. Maybe it did matter what his kitchen looked like. "You get used to it." And he had. It took a few months, but he was used to it. "You should see the bathroom."

He still was not quite used to the pink toilet.

She held up an empty cake wrapper.

"Guilty pleasure," he said, and grabbed it from her and started frantically collecting the rest of them. He shoved them in the garbage can under the sink, and when he turned back around, she was unpacking her bag.

Onions, mushrooms, zucchini . . . it looked like she had robbed a farm stand.

His stomach growled.

But wait. Had he even invited her in? How was she suddenly rooting through his kitchen drawers, pulling out knives and peelers and things he had forgotten he even had?

"I could have other plans, you know."

She froze, knife in midair.

He could have timed that better.

And the look on her face told him that she did not get the joke.

Also, the fact that she unfroze and started tossing the vegetables back in the bag, muttering apologies and curses.

"No! I was kidding. I don't have plans. Please, make me dinner."

She looked at him with narrowed eyes. "It's fine, I get it. I shouldn't have just—"

He grabbed her shoulders. "Please, Joanna. I want you to stay."

Well, that was definitely not open for interpretation.

Joanna tried to calm her gut instincts, which were still in the fight-and-also-flight mode she used in awkward situations. First, throw in a few angry jabs, then run away. It was her patented method of conflict resolution.

Well, not so much of resolution. But it was the best way she had found to deal with conflict.

Well, not the best way. But it was her way, dammit.

But then there was Liam. Liam who didn't react to her fight with more fight, and who expressed clearly and with words that he was not into her flight. Her guts were telling her that there was some trick here. People didn't just say what they meant. What was he, mature or something?

His eyes, at least, were sincere. And blue, and clear, like the desert sky. He had nice eyes, this librarian. And his eyes said they meant it. His were the eyes of a guy who did not have a lot of practice saying what people wanted to hear so he could get what he wanted.

Unusual eyes.

She took a deep breath, willing her guts to chill the fuck out. "Okay," she said. "Sorry about that."

"You don't have to apologize for my bad joke."

He let go of her, just when she was thinking it would be a good idea to lean into him. Of course, she was still holding a knife.

"So," he said, taking a further step from her toward the counter. "What culinary masterpiece do you have planned?" He lifted a set of . . . were those cabinet doors? Also, were those his biceps?

She shook off her haze of attraction. *Come on, Joanna. The librarian? Get real.*

"That's probably overstating it," she said.

"Masterpiece?"

"And planning. I just kind of bought what looked good. And pasta."

"I like pasta. And cheese," he added, holding up the block of pecorino.

"Well, good." She started unpacking the vegetables, briefly reconsidering the onion. But no. No reason to get her hopes up. What was she even thinking about, hopes?

Liam knew he shouldn't get too excited when he saw her hesitate with the onion. Because no onion meant good breath, which meant smoochin'. But that was ridiculous. She'd come over here to apologize and cook him dinner, not to make out. Besides, Joanna did not strike him as the sort of person to go for a subtle suggestion. He imagined that if she wanted to make out with him, she would grab him by the collar of his shirt and just—well. He didn't need to worry about that. Not when she was holding a knife.

Never mind the fact that watching her leaning

over the kitchen counter like that filled him with the sudden image of her there, waiting for him, wearing fewer pants.

"Are you gonna help, or just stand there and watch me?"

That was Real Joanna, not Naked Fantasy Joanna. He stepped up to the counter and awaited instructions.

Dinner wasn't terrible. She'd made the dish hundreds of times before. "Dish" was probably too formal a word for it. She just picked up whatever vegetables looked good, sautéed them, threw on some tomatoes and whatever Italian-ish cheese was on sale, and tossed it over pasta. Tonight it was zucchini and mushrooms and, in the end, onion. The pasta came out perfectly al dente, despite the fact that Liam, who was in charge of the pasta, was sort of dreamily watching her stir the veggie pan. If this guy had fantasies of domestic bliss, he was barking up the wrong tree.

And yet, she liked feeding him. She liked the appreciative sounds he made when he was eating, and she liked that he went back for seconds, and thirds. Nobody ate three helpings of something they were only pretending to like.

Now he leaned back in his chair with his eyes closed. "Can you come over and cook every night?"

She snorted. "This is pretty much my specialty. You'll get sick of it after a while."

"Doubt it." He leaned in and grabbed another

piece of bread to soak up the last drops of sauce on his plate.

"Maybe you should cook next time."

"Okay. I hope you like pizza."

"Homemade pizza? Love it."

"What if it's homemade in a pizza shop? And I pay the nice man who delivers it to us?"

She laughed. "Depends on the pizza shop."

"You look really pretty when you laugh."

She froze, fork in the air, mid-laugh. "Are you going to tell me I should smile more often?"

He held up his hands. "No. Just that you look pretty when you laugh."

"What the hell is that supposed to mean?"

"Uh. Just . . . that . . . you look pretty. When you laugh."

"Hmph." She shoved her forkful of food in her mouth before she got even madder. Because, really, it was a compliment. He couldn't know that people telling her to smile more was a major pet peeve.

"Will you kill me if I also tell you that you look really pretty when you scowl?"

"Maybe," she muttered.

"Okay. Then I won't."

"Good."

He was smiling at her. Usually when guys smiled at her prickliness, she felt patronized and, as a result, got even more prickly. Only Liam seemed to be, she didn't know, just enjoying watching. And he enjoyed talking to her. And he enjoyed her cooking.

Joanna's palms started to sweat. She looked for Starr, who would maybe need a walk or a swift return to the real world where people did not find her charming.

"So. Do you want to watch a movie or something?"

"A movie?"

"Yeah, or listen to some music?"

"Music?"

"Sorry, is that a sore subject?"

Oh, God, he knew, too. She shouldn't be surprised. With the entire town itching for her to fail, someone was bound to share it with the beloved librarian.

But, what? She wasn't ever going to listen to music again? Or talk about it?

"Okay, music. Anything but Bunny Slippers."

"Ha." He stood up, then took her hand and led her to the living room. Starr lifted her head, then put it back down again, apparently unfazed by the total weirdness of Liam holding her hand.

All the weirdness stopped when she looked up to see a massive bookcase. How had she missed that when she came in? Because it wasn't a bookcase at all. It was an entire wall of shelving, full of CDs and records.

"Whoa."

"I know. Trina built them for me."

Trina had? Why hadn't she said anything?

But then, why would she?

"What do you feel like listening to?"

"God, how will you find it?" She pulled out a record. Otis Redding. Cool. Then she looked closer at the collection. "Oh my God, are these in alphabetical order?"

"How else am I supposed to know where anything is?"

"I don't know, but I still want to laugh at you."

He threw his hand over his heart. "You wound me."

She bumped her hip with his. He didn't move away.

"Oh! How about this?" He leaned down and pulled a Patti Smith album out.

"Yes, I love her."

"You kind of remind me of her."

"And now I love you."

She was just joking, clearly. She didn't love him. But that didn't stop her from looking at him a little too long, to see what he would say.

"My plan worked," he said, and he turned to put the record on.

Six hours and many records later, Joanna started to feel tired. She looked over at Liam, leaning into the corner of the couch, eyes closed, Starr on his lap.

He'd been like that for a while. She'd thought he was getting into the Magnetic Fields, but maybe he was just asleep.

"Hey." She gave his knee a gentle shake. He bolted up. Yup, definitely asleep. "I'm gonna go."

"Okay." He rubbed his hand across his face. "Okay. God, sorry about that."

Part of her—a big part of her, the part with hormones—wanted to suggest that, *hey, maybe I could just stay.*

Wouldn't that be perfect? Troublemaker Joanna comes home and throws herself at the poor, innocent librarian.

"Come on, Starr. Let's go for a walk."

"You walked?"

Joanna shrugged. "I know kung fu." She winked and punched his arm.

"It's kind of late."

Ha. Clark was such a city boy. She hooked Starr onto her leash and waited while the dog finished a massive yawn-and-stretch. Then she opened the door, turning just to give him a parting joke. "This is Halikarnassus. All of the criminals are long abed."

"Or they're about to get up. It is technically morning." He followed her out the door, shutting it behind him.

"I can take care of myself." She started walking. He started walking beside her. She guessed that meant he was walking her home.

"Oh, I have no doubt of that. But don't you want my big, intimidating presence to ward off any would-be attackers? So you won't even have to take care of yourself."

"You better take off your glasses for that, Clark."

"Clark?"

"Uh . . . nothing." Oops. That was supposed to be an inside-only joke.

"You do know my name is Liam, right?"

She shoved him playfully. He barely broke his stride.

Strong librarian.

"Yes. Liam Byrd." *It's a Byrd, it's a plane . . .*

A short, companionable silence fell between them.

"Not gonna tell me?"

Joanna kept her mouth shut. For once.

But only because she did not want to admit to any fantasy life involving the hot, strong librarian with excellent taste in music.

Man, in her dreams, though. He was a great kisser.

She was so lost in her thoughts of dream-kissing Liam the Librarian that she barely noticed climbing up the three steps to Granny's front door.

"Hey," she said stupidly. "We're here."

"Where did you think we were going?" His eyes were all scrunched up in confusion, but he was smiling. Damn, he was cute.

Good thing she didn't do cute.

Except in her dreams.

Sigh.

"And see? My tall, manly presence warded off potential attackers."

"You can't prove that."

"Did you get murdered on the way home?"

"You have a point. I am alive."

He bowed gallantly.

"This isn't going to be a thing, is it?"

"Chivalry?"

She gave him a bitch-please look. "You're not going to, like, make me your personal mission? To save me from myself so you'll be sure I never walk home alone again? Because I laugh in the face of danger, but really it's because I can tell when there's danger, and there has probably never been danger in Halikarnassus."

"Uh . . ."

She opened the front door to let Starr in before she barked the whole neighborhood awake. "Because I can take care of myself, you know. Everyone has this idea that because I was a screwup in high school, I'm automatically an incompetent adult. Just because I'm not 'financially successful,' it doesn't mean I can't cross a baseball field at night. I've crossed that field hundreds of times, and I'm sober this time." Her rant was spiraling quickly into a pity party, and as she spoke, she couldn't seem to stop it. "God, you break a few rules when you're sixteen and you're an incompetent for the rest of your life. That's why I hate this town. That's why I never wanted to come back here. It's been ten years, ten years! Do you know how much can change in ten years? A lot! A lot changes! If other people can get married and have kids, why can't I—"

Her rant was abruptly stopped by Liam's mouth.

This was good because she was getting majorly off track with her point about . . . well, she couldn't remember the point. It took her about three seconds to go from rant to surprise to OMG. His lips were gentle, but they were packing some kind of wallop. He had her face cupped between his big hands, and she tilted with his guidance, letting the kiss deepen. She was just reaching for his arms to steady herself.

And then he was gone.

"Sorry. Oh, God, sorry." He was flushed and his eyes were dark and his hair was flopping across his forehead and Joanna had never been into cute before but this guy was seriously changing her mind.

"Whu?" she asked. In stopping her ranty spiral, he had also robbed her of all speech.

That kiss. That was . . . that was even better than Dream Liam. And Dream Liam was pretty damn great.

"You were talking. That was rude. But I . . . uh. I don't have a good explanation, I just kept watching your lips and—"

Joanna knew the start of a good verbal spiral when she saw one. And maybe it was rude of him to kiss her instead of listening to her babble about the same old shit she always complained about. But mostly she was just concerned that that was going to be their only kiss, that short, intense, midsentence kiss. They could do so much better.

So she threw herself at him.

He caught her, his arms going tight around her waist as she flung hers around his neck. He recovered fast, that Liam, and before she could tell him to shut up, his mouth was on hers again, hot and insistent, and she battled his tongue as it snaked into her mouth. His hands at her waist tightened and she shifted her pelvis up and into his. He moaned, or she moaned, somebody made some kind of noise.

And then the porch lights came on.

And Starr started barking.

Joanna stepped back, grateful that Liam kept his hands on her hips because she was pretty sure that was the only thing holding her up right now. She wanted to melt into a puddle of desire, and she guessed by the dark look in Liam's eyes that he was totally willing to take a dive in.

She was about to suggest that she walk him home, for safety, when the front door opened and there was Gran, balancing on her crutches and squinting out into the night.

"Jo Jo?" she asked, confused and rumpled. Joanna marveled at how fast burning desire could cool to molten shame. She still wanted to melt into a puddle, but this was more a disappearing puddle. Anything so her grandmother, disheveled and confused by sleep, wasn't standing at the door in her nightgown watching her grope the librarian.

"Gran, you should be in bed." Joanna opened the screen door, edging around Liam to get hold of her grandmother before she noticed.

"Starr was barking."

"Starr barks at everything," Joanna said with more levity than she felt. Since she felt no levity at all. Just melting.

"Is there someone else out there?" Gran asked, leaning around Joanna's shoulder. Joanna caught her before she tipped herself over.

"Hi, Peggy," Liam said and Joanna wanted to kick him. Instead, she shot him a dirty look. He just shrugged. And he looked cute doing it, damn him.

"Liam? What are you doing here! Come in for a cup of tea, won't you?"

"No, Liam was just leaving."

"But what is he doing here?" Gran asked Joanna. "Why are you blushing?"

This was definitely not a conversation Joanna ever wanted to have with her grandmother, the one where she explained that she was in fact a sexual being and she was being a sexual being with the librarian on the front porch. She especially didn't want to have the conversation on said front porch, with the door open and the lights on for all the neighbors to see, with said partner sexual being standing awkwardly by with a pretty visible erection.

There had been plenty of times in Joanna's life when she was wrongfully ungrateful for Gran's hospitality. Glancing down at the crotch she was just shamelessly grinding against, she realized this was another one of those times.

She shot Liam an apologetic look and closed the door gently in his bemused face. Hopefully, Gran would just forget all about this by the time it was actually morning.

Ha.

Chapter Fifteen

"You're up early," Gran said to Joanna as she stumbled into the kitchen. Gran, Joanna noticed through bleary eyes, was neatly dressed and had clearly been up long enough to brew a pot of coffee. Joanna knew for a fact she was not up early.

She also knew, based on Gran's smirking tone, that the woman had not forgotten last night. Which meant that this time, the kiss was not just a dream and that Liam was, potentially, an actual sex machine. It also meant that Granny was going to give her so much shit about it.

Also, Joanna felt like she had a hangover.

It wasn't like she'd had that much to drink last night. A few beers with dinner, which was nothing for her, even in her new nunlike existence in Halikarnassus. And she'd drunk a big glass of water after she'd put Gran back to bed. Then she'd let the dog out again. Then she'd drunk more water. Then she ate some toast. Then she flipped through channels on TV. Then she peeked in on Granny, who was snoring like a champ. So was Starr.

Then she wiped up the nonexistent crumbs on the kitchen counter. She straightened a pile of books in the living room. She fluffed the throw pillows. She came back to the kitchen and thought about organizing the junk drawer. She realized that she was not the sort of person who took pleasure in organization, so she took herself to bed where she did what she had been avoiding all night, which was staring at the ceiling, thinking about how good Liam's hands felt on her waist and how good they would probably feel all over the rest of her.

She was just hard up, that was all. She got tons of booty in LA. That was one of the benefits of being in a band. Guys thought it was cool to bang a chick who could play guitar, and she got her rocks off without anyone getting too mushy about it.

That was all she was doing with Liam. She was trying to relive a little of that rock-star cool she used to have, back when she was in a cool band and not a total failure who was so concerned with not selling out that she was now living in her childhood bedroom in a town she hated. Liam was into music, and he clearly liked the idea that she played.

The only thing missing was her actually getting her rocks off. Nothing like a little Grandmother Interruptus to spoil the mood.

Spoiled it in her brain. Her body needed some convincing. Even this morning, faced with a bright-eyed, clearly curious Gran, Joanna's body couldn't quite forget that she had some unfinished business with Liam and his hands.

Whoever said you can't go home again was wrong. You can go home again. It's just always a terrible idea.

Not that being home didn't have its benefits. Gran, for example. And if no one was around to hear her say it, Starr, who was watching Joanna from atop the pile of newly fluffed throw pillows.

Joanna took the mug of coffee Gran pushed across the island to her.

"You shouldn't be doing this stuff," Joanna scolded. It didn't carry much weight, though, tinged as it was with her gratitude for the ready-made coffee.

Gran waved off Joanna's halfhearted scolding and hobbled to her crutches, leaning against the counter. "I am capable of making coffee, you know."

Joanna took a sip of the coffee. It was too hot, just the way she liked it. It burned on the way down her throat, waking up her internal organs.

Fortified enough to be helpful, she picked Starr's leash up off the island. "I'm taking her for a w-a-l-k."

Starr looked up from her cushion on the living room floor, ready to bolt. Starr hated her morning walk. It was bad enough that her warm Gran-body pillow woke her up by moving, and she was only happy again when she could retire to her living room cushion that caught the morning sun. The fact that she had to bear the indignity of taking several extra steps—attached to a leash, no less—was an interruption to her morning routine that she did not suffer easily. Left to her own devices, she would hide under the bed. Joanna had learned that you had to sneak up on her, and you could not say the word "walk" or she'd dart into the bedroom and not come out.

The dog must have a bladder of steel, Joanna thought. Or just a will of iron that let her quest for sunny comfort outweigh her need to go to the bathroom. Or she went in the house in a place neither of them had discovered yet.

Joanna was really starting to love this crafty, cranky dog.

"I took her out already," Gran said as she made her way to the couch while Starr kept a watchful eye on her in case the possibility of a lap to sit in appeared. It did, and Starr abandoned her sunny spot for Gran's lap.

"Gran! How?"

"Oh, don't worry, I didn't take her on a marathon. I just let her out the back door."

"What if you got tangled in her leash? What if she tripped you?" Starr had a hilarious habit of bolting to or away from any potential stimulant, which usually resulted in the walker being tangled in tiny dog leash. It was a safety hazard, clearly. And Joanna wasn't on crutches.

"I don't know what you're talking about. She's a perfect lady, aren't you, Miss Starr?"

Starr lifted her head to receive her lady-ear scratches.

Joanna shook her head. "You're going to hurt yourself—again."

"Drink your coffee, crabby pants," Gran told her.

"I'm not crabby," Joanna mumbled, crabbily. But she did as she was told, then went to refill her mug. "How about some breakfast?"

Gran didn't say anything. Joanna looked at the

empty plate in the sink and the dirty pan on the stove.

"Gran."

"Hmm?"

"Were you cooking?"

"No!"

"You're supposed to be resting!"

"I am! Look! I'm even elevating my leg!" She shifted around to lean against the arm of the couch, her leg perched on a pile of pillows. Starr held onto her lap for dear life, and was not displaced.

Joanna watched the dance, amused until she saw Gran wince. "Here, let me," she said, moving into the living room to fluff Gran's pillows. Since she was Halikarnassus's premier pillow fluffer.

"Thank you, sweetheart."

Joanna sat on the coffee table and faced her grandmother. This was her third official week as Gran's nurse. So far, Gran had allowed her to help with precisely nothing. She needed to have a talk with the woman if she was ever going to recover.

But Gran was pale and a slight sheen of sweat was forming on her brow, so Joanna had mercy.

A little bit of mercy.

"Gran," she started.

"I know, I know, I overdid it."

"Yes. You need to rest so you can recover; then you can go back to your superhuman feats of strength."

"I hate just sitting here. I'm fine!"

"You are not fine."

"It's just my leg. Everything else is fine."

"Gran—"

"You know I can't sit still. Am I supposed to—"

"Because sometimes life isn't fair, buttercup," Joanna told her, just like Gran had told her so many times when she was a kid, railing against the rules and common sense that meant she couldn't do whatever she wanted whenever she wanted to.

That got Gran to smile. She reached over and squeezed Joanna's hand. "You're a good girl, you know that?"

"Your pain is making you delirious."

"I'm glad you're here."

"Me, too," Joanna said, squeezing Gran's hand back. In that moment, she almost meant it. "Now let me give you something for the pain."

"You just want me to stop complaining."

"I'm not going to lie," Joanna said, getting up to grab the pills from Gran's bedroom. "That is a pleasant side effect."

When she got back to the couch, Gran took the pills and the glass of water without complaint, which was how Joanna knew Gran was really hurting. She took the empty glass back and fluffed her pillows again, which was her duty as the reigning expert. "Better?"

"Thank you."

"Good. Now can I leave you to take a shower, or are you going to start moving furniture as soon as I leave the room?"

"I did have some ideas . . . no. I promise. I'll be good."

"Good."

"And when you've showered, you can come down and tell me all about what you were doing on the porch with Liam last night."

Damn. She almost got away with it.

"Rest," Joanna ordered her grandmother, and she escaped to take a shower.

Liam fumbled twice with his keys before he got the door to the library unlocked.

"'Morning, boss."

He turned to find Marcel, the night janitor, on the other side of the door.

"Hi, Marcel."

"Something wrong with your key?"

"No, just my head. You're still here?"

"Mimi had a night off, so I came in early instead of overnight. That's okay, right?"

Marcel's wife worked as an overnight home health care nurse, relieving the dinner shift for clients who required round-the-clock care. They also both had day jobs, and Liam knew that a precious night off meant the rare dinner and a movie date for the couple. And more, which Marcel often hinted at with wiggling eyebrows. Liam didn't need to know the details of the sex life of his night janitor, or any of his employees, really, but he certainly didn't begrudge the guy a little spontaneous schedule adjustment. Especially since he knew Marcel would never leave a job half-done. This wasn't the first morning he'd come in to find Marcel on his way out the door, but it had been a while. It was good to see the old man smiling.

"It's no problem. Whatever you need to do—"

"So long as the job gets done. Got it, boss."

It was Liam's management mantra, one that had

taken the staff a little while to get used to. Mrs. Pratt had been more of a benevolent-ish dictator. Liam didn't have it in him to look over people's shoulders every second of the day.

Besides, who was Liam to begrudge anyone a little smooching? Especially since he himself was here a little late, and a little worse for wear?

He'd tried to go to bed as soon as he got home last night. But no matter how many times he brushed his teeth, he just couldn't get the taste of Joanna out of his mouth.

That sounded a little gross, now that he thought about it. It didn't feel gross last night. It felt hot. And a little frustrating.

And to be honest, a little embarrassing. When was the last time he got caught making out? High school, at least. And on Peggy's front porch? God. He'd never live this down.

Maybe she'd forget. Maybe she was high on pain-killers and didn't notice who Joanna was making out with.

Ha. Or maybe he could deal with the reality of Halikarnassus and get used to the idea that, by the time the library was open to the public, everyone would know that he and the town badass were caught making out like teenagers by her ailing grand-mother.

"I got another supply order ready for you," Marcel told him, waking Liam from his shame reverie.

"Great, I'll do that today."

"Goin' through a lot of toilet paper."

Liam sighed. He was well aware that spare rolls of toilet paper left out in the bathrooms often went missing before they could be put to good public use. But he just couldn't bring himself to keep it behind the service desk, as Mrs. Pratt had. That felt . . . well, that didn't feel like good public service.

Besides, he'd rather people stole rolls of cheap, institutional toilet paper than DVDs. And since DVD theft had gone down since he'd started hiring the after-school kids to shelve instead of making them pretend to do homework while they generally caused adolescent mayhem, he'd happily spend a little extra on supplies.

Who said being the boss wasn't glamorous?

"Thanks, Marcel."

"Okay, boss. See you later."

"Any chance you'll call me Liam?"

Marcel clapped Liam on the shoulder. "Naw, man. You're the boss."

"Say hi to Mimi for me."

Marcel waved and then Liam was alone in the library.

He knew it wouldn't be for long. The summer reading program kickoff party was today, and Toni was always a mess of nerves that something terrible would go wrong. It never did—Toni could plan the hell out of an event, with backup plans for backup plans. All Liam had to do was await instructions, follow said instructions, and everything would be great. He barely had to use his brain, which was good because his brain was having a hell of a time focusing on anything other than the feel of Joanna's mouth on his, her hips pressed into his . . .

"Morning, Liam."

Liam practically jumped out of his skin.

"Sorry," Toni said. "I thought you heard me honk when I pulled in."

He took a box overflowing with streamers and balloons from her. "Just a little out of it this morning."

"Well, get back into it—it's gonna be nuts today."

"Yes, ma'am." He followed her back to the children's area and awaited further instruction.

Chapter Sixteen

Everywhere she looked, there were . . . children.

Were there even this many children in Halikarnassus? Were they being bussed in for some secret library-destroying project? Had Hal sicced them on poor Liam?

This was a terrible day to bring Gran back to the library. Not that Joanna had brought her. It was more like Joanna was being held hostage and forced to drive Gran's boat while Gran complained that if she didn't leave the house, she was either going to die of cabin fever or kill Joanna. So, really, this was a lifesaving mission. For both of them.

Except who were all these children?

Joanna hovered near Gran, even though Gran hated hovering. The woman had refused a wheelchair and was hobbling around on a walking cast with a cane. At least she had a weapon she could use to defend herself, should the mini-hordes become too unruly.

"Aren't they just precious?" Gran asked Joanna.

Joanna assumed it was rhetorical. They were not precious. They were loud. Ear-piercing. And Joanna used to be a rock star. She should know from ear-piercing.

"Why're there so many of them?"

"Peggy!"

As if this day couldn't get any worse, there was the literal man of her dreams, standing in front of them in jeans and a T-shirt that said SPLISH SPLASH READ.

He looked good in blue.

Not that she cared.

Although there was a big part of her that wanted to jump in his arms so they could pick up where they'd left off last night. Probably not appropriate in front of all these children.

Joanna stepped back as Liam leaned in to give Peggy a hug, which seemed very unprofessional to her. Because Joanna Green was definitely the arbiter of professional behavior.

"I'm so glad you're up and moving," he told Gran.

"I'm glad you're wearing pants," Joanna muttered.

"Sorry?"

"Nothing. Hi, Liam."

"Hey, Joanna. Peggy, can I get you a chair or something? It's a little chaotic here today."

"Oh, pish, I'm fine. I just came to browse the new books."

"Oh! Great! I thought of the perfect book for you this morning when I was shelving. Let me grab it for you. Atticus! Walk, please!" Liam's excellent customer service was interrupted by a moppet torpedo who threatened Gran's stability.

"Maybe I should sit down," Gran said, and of course

she did. She did what Liam said. He'd only caused her to break her leg with his hotness. What her own granddaughter suggested didn't mean anything at all.

Liam shooed a set of twins out of the nearest comfy chair and ushered Gran into it. Joanna stood by, bouncing on her heels. Maybe she could go, since Gran was being so well taken care of. Except she sort of wanted to see the book Liam picked out for Gran. Also, she was trying to be a good granddaughter. Abandoning Gran in this chaos was probably not a great move.

"Who are all these kids?"

"Joanna," Gran scolded.

"School's out and summer reading begins today," Liam explained. "We're having a big party. Well, Toni is having a big party. I'm just helping."

"Oh, summer reading! Joanna, you used to love that."

Great. Next thing she knew, Gran would pull out pictures of her naked in a bathtub.

Actually, Joanna had a few recent ones of those. Huh. Full circle and stuff.

"Yeah," she said noncommittally as a child wailed in her ear.

"I should get back," Liam said. "Toni has a bunch of volunteers, but . . ."

"Mr. Liam!"

"Oof," he grunted, as his abdomen was struck by several flying children. "Yes, I should go."

"Liam! There you are."

"Toni? What's wrong?"

The children's librarian looked . . . well, she

looked frazzled. There was no more polite way to say it, even with Joanna's new personality.

"Bouncing Bob isn't coming."

"What?"

"Who?"

"Bouncing Bob, the guy who's supposed to sing goofy but educational songs to entertain all these hooligans," Toni explained.

"Why isn't he coming? He signed a contract," Liam said. His face looked hard and serious. Joanna hadn't thought his face was capable of it. Must be his Director Face.

"He had a heart attack."

"Oh."

"He's not dead. Just in the hospital."

"And we're just finding out now?"

"Well, he is in the hospital."

"Joanna is a musician," Gran said from her comfortable chair.

Oh no. No no no no no no no. Joanna was a musician, sure, but she'd given up on music. And even if she hadn't, she didn't know any goofy but educational songs. All the songs she knew were about sex and heartbreak. Which could be educational, she thought, but probably not what Toni had in mind.

"Yes! Joanna!" Toni exclaimed, looking at Joanna as if she was the second coming of Bouncing Bob.

"I don't have a guitar," Joanna said, relieved to have found an excuse in her back pocket.

"I have one. It's pretty crappy. I usually just use it for storytime."

"Joanna learned to play on a pretty crappy guitar," Gran said, helpfully.

"I don't know any songs that are rated G."

"Can you just make something up?"

"You used to make up songs all the time," Gran said. Really, really helpful. "Remember that one you used to sing to Doris's cat? How did it go? 'Where'd you get such a fluffy fluffy butt, fluffy fluffy butt, fluffy fluffy butt—'"

"I remember! Jeez, Granny," she said, sounding nothing at all like a petulant child. Maybe she should stamp her feet and throw herself on the floor, go full-on temper tantrum.

"Toni, she's not prepared. Can't you just play?" Liam, bless him, jumped in to her defense.

Except why did he think she couldn't do it? She could totally do it. She grew up improvising fluffy dog butt songs.

"They didn't come here to see *me*," Toni said desperately.

"Well, we're not going to be able to pretend that Joanna is Bouncing Bob."

"Who's going to corral the volunteers and sign the kids up and prepare the snacks and . . ."

"I can do that," Liam said.

"Then who's going to watch the rest of the library? Please, Liam, don't make a stressed-out pregnant woman cry."

Liam turned to Joanna. "Are you sure this is okay?"

Joanna didn't remember agreeing to do anything, so she wasn't quite sure what Liam wanted her to confirm.

"Joanna," Toni said, looking desperately into Joanna's eyes. "Joanna. I hate to use the hormonal card twice in one conversation, but I am very pregnant and very stressed and I need someone to sing stupid songs to these kids. At this point, I don't care what you sing, as long as you don't curse. Please. I'm begging you. Don't make a pregnant woman get on her knees and beg."

"Oh, you don't have to beg," Gran said from her comfortable chair where she was not being asked to suddenly play songs she didn't know in front of a crowd of hyped-up kids.

Toni looked at Joanna beseechingly.

Gran looked at her hopefully.

Liam looked at her like he was getting ready to tell Toni that her beseeching looks weren't going to work.

Joanna took a deep breath.

"Fine. I'll do it."

Liam hadn't thought Joanna could sing.

He still wasn't quite sure.

Bouncing Bob was supposed to come with his own PA system, so he and Toni set Joanna up with the crappy one they used for author talks and board meetings, the one that he was currently writing a grant for the money to replace.

It didn't do much to amplify her voice. This might have been a good thing.

Except that the kids were getting restless. It was still pouring rain outside, so the only place for them to burn off that last-day-of-school energy was by bouncing along to Bob, or, in this case, Miss Joanna and her Magical Guitar.

One thing that did not help was that the first thing Joanna said when she got up to the mic was, "This guitar isn't magical, you guys."

Maybe she still had anxiety about performing. Her meltdown had been pretty spectacular—or so he'd heard. He still hadn't watched the video, no matter how sorely he'd been tempted.

It felt a little different now, watching the breaker-upper struggle with a crowd of unruly children.

He was tempted to step in. Toni, who was supposed to be working on all the other stuff she needed to do, was standing at the back of the room, nervously biting her fingernails. That wasn't a good sign. Liam half expected her to run up on stage and rip the guitar out of Joanna's hands.

If she didn't, he might.

"You suck!"

The crowd was definitely getting restless, as evidenced by the fact that one of the older boys was being heartily shushed by his mother. But the heckle seemed to do something to Joanna. It was like she woke up from her nervous stupor. All it took was someone to tell her she sucked, and she came alive.

"Hey, guys," she said into the mic, and her voice sounded clear and strong.

"Uh-oh," said Peggy, who had hobbled up next to him.

He was distracted by getting Peggy a chair, so he didn't quite hear what Joanna said next, but it must have been hilarious because every kid in the audience was cracking up. The parents, not so much. He was definitely going to get angry e-mails about this.

"How many of you have a dog?"

About half of the kids raised their hands.

"Yeah, me too. Well, it's my gran's dog, but she's pretty cute. How many of you sing songs to your dog?"

Pretty much the same hands stayed up.

"Here's a little song for my gran's dog. It's all about my favorite part of her, her fluffy butt."

The eyes of a good portion of the parents in the audience went wide—apparently "butt" was not a very nice word—but the kids were suddenly rapt. A grown-up singing about dog butts. This, they could get into.

The song . . . well, it wasn't terrible. Certainly it wasn't any worse than the greatest hits of Bunny Slippers. It was maybe even a little more intelligent. It used metaphors and clever rhyme schemes, and lots and lots of repetition of the phrase "fluffy butt." With every rousing chorus, more of the kids joined in, and soon the entire library was singing its devotion to Starr's fluffy butt.

"Well, that's the only song I know that's not about making out," Joanna said.

"Eww!" said every preadolescent in the crowd. Liam caught Toni's look of abject horror. She, too, could imagine the angry parental e-mails.

A little girl in the front of the crowd said something Liam couldn't hear and Joanna said, "Oh, really? You wanna come up here and sing it?" Then the girl was taking the one step up to the stage while Joanna fiddled with the fragile mic stand so it was kid-height.

Liam couldn't hear most of what was so song-worthy about the little girl's cat—he had to show someone how to use the copier—but what he could hear sounded remarkably like Starr's Fluffy Butt song. Which was good, he supposed, since Joanna already knew that one.

Then Mrs. Altman needed help printing out pictures of Whitney Houston (again) and he helped Mr. Johnson find a Jack Reacher book he hadn't read yet, and before he knew it, the hour had practically passed and there was still raucous music coming from the children's room. So either Joanna was still playing on the stage or the PA system had been taken over by the audience.

He poked his head around the corner. It was both. The stage was full of kids, so many that there were barely any left in the audience. The grown-ups were close to the stage, too, clapping along. He saw Trina up front, waving her hands along with the beat.

Joanna was there somewhere, he was sure. He could hear the guitar, barely, over the din of little voices. Then the sea of stage children parted, and Joanna emerged, leaning into the crappy acoustic guitar while her fingers flew over the strings. Liam couldn't help the smile that crossed his face or the bob that dipped his head. Even on a barely-in-tune piece of junk, on a stage covered with children she professed to dislike, she was wailing.

Then she threw her head back, raised the guitar above her head, and howled. The kids howled with her. He was definitely going to get some angry e-mails about the ruckus, but he didn't care. The kids were having a great time, and he'd bet none of them would ever forget the time they were rock stars at the library. Then Joanna let her guitar down, grabbed the mic, and shouted, "Don't forget to read!" and he could have kissed her.

Instead, he just girded the circulation desk for the onslaught of checkouts to Halikarnassus's newest batch of budding rock stars.

Chapter Seventeen

"You were amazing!"

Joanna was starting to get embarrassed at the way Toni kept following her around the children's room, rehashing her favorite moments of the impromptu concert that had happened literally five minutes ago. Fortunately, they were interrupted by frequent hugs and high fives from her new adoring fans. Joanna even signed a few autographs.

This was always her least favorite part of rock stardom—the stardom part that took away from the rock part. Sure, she wasn't the most famous member of Bunny Slippers—well, maybe now she was—but there was still an element of fan schmoozing and adoration that she just could not get behind. She just wanted to play.

She missed playing.

That was the only way to explain that the most public fun she had had since she'd moved back to Halikarnassus was on a stage taken over by rock moppets singing about fluffy butts. There was something about the innocence of their anarchy that made her nostalgic for when she used to be an actual badass, before her band sold out and then watched that bridge as it burned to the ground.

"You should consider playing children's music," Toni said, and Joanna was very proud of herself for not laughing in the poor woman's face. "A lot of rock stars are doing it now, you know."

"I think this was just a one-time thing," Joanna said.

"Even if I get hundreds of requests to have you back?"

"Even if all the kids in the town offer to sell their souls to rock and roll for the chance to hear me play again."

"See? Even that sounds like a rock song! You have to!"

"No."

"Fine. At least let me thank you in some way."

"Oh, Joanna, that was wonderful!" Granny hobbled up from the back of the room, weaving her way around discarded juice boxes. "I knew you could do it."

"You always knew I could entertain a crowd of toddlers."

"You can be as sarcastic as you want to be." Granny leaned in and kissed her cheek. "I'm still proud of you."

"Thanks, Gran."

"Now will you convince her to come back?" Toni asked.

Granny snorted. "Honey, if I could convince Joanna to do anything . . ."

"It's true," Joanna said. "I'm an adult woman."

"Can I treat you to lunch?" Toni asked. "I'd say

dinner, but we have a deal that while I'm pregnant, my husband cooks, and I want to take advantage of that. I would invite you over, but . . . he's still learning."

"Calvin always was such a sweetheart," Gran said.

"Really, it's fine," Joanna said. "It was just a favor. Let's just . . . let's just pretend it never happened."

"I don't know if you realize the long memory that children have. We'll be hearing fluffy butt songs for months. And when you invited them onstage? Girl, you made them feel like rock stars. They won't forget that any time soon."

"It was amazing." Liam came up from behind her and joined the group. She stiffened. She didn't know why. He didn't make her nervous or anything. "Best accident ever."

"Yes, I'm so glad Bouncing Bob had a heart attack," Joanna said.

"Oh, that's not what he meant and you know it," Gran said, ruining Joanna's perfect moment of ruining Liam's moment.

"Did Toni talk to you about payment? We did budget a performer for this."

Joanna tried to picture what Gran's face would look like if she took money from the public library. Then she looked over at Gran, and she didn't have to imagine. There it was. "No, it's fine, really. It was just a one-time, volunteer thing that will never happen again."

"Even though you were a huge hit?" Toni asked.

"Especially because I was a huge hit." That was how the whole trouble started with Bunny Slippers. They became a huge hit, then they became terrible.

Only they didn't notice because they were too busy being a huge hit.

She was done selling out.

Even if it meant living with her grandmother in a town she hated.

At least she wasn't playing gigs for kids' parties.

She wasn't that desperate.

Yet.

"Let us buy you dinner, at least," Liam said. "We're closing in a couple of hours, and I don't know about you guys, but I could use a beer."

"Hmm. I could definitely use a beer," Joanna agreed. A beer or two or six. Even though this wasn't a real gig, she was starting to feel the post-gig adrenaline crash. Always best to pour a little booze on that.

"No beer for me," Toni said, patting her baby stomach. "And no dinner for me, either. Calvin's cooking."

"I'm wiped out," Gran said. "You kids go. Joanna can take me home and you can come pick her up?" she asked Liam.

Jesus. Granny was trying to set her up with the librarian.

Probably just so she could look at his legs more often.

Yikes. That was a terrible thought.

Either way, this was decidedly not a date.

"I'll just meet you," Joanna said with a pointed look at Gran. "Where?"

"Um . . ." he said, clearly thinking. Smooth guy, this librarian.

Not.

Oh, God, her inner monologue was reverting to her teenage sense of humor.

She needed a beer.

"How about that new place on Main?" Toni asked. "I've never been there, but I heard it's great."

"Uh . . ." said Liam, clearly trying to think of a way out of it. Joanna tried to think of what the new place on Main was.

"The Wine Bar?" she asked. "I thought we were getting a beer."

Toni waved away her objections. "You deserve something more fabulous than beer. Besides, you refuse to be a rock star, so you might as well go classy. Right, Liam?"

Joanna tried to ignore the pained look on Liam's face, but there it was. No matter how much she saved his great ass, going to a fancy wine bar with the town troublemaker was clearly not high on the library director's list of Friday Night Fun.

Well, screw him. He was going to take her out, dammit. He was going to buy her a damn drink.

"Right," he said, then turned to face Joanna. "Right."

One of the things that Liam loved about upstate New York was the food. He grew up in places where "greasy spoon" meant you sent your plate back to the chef. Here, he could get eggs and hash browns any time of the day, or the best burger in the world, or grape leaves and hummus with a cannoli for dessert, all in the same place.

This was not the case with the Wine Bar.

At the Wine Bar, one could have wine and a small plate of vegetables cut into fancy shapes without taking out a second mortgage on one's house, but that was about it. He tried not to think about how there was perfect French onion soup at Hallie's, and Hallie's also served beer, which he preferred to wine, just like he preferred not wearing a tie, which he would never have to wear at Hallie's. Ties reminded him of board meetings. This was supposed to be fun.

If the look on his companion's face was any indication, he was going to have to have enough fun for both of them tonight.

But, no, it wasn't about fun. It was about gratitude. Joanna had saved their butts totally and completely this afternoon. As they walked toward the bar in the back of the restaurant, several people had stopped him and told him how much fun their kids or grandkids had had at the library party today. He only got one complaint about the repeated use of the word "butt," and the parent was assuaged by the fact that Liam assured him Joanna would never perform at the library again. Not by Liam's choice, of course. In fact, Liam had hoped to use tonight to persuade Joanna to give summer music another go. Maybe if she had time to learn some nonanatomical songs . . .

"When I was in Italy, someone told me to always order the house red because it was usually the best. Do you think that will work here?" Joanna said when they finally reached the bar.

"You were in Italy?"

"On tour."

"Wow, I didn't realize you toured internationally."

"Don't get too excited. It was the same as our tours here, before we got big. Crappy rented van, sleeping on people's couches, that kind of thing."

"But still."

Joanna shrugged. "It was fun."

"And the house red?"

"Always the best. Of course, I'm no wine snob."

"Good," Liam said, with what he hoped was not a ton of enthusiasm. He was the library director, and his pay was okay, but the idea of spending a high percentage of his disposable income on a glass of wine was not appealing to him. No matter how grateful he was to Joanna.

The Wine Bar was the only restaurant in Halikarnassus that had a dress code. No jeans, no hats, jackets and ties strongly suggested. So Liam, not wanting to cause a scene, wore a jacket and tie and non-jean pants.

Joanna . . . well, she wasn't wearing jeans.

She was, however, wearing leggings with a hole in the knee, a very short black skirt, and motorcycle boots that, while kick-ass, definitely did not meet the unspoken sartorial criteria for the Wine Bar.

She looked really hot.

Not that Liam was thinking about that, of course. This was a professional obligation, a thank-you-for-your-service meal. He did question Toni about her choice of venue—he didn't take any of the other volunteers out for drinks. But Joanna liked drinks, Toni explained, and she wasn't a regular volunteer. She was a lifesaver. She deserved a fancy drink.

If Liam was a suspicious kind of guy, he might have thought that Toni was trying to set him up with Joanna.

Good thing he wasn't a suspicious kind of guy.

Besides, even if Toni was playing matchmaker,

Liam didn't think his fragile ego could take another rejection from badass Joanna Green.

Despite how much that short skirt made him want to try.

Good thing this was work-related. Otherwise he would really make a cake of himself, as Georgette Heyer said.

"Thanks again for this afternoon."

"Seriously, if you thank me one more time, I'm going to pour this overpriced glass of wine over your head."

"Please don't do that."

"I won't. It's delicious."

"I appreciate that."

"Well, I'm a really good person, it turns out."

"You keep saying stuff like that," Liam said. "Why?"

"Why what?"

"Why should I be surprised that you're a good person?"

"Wow. Maybe my reputation doesn't precede me."

"Oh, it absolutely does. Did you know I was encouraged to bar you from the library?"

"Dang."

"I think that had more to do with the defacement of a book by Rush Limbaugh."

"Oh yeah. I forgot about that."

"What was it about? All I know is that, when you returned it, it could never be checked out again."

"Listen, this guy was arguing that women shouldn't play music, that they should just focus on being groupies. He was gross."

"I know his work. He is gross. Still . . ."

"So I may have cut the page every time he used a misogynistic term."

"Oh . . ."

"It turned into quite the beautiful snowflake of a book."

Liam tried very hard not to laugh. Defacing library property was no laughing matter. But picturing young Joanna practicing civil disobedience with safety scissors . . . it was quite an image.

"I returned it," she said.

"So I've heard."

"Anyway, I don't cut up library books anymore."

"That's what I told the person who wanted to bar you."

"Do I want to know who it was?"

"Nope."

"It wasn't Granny, was it?"

"No, and if your grandmother had been there, she probably would have kicked this woman's ass."

"Kicked her fluffy butt."

She laughed, and he did not point out that she looked beautiful when she laughed since she didn't like that. He just admired her silently.

"Liam, what are we doing?"

"What?"

"This." She waved a hand between them.

"I'm just thanking you for helping us out today."

"Oh. So this isn't . . . more?"

"Do you want it to be more?"

"No!"

Well, that was great for his ego.

She sighed. "Sorry. That came out wrong. I just mean . . . I mean, less than twenty-four hours ago you had your tongue down my throat."

That was true. It didn't sound quite so romantic when she said it, but technically, she was right.

"I was just following your lead," he explained. "You didn't seem to want to talk about it."

"I don't."

So . . . no chance for a repeat performance, then.

"It's just . . . I hate this place."

"Yeah, it's not great. A little too rich for my taste."

"No, I don't mean this *place*, I mean this town. Halikarnassus. I hate it."

"So you've said."

"And I don't plan on sticking around. Once Granny's better . . ."

"I know." She'd leave town and never look back. It was a bummer, but it wasn't the end of the world. Probably.

"Here's the thing," she continued, leaning over the table. "I . . . oh, God, okay. Listen. Don't laugh."

"Okay."

"I want you."

Well. He didn't know why she thought he would laugh at that. Spit his wine out in surprise, maybe. But definitely not laugh.

"But I'm leaving."

"O . . . kay?"

"So I don't want you to get too attached."

"Okay." There seemed to be something wrong with his vocabulary.

"You seem like a nice guy, that's all."

"Thanks?" he said, because that sure didn't sound like a compliment.

"And despite what people say, I'm not a total monster. I don't want to hurt you. But . . ."

"But?"

"But I can't get over this urge to climb across the table and jump you."

"Check, please."

"Liam—"

"Listen, Joanna. Listen to me. You've just said that you want me. That's very convenient, because I am having a hard time keeping my hands off you. I understand that you're not here to stay. I get it. I'm not trying to change your mind. But . . ."

"But?"

The bartender came over with his card. Liam signed the receipt, leaving way too much for the tip, but he did not care. He was on a mission.

"Let's go."

Chapter Eighteen

Joanna used to think Halikarnassus was a small town. The drive from the Wine Bar to Liam's house was proving her wrong. It was taking freakin' forever.

"I'm going to apologize in advance for the state of my house," he told her. She watched his hands as he drove—how smoothly he held the wheel, the quick flick of the blinker. God, he even drove sexy.

"Cabinet doors everywhere?" she teased, mostly to distract herself.

"Didn't you know that open cabinets are the latest concept in kitchen design?"

"Are they now?"

"Yes. And the doors look very good stacked in my garage."

And then there they were, pulling into his driveway with the garage full of cabinet doors.

She did not give one iota of a crap about the cabinet doors.

As she followed him up the short path to his front door—watching his butt the whole time, natch—she tried not to think about how much she wanted this.

It wasn't like she'd never had sex before—ha—but she'd never felt such a specific attraction before. Like, if she couldn't have Liam, she wasn't going to bother.

That was undoubtedly going to be a problem. Then he fumbled his keys, and as he bent to pick them up, she decided she did not care.

"Just . . . I didn't know I'd be having company," he said before he opened the door.

"You're making it sound like there's a crime scene in there or something."

"No, I cleaned up all the body parts. It's just that bloodstains are hell on furniture, you know?"

"I do. Liam." She leaned around him and pushed the door open. "I do not give a shit what your house looks like."

He gave a weak laugh and held the door open for her.

Well, it wasn't the neatest place she'd ever seen.

But it definitely wasn't the worst.

And as she looked at the mess, she realized it was mostly records.

"What happened?" she asked, thinking he must have been robbed or hit by a flash tornado or something.

"I decided to rearrange," he said, walking over to the shelves. He picked up a few albums and put them in a neat pile on the floor.

"I thought they were alphabetical?"

"Yeah. I thought it would be interesting to put them in chronological order, by release date."

"Oh." This man had a lot of time on his hands.

"The problem is, only the year is listed, so I had to look up each one to see the exact date to get an accurate picture of a year in records, you know? Then I found that some are reprints, and so the date on the sleeve is not the date it was—"

Because she did not care about how he organized his albums—or at least she did not care right now—Joanna stepped between Liam and his record collection, grabbed his tie, and kissed him.

It was just like she remembered, hot and sure. He took over almost as soon as their lips met, fisting one hand in her hair and tilting her back to get even deeper. She moaned into his mouth and held on.

"Hold on," he said, his breath coming fast. "Let me make sure my bed is made."

"Why?" she asked. "Aren't we gonna mess it up?"

"I don't want you to have a bad opinion of my housekeeping skills."

"Liam, until a year ago, I essentially lived in a cargo van. I do not have high expectations for housekeeping. I'm just impressed that you have furniture."

"Oh yeah?"

"Yeah, baby. I just love that big, hard sectional."

He tilted his head up and laughed. She leaned in and breathed. He smelled like oranges.

"Did you just sniff me?" he asked.

"Shut up," she replied, and pulled his shirt out of his dress pants, and ran her hands over all that smooth muscle.

"Okay, forget it," he muttered, and she squealed as she was lifted off her feet. He hiked up her skirt so she could wrap her legs around his waist, and then they were walking, her holding onto his shoulders, and maybe leaning in and smelling his neck a little more. Then she licked it, and she felt him lose his footing. Because she was a jerk, she licked him again, then grazed him with her teeth.

"Why are you wearing a tie?" she asked, and started pulling the knot free. She tossed it aside just in time for him to put her down on the floor of his bedroom.

The bed was not made. But it was big and Liam was reaching under her shirt and kissing her neck, so she did not care. She pushed him off, just for a second, so she could tear her shirt over her head. He grinned and grabbed her, but she held him off.

"Too much shirt," she said, and started undoing his buttons. He worked on his cuffs, and once they were open he took over, and soon he was just Liam.

It was kind of like in her dream, except in her dream he was slick and shiny, and in real life his pecs were covered with a dusting of hair. It didn't matter. He looked strong and defined, all those lean runner's muscles, and she was so busy admiring them that she almost missed him pulling off his belt, then dropping his pants.

Oh, those runner's legs.

He tilted his head toward her, and she realized that she was unfairly clothed, so she grabbed everything at her waist and pulled it down—skirt, leggings, panties. All of it. Then, just for good measure, she reached around and unhooked her bra.

"Holy shit," he murmured and stepped closer. "I want to take it slow and savor all of this," he said, running his hands over her shoulders, her hips, her breasts. "But I don't think I can."

She reached for the waistband of his boxers—which were plaid and very dorky—and shoved them over his hips. He hissed a little, but then his cock sprang free and she was too wound up to apologize.

He kissed her again, and she felt it in every inch of her skin, and he lifted her again, but this time he tossed her, right into the middle of his unmade bed.

She wanted to tease him, to scold him, but the look on his face as he loomed over her made her lose all interest in joking around.

"You look so serious," she panted as his hands moved up her legs, between her thighs.

"I am seriously going to make you come," he growled, and that made her breath hitch, and then his fingers moved and then he kissed her neck and she tossed her head back and shouted out his name.

She blinked, hard. "Whoa," she said, because, whoa. "That was . . . Jesus, you really know what you're doing."

"Why does that surprise you? Never mind, I don't care." He kissed her again, and she felt herself melting into the bed.

But this was no good—he couldn't do all the work. So she pushed and rolled until she was on top of him, pressing his erection against her belly. His hips jerked and he said "condom" and pointed desperately toward the nightstand, so she leaned over and opened the drawer and there they were, right on top. "Good Boy Scout," she said, and tore the foil open with her teeth. He opened his mouth and said "Wha—" but before the word was finished she had him sheathed and positioned and she was sliding down, as slowly as her jelly legs would let her.

"Oh, God, Joanna," he said, and it sounded like a prayer. That wasn't right; she was no angel. But he put his hands on her hips and she started to move, and his hands moved over her breasts and she felt worshipped. She put her hands on that beautiful chest and ground against him. He grunted in response. She twisted her hips. He cursed. She put her hands next to his head and kissed him and they both gasped. His hands fumbled for hers and he twined their fingers together and she held on as they rode it out together.

She was out of breath. Totally winded. She needed to start working out if she was going to keep up with Liam. Not that she needed to keep up with him. She wouldn't be sticking around long enough to keep up with him.

Don't think about how you just had the best sex of your life with a librarian. That would lead to thoughts of doing it again, and tomorrow, and for many days after that. Many days from now, she would be gone.

But for now, she was here, and Liam was strong and warm and his arms were loose around her waist and his breathing was deep and even. He was probably asleep. He probably wouldn't even notice that he was cuddling.

Chapter Nineteen

"Tell me something embarrassing."

Liam started from his post-bliss blissing out. Something embarrassing? Like about how he was falling for her? Maybe that was just the sexual bliss talking. And it was talking loud, because he had no idea what she was talking about.

He felt her shift. He opened his eyes and found himself face-to-face with a mussy-haired, kiss-swollen Joanna and it was all he could do not to grab her and ravish her like in those old-school romance novels he got from interlibrary loan for Mrs. Wilson. Instead, he listened.

"There must be something wrong with you," Joanna said, sliding a finger across his chest.

There were many things wrong with him. He was a terrible listener. Or he had forgotten how to speak English. What was she talking about?

"You have your shit together. It makes me feel inferior."

That got his attention. He started to sit up, but she put a gentle hand on his chest and he stayed down.

She settled her head on his chest while her fingers continued their wandering. He put one arm behind his head and the other on her hip. He heard her sigh and felt her sink deeper into his side. He forgot all about her feeling inferior. He just loved this.

"There must be something wrong with you," she said. "Tell me."

"I can tap-dance."

Her fingers stopped. Her head came up. "Really?"

"Not very well. Probably not at all anymore. But I used to take lessons when I was a kid."

She snorted into his chest hair.

"Hey, my mom wanted me to."

"Oh, so you didn't have dreams of being a big-time hoofer?"

"You laugh, but look at Gene Kelly."

"Yeah, Gene Kelly was hot, but that was, like, a hundred years ago. If I was a hundred years old, I would have hit it."

"Or Channing Tatum?"

"Channing Tatum is not a tap dancer." Pause. "Wait, can you dance like Channing Tatum?"

He lifted his arm and attempted a pop and lock robot.

"So . . . no."

Joanna thought about the other guys she had dated. The last one, Troy, wouldn't even get on the dance floor with her because he thought it was too . . . well, when he said what he thought it was, she probably should have dumped him right there. But she was determined to convince him that dancing could be sexy, that it could be like sex, but with clothes on and in public. No good. And Bobby, who got pissed when she even suggested going to see a touring musical with her. She told him she didn't expect him to enjoy it, and she promised copious oral sex afterward. That was quite a blow to her self-esteem, that he would rather forgo blow jobs—plural!—than be caught in a dark theater watching a musical.

Then she thought about little Liam in tap class, surrounded by girls in frilly skirts. Maybe he wore a sparkly vest and bow tie. And a jaunty cap. And the idea of his earnest face—the same one he used to chop tomatoes—concentrating on the steps and keeping time with the music, it filled her with so much glee that she had to lean away from him and put her hand over her heart lest it beat out of her chest.

"Are you laughing at me?"

She wiped her eyes and took a deep breath. She hadn't even realized she was laughing. She thought she was having a cuteness overload heart attack.

"No," she gasped. "I mean, sort of. But in a good way."

He leaned over her. "How is this a good way?" He narrowed his eyes at her, but he wiped a tear off her cheek and her heart melted.

"I'm just picturing little Liam in his bow tie . . ." She couldn't finish. She was dying of laughter.

"Hey, I never said I wore a bow tie."

"I know, I just . . ."

"I mean, I did wear a bow tie. And suspenders."

Suspenders! She threw her head back. She couldn't breathe. Suspenders!

"Hey, now," he said. But she couldn't stop laughing. Every time she looked at him, all she could see was that sweet, earnest face highlighted by a sequined bow tie. His eyes narrowed, and she tried to stop, really, she did, but then he threw the covers off them and nudged her legs apart and finally, finally she stopped laughing.

"Now you tell me something."

Joanna didn't want to talk. Her muscles were rubber. Moving her jaw was too much work.

"I know you're not asleep."

"Yes, I am," she muttered into his chest.

"I can feel you thinking."

She sat up, pulling the sheet with her. She wasn't sleepy, just a little dead. She crossed her legs, and he put his hand on her knee.

"Tell me something embarrassing," he said.

"Where to begin . . ."

"Tell me about Bunny Slippers."

Her head dropped to her chest. Of course he wanted to know that. "You don't already know?" She felt his thumb rubbing a lazy circle on her leg.

"I want you to tell me."

She took a deep breath. What did it matter? She'd be gone soon anyway.

"We recorded one album ourselves. It wasn't great."

"Yes, it was," he said. "I have that album. It's raw and loud and great. It makes me want to smash things."

"Yeah, okay. It was pretty great. And it was so fun to make. God, we tore up that studio. Not literally, of course."

"Of course."

"We were just touring around, working crappy day jobs, nothing major. But Mandy—the lead singer—

she was talking to this record company guy. He came to one of our shows . . . We had a lot of band meetings. God, so many meetings. I didn't want to sign, Mandy did. I thought this guy wanted us to tone it down way too much; Mandy said it wasn't a big deal. So we signed with him. It all happened so fast, but I barely noticed the change. It would just be little things—tone down Mandy's shouting vocals, cut my damn guitar solo."

"That's cruel."

"I know. I'm a damn rock genius."

"Your guitar solos are the only good thing about Bunny Slippers."

She looked down at him. He was serious.

God, he was sweet.

"So, okay. He got us on this tour with the Penny Lickers. At first I thought he was joking. I mean, those guys are nothing like us."

"They're terrible, for one thing."

"Yeah, and it's just a totally different sound, you know? They're more traditional rock, and we're, like, the second coming of Sleater-Kinney."

His thumb kept circling the spot right above her knee. It was comforting. And she needed comfort, because this was the worst part.

"So it's the night of the first show. I'd been feeling like this really wasn't all it was cracked up to be, but I'd signed the contract, right? So I had to do it. Then, just as we're about to go onstage, Jeff gives us these . . ."

"These what?"

"It's too embarrassing."

"More embarrassing than a sequined bow tie with matching suspenders?"

"Yes."

He tugged her down so her head rested on his shoulder. He snaked his hand through her hair and massaged her scalp. She got goose bumps, it felt so good.

"Bunny tails."

He stopped massaging. "Bunny tails?"

"White fluff balls. They attached with Velcro. To our butts."

Her head was shaking. She realized it was because Liam was shaking.

"Are you laughing?"

"No," he said, but then he snorted and rolled on his side away from her.

"Stop laughing at my pain!"

"I'm sorry. I shouldn't. I can't. Bunny tails?"

She shoved him farther to the edge of the bed, but he caught her arms and held on.

"Okay, okay, I'm done laughing. Tell me the rest."

She settled back onto his shoulder and closed her eyes. She could still feel it, all these weeks later. The adrenaline as they stood in the wings, the roar of the crowd pulsing through her veins when they stepped out onstage. The thwack on the ass Jeff gave each of them right before they went on.

Not a thwack on the ass. A thwack on the tail.

Mandy was eating it up. She paraded out onto the stage, her arms outstretched, taking in the screams. As Joanna and the others followed her, she bent down and stuck her tail in the air. "How do you like our new look?" she shouted into the mic. Deb and Harlow gamely turned and wiggled. Joanna looked out over the deafening crowd. This was the biggest show they'd ever played, exponentially bigger. This would expose them to thousands and thousands of new people who would download their album and make them stars.

"All I had to do was get onstage and shake my tail," she told Liam.

"And it didn't feel right?"

That was exactly it. It wasn't that she didn't want to—although she didn't—it just wasn't who they were as a band. It wasn't who she wanted to be as a musician. Women in rock had a hard enough time being taken seriously as musicians, and now Jeff wanted them to have a piece of fuzz up their asses?

"It's because I saw this girl in the front row. I don't even know how I was able to pick her out. The lights were blinding, the whole thing was sensory overload. But there she was."

"The girl in the front row."

"She was wearing a Bunny Slippers shirt, one of our old ones. Those were the ones that Mandy screen-printed in her dad's garage, one at a time. They were so crappy, these cheap white T-shirts that just said 'Bunny Slippers' in this crazy font that was totally illegible. But I knew that shirt. I'd sold those shirts at the merch table in many crappy bars."

"A real fan."

"Yeah. Only she wasn't smiling. I'll never forget it. All these people jumping and screaming around her, and she's just standing there, staring at me and my fluffy tail, like I'd betrayed her."

"Not very nice."

"That's when I knew. That's when I knew this had all gone too far, all the little compromises we made to be palatable to all these jumping people made us look like fools to the people who cared about our music when no one else did. And I was one of those people. I didn't care that this was going to be our big break. If this was what we had to do to get big, I didn't want to do it. So I didn't."

"So, what, you just left?"

"Didn't you see the video?"

"No. I wanted to, but . . . I don't know, I thought I'd just wait for you to tell me."

"This would probably be easier if you'd seen the video."

He reached around her for his phone, charging on the nightstand.

"Wait, really?"

"You said I should see it."

She took a deep breath and Googled.

She was relieved to see that it wasn't the top result for Bunny Slippers. First, there were news stories about the album making the charts and the hot new guitarist who wore ears *and* a tail. Finally, she found the video and handed the phone to Liam.

"You don't want to watch?"

She shook her head, but then she lay back down on his shoulder where she could see his face and the screen.

There it was: the screams and the tails, and Joanna, frozen on the side of the stage. There was Mandy, giving her a playful wave. Then Joanna shaking her head, and Mandy shouting something the mics didn't pick up. Then Joanna walking off the stage while the guy taking the video said "Holy shit, she just left!"

And that was it. The end of her rock-and-roll career, over in a minute and thirteen seconds.

Liam made a funny sound in the back of his throat. "Have you seen this before?"

She shook her head.

"Don't read the comments."

"Ugh. Let me guess: that fat chick with the guitar is a total loser."

Liam put the phone down. "Never mind."

This time, he didn't go back to his side of the bed. Instead, he hovered over her, pushing her hair out of her face.

"So. That's your most embarrassing moment."

"So far."

"It's a pretty good one."

"Thanks."

He leaned down and kissed her. It was soft and sweet and it kind of made her want to cry. "Thank you for telling me," he whispered in her ear.

This guy was strange. She peeled back her skin to show him the darkest layers of her soul, and he said thanks.

If she wasn't careful, she thought as he leaned down to kiss her, more thoroughly this time, she was going to be in real trouble.

Chapter Twenty

Joanna pulled up to Trina's house and noticed that she was no longer grateful that Trina lived in the wide, unobstructed country where she was never in any danger of hitting other cars or people. Not that she wasn't grateful, she just wasn't, like, obsessed with it.

She was getting good at driving Granny's boat.

She got out of the car and went around to unbuckle Rosetta from the front seat. She knew it was weird and unnecessary, but she didn't care. It was too hot to put Rosetta in the trunk. Which was not technically true, but again, she didn't care. She was a weirdo for her guitar, even more so now that she was actually playing it.

All she needed to do to get back into music was play a crappy gig in front of a hundred kids at the library. Who knew?

Truth be told, it wasn't the worst gig she'd ever played. And it wasn't even the least she'd gotten paid.

She got a pretty nice dinner out of it, and afterward . . .

Afterward she'd smooched the hell out of the librarian. Or had he smooched the hell out of her? And then there was last night . . . She'd have to watch herself or she'd start to like him.

She walked in Trina's front door—because this was Halikarnassus, where nobody locked their doors—and headed out back to the barn. Rick and the kids were in the yard, kicking a ball around. Or Rick was trying to kick the ball around; the kids were working on their cartwheels.

"Hey, guys!" she shouted, because she was in a good mood, dammit.

"Joanna!" Max shouted back.

"Fluffy butt!" Hazel added.

"I'm gonna kill you for that song!" Rick shouted.

"Sorry!"

"No, you're not!"

"I know!"

"Quit shouting, would you?" Trina shouted from the door to the barn.

Rick jogged over and gave Joanna a quick peck on the cheek. Then she almost hit the ground because Max and Hazel gave her a stealth leg-hug attack that she was not expecting. She held up Rosetta protectively.

"Watch the guitar, monkey children," Rick warned his kids.

"Monkey children!" they shouted, and ran circles around each other until they fell into a giggling heap.

"Seriously, whose kids are those?" Rick asked Trina.

"I don't care as long as they take a nap later."

"What do you care, you'll be out here blaring your rock and roll. You guys! You're getting the band back together!" Rick was possibly more excited than Trina and Joanna about their decision to revive Delicious Lies, if only for the summer. They both missed playing music, although Joanna had a feeling Trina was doing it more as a favor to her than anything else.

Whatever, she was itching to play. She was still feeling a little gun-shy on account of the record deal with the devil, but that didn't mean she was ready to retire Rosetta. Messing around in a barn with her best friend sounded good to her.

Rick joined the kids in their cartwheeling contest, which was an alarming sight, but, she had to admit, kind of charming.

Charming. God, she was getting soft.

"Before we start, there's something I should tell you." Trina was standing in the doorway to the barn, her arms outstretched as if she was blocking Joanna's path.

"What? Did the kids destroy your drums?"

"No . . ."

"Did *Rick* destroy your drums?" Joanna had a hard time imagining that happening and Rick still standing. Although at the moment, he was lying in a post-cartwheel heap on the grass. But still, they hadn't acted like a couple that just had a major blowup because one of them decided to destroy the other one's dreams.

Not that music was Trina's dream. But still. It was, like, a hobby.

"Okay, stop thinking about ways to kill Rick and let me finish," Trina said.

"I wasn't!" Joanna protested, even though she was

pretty sure that was the next path her thoughts were going to take.

"Just listen. I invited someone else to play with us."

"Okay."

"Really?"

"Is it Hitler?"

"Yes, Joanna, I resurrected the ghost of Adolf Hitler and asked him to join our band."

"Not cool, Trina."

"Shut up. This is a real person."

"Hitler was real."

"A not-dead person. Jesus, what is with you today?"

"What do you mean?"

"You're, like, giddy or something."

"I am?" Oh, God. Did she have a postcoital glow? Granny hadn't said anything when Joanna snuck into the house early that morning. But then, she didn't have to because Joanna was sneaking into the house early in the morning.

"It's weird. But . . . listen, I want you to hold on to that giddy feeling, okay? This is not, like, a permanent addition to the band. We're just jamming."

"Okay, geez."

"Do you promise?"

"I promise to hold on to that giddy feeling."

"Just . . . just don't freak out, okay?"

"Fine! I promise not to freak out!"

"Thank you. Come on."

Trina led her inside the barn. As they climbed up to the loft, Joanna half expected Liam to be there. She wasn't sure why; she was pretty sure he didn't play. And she wasn't sure why Trina would expect her to freak out at that, except that Joanna was a generally unpleasant person who didn't react well to change that she did not initiate herself. This was an unfortunate truth about her, but clearly Trina knew it and accepted it and prepared for it.

Besides, playing with Liam wouldn't be terrible. I mean, it wouldn't be terrible to spend more time with him, dork that he was. He probably had a whole pile of sheet music he practiced from.

Thinking about Liam's dorkiness made her smile, so she was smiling as she climbed the oversized ladder to the loft with Rosetta strapped to her back.

Her smile froze on her face when she saw who was up there waiting.

She'd promised Trina she wouldn't freak out.

Every fiber in her being wanted to throw a fit. It was all she could do not to just back down the ladder.

Standing next to Trina's drum set, a bass guitar strapped to her chest, was Kristin Klomberg.

"Are you kidding me?" Joanna asked in a tone that she hoped relayed that she was not going to freak out, as promised. She was pretty sure it didn't. Because she really, really felt like freaking out.

"I knew she wouldn't go for it," Kristin said to Trina.

"What, you guys are like best friends now?"

"Jesus, Joanna, relax. Kristin's been learning electric bass, so I thought she could join us."

"There's no bass in Delicious Lies."

"That's because we didn't know any bass players in high school."

"I thought you played the cello." Joanna had distinct memories of Kristin bragging about private lessons and how she didn't have time for the Halikarnassus Concert Band because she was in the state youth orchestra program, which was a much more worthwhile endeavor than playing in some crappy band. "I thought you were Miss Fancy Orchestra Pants," she added, because she really knew how to sling an insult. Dang, she was getting soft.

"Nice. For your information, I gave up orchestra after high school."

"Why, you weren't good enough?"

"Are we really going to do this?" Kristin asked Trina.

"Joanna—"

"No! No, it's fine. I promised not to freak out. I'm not freaking out that my best friend decided to include a prissy orchestra chick who doesn't even play the bass to join our band."

"Okay, first of all, we're just messing around here. It's not like—"

"Prissy orchestra chick! Grow up, Joanna. Don't you think it's time you let this whole mean girl thing go?"

"I'm the mean girl? I'm not the mean girl! You're the mean girl!" *And whatever you say bounces off me and sticks to you*, Joanna wanted to add. But she didn't, because that would mean she was freaking out, which she definitely was not.

"Very selective memory, Joanna. You terrorized me as soon as I got boobs!"

"Are you kidding me? You had people calling me 'Flat Stanley'!"

"I only said that because you would run through the halls calling me 'Titson Walsh'!"

That was true. Joanna used to take a lot of pride in the cruel puns she came up with for Kristin's perfect figure.

"I did not!" She denied it anyway.

"Joanna." Trina was standing there with her arms crossed, clearly on the side of Titson. "You were pretty mean."

"Yeah, but . . . what did that matter! Nobody liked me in high school! They didn't care what I thought!"

"What? Joanna, you're crazy! People picked up on all the terrible things you said."

"Yeah, but . . . what do you care? You were cool and popular and your little minions were always saying shit about me!"

"Girls!" Trina stepped between them because somehow, they had each stepped forward and were shouting in each other's faces. "Time out, okay?"

Kristin stepped back, like the Goody Two-shoes she was.

"Thank you. Can we just agree that you were both terrible people in high school?"

"I wasn't—"

"Yes, Kristin, you were. Accept it."

Kristin huffed and crossed her arms. Joanna smirked in victory.

"You weren't any better, Joanna. You think just because you weren't popular that your jerkiness didn't matter, but you said some really mean stuff."

Joanna huffed and crossed her arms. Then she realized she was standing the same way Kristin was, so she uncrossed them.

"Here's the thing. High school was a long, long time ago. We've all changed a lot since then, right?"

"She hasn't changed," Joanna muttered. "She's still Little Miss Perfect."

"You don't know anything about my life," Kristin said.

"Oh, really, miss First Lady of Halikarnassus?"

"My husband wants me to do nothing but look good in photo ops and raise our son to be a football star. I do nothing just for myself. When I told Hal that I wanted to come over here and play, so could he clear his schedule to watch Kale, do you know what he said? He said he shouldn't have to spend his weekend babysitting. Babysitting! His own son! Do you know how lucky you are? You never let anything stand in your way. You wanted to become a rock star, so you did. I know I'm not cool like you are, but I love to play, and I'm going to do it. It's not babysitting if it's your own kid!"

Joanna looked at Kristin, who seemed to be on the verge of tears. Crocodile tears, she wanted to say. Poor little rich girl.

But Hal was an asshole. Joanna had thought he was just an asshole to her because he had some weird thing against girls who didn't fall at his feet and worship him.

But then, she'd also conveniently misremembered how she'd terrorized Kristin as much as Kristin terrorized her.

Plus, Joanna wasn't exactly living her most authentic life at the moment.

God, she really was going soft. She was starting to see Kristin as, like, a human being.

"Okay, fine. Don't start crying or anything."

Trina looked back and forth between the two of them, a little unsure. "Are we cool?"

Kristin tossed her hair back in that way that used to annoy Joanna no end. It still sort of did. "Yes, we're cool," she said.

Joanna wasn't sure if she was ready to commit to being cool with Kristin. It was a lot to process, finding out that the neat little box you've smashed someone into isn't really the appropriate box at all. She couldn't just shake off the whole Kristin-as-mean-girl thing. But she also couldn't quite wrap her head around the Joanna-as-mean-girl thing. Sure, she was rude and a badass, but being a mean girl implied a certain amount of social power that Joanna was not aware she had ever wielded in high school.

It was a lot to process, especially now that she was going soft. Maybe she'd sit under a tree and journal about it later. For now, she just wanted to play.

"Let's do this," she said, and pulled Rosetta out.

Chapter Twenty-One

Liam looked sadly at his peanut butter and jelly sandwich.

It wasn't that he couldn't cook. He could. He just wasn't very good at it. And even if he were, the summer library kickoff party had drained all the cooking out of him. That, and the copious amounts of sex he was having with Joanna Green.

Thinking about Joanna was too distracting for work. Instead, he thought longingly of Peggy's freezer full of homemade casseroles. Joanna said they weren't very good, but if she was faced with the tragedy of this PB&J, would she think differently?

Probably not. He got the sense Joanna stuck to her guns.

He'd like to stick her to his guns.

Wait, what?

Clearly, he was suffering from tragically low blood sugar. He took a big bite of the sandwich.

"Boss, the mayor's here." Dani stuck her head in the break room door just in time to see her respected director boss almost choke on a too-big mouthful of sandwich.

"Does he want to see me?" Liam said, rudely, with a full mouth. He couldn't help it. Hal made him panic.

"No, he's here with his son. I think he's just being a patron."

"That's weird."

"I know. That's why I'm telling you. Sorry to interrupt your lunch."

"That's okay," Liam said. He could finish his sad sandwich later, when the mayor wasn't here for suspiciously no reason.

Hal was hanging out by the new books shelf while Kale toddled around, touching all of the books he could reach but not pulling them off the shelves. Kristin had trained him well. Kale was mumbling toddler nonsense, as if he was reading the spines. Hal occasionally put a hand on his son's head, as if making sure he was still there, while he perused.

"Can I help you find something, Mayor?" Liam asked, hoping his breath wasn't too peanut butter-y.

"Big, how are you?" Hal gave Liam's hand a vigorous shake. "I'm just admiring the books."

"Great. Can I help you find something in particular?"

"No, no, I don't read."

Liam winced.

"You sure got a lot of books over here."

Liam turned and looked at the half a bookcase that made up the New Books area. It was less than half-full. More than half-empty. And that was only because Liam left the new books out for a year, well past their "new" dates. But if he moved the books into the regular stacks any sooner, the shelves would be empty. All the new-new stuff was checked out.

Hal picked up a book with a bright red cover. Liam hadn't read the whole thing, but he'd skimmed it enough to get the gist: The Internet was making us all stupid and we needed to read more. It was the first time he'd seen it on the shelf—it was usually checked out.

"That's a pretty interesting book," Liam said. "The author talks about how our social interactions have changed since—"

But Hal had put it back—in the wrong place—and picked up a book with a pink cover featuring a woman driving a convertible with her scarf waving out dangerously behind her. "What's this one?"

"That's a memoir. The author's husband had an affair, so she sold their house and bought a convertible and took a yearlong road trip around the country."

"What, like that *Eat, Pray, Whatsit?*"

"*Eat Pray Love?*"

"Yeah. Kristin loves that shit. Has she read this one?"

"I'm not sure . . ."

"She comes in here often enough, I thought you'd know."

"Well, I'm not here all the time . . ."

"Big, I'm gonna level with you." Hal tucked the memoir under his arm and turned to face Liam. "The council's decided to table the budget discussion for now."

"Oh?"

"I think it's a shame. Those kids up at the high

school could use the money, you know? But it'll still go to buying stuff like—" He picked up a paperback, a paranormal romance featuring a shapely woman in leather pants with an enormous lower back tattoo. He tucked that one under his arm, too. "I mean, why do you have two copies of this one?" He pointed to the next-to-newest James Patterson title. They actually had more than two copies of that book; the others were checked out. And they had even more of the newest one. Also checked out. "See, that's what I'm talking about," Hal continued. "Wasteful. If you just spent your money a little more carefully, it'd go a lot further."

It took every fiber of Liam's professional being not to roll his eyes. "Noted," he said.

"I can't promise I'm not going to go after that money in the future," Hal said.

"Fair enough." *And I'm going to fight you for every last penny.*

"I mean, nobody's even in here."

That wasn't true, there were several dozen people in the library. It wasn't many, true, but it was a gorgeous summer afternoon. Most people were out enjoying it.

"Doughy Deh!" Kale said, pulling on his dad's shorts.

"Oh, right, the book. Listen, Kristin sent me to get a book for him—I guess it's his new favorite. I don't know what the hell he's saying, though. What's the book called, buddy?"

Kale's face got very serious. "Doughy Dey," he said, stretching out every syllable so his dad would understand him.

It didn't work.

"Do you know the Doughy Day book?"

"Do you mean *The Snowy Day*?" Liam asked Kale.

"Doughy Dey! Doughy Dey!" Kale shouted, clapping his hands.

"At least someone understands the kid," Hal said. "So, you got it?" He looked around the new books shelves, as if a classic children's picture book would be there.

Not that he would scold Hal about that. Not to his face, anyway.

"It would be back in Children's, but let me check if it's in." Liam walked over to the catalog computer and looked it up. "Oh, it looks like it's checked out. Sorry, buddy. How about another book about snow?"

"You don't have that one?"

"We do, but it's checked out."

"You only have one copy?"

Liam sighed.

"You don't think I'm a jerk, do you?"

Starr lifted her head from the throw pillow to look at Joanna.

Joanna smiled at her from where she lay, inches away from the dog's face.

The dog blinked.

"I'm going to take your non-answer as a no and that you think I'm perfectly delightful."

Starr reached out her paw to bat at Joanna's hand. In any other dog, this would have been seen as an adorable sign of affection. For Starr, it meant that you'd better start petting her soon or she was going to unleash her mighty bark.

Joanna sat up and scooped the dog with her, cuddling Starr close while scratching her belly. Joanna had found that Starr didn't mind cuddling as long as you were also petting her.

Good thing Granny wasn't home to see this.

"Yes, our granny left us to fend for ourselves," Joanna explained to Starr, who did not care. She preferred Granny's company, sure, but Joanna had found that as long as there was someone to scratch behind her ears, she didn't really care who it was.

Starr also didn't care that Joanna was an asshole, and had been her whole life. It wasn't that Joanna didn't know that she'd said a lot of mean things about Kristin when she was in high school. She just didn't think that Kristin noticed, or that she cared. But of course she would care.

Joanna just didn't like to see her as a person with feelings.

Which made her feel ashamed of herself, which made her want to double down on her dislike of Kristin so she didn't have to deal with the former mean girl or the feelings of inadequacy she brought up.

"I have a very healthy emotional life," she told Starr. Starr stood up, walked in a tight circle, then lay back down again, facing away from Joanna.

"Great." Joanna threw her head back on the couch. She was a bully, her grandmother's dog hated her, and now she was throwing a temper tantrum because things were not going her way.

Not that they ever went her way.

"Oh, good, a pity party on top of a temper tantrum." She had to get out of the house. She'd also promised

Granny she would keep Starr company, even though Starr didn't seem to want her company.

"That's it. We're going for a walk."

Starr's left ear rose.

"You heard me. Walk."

Starr's left ear went down again.

"Quit pretending to be deaf, I know you heard me. And I know you know what 'walk' means." She scooped up all ten fluffy pounds of Starr, grabbed the leash, and went out the door.

It was a perfect day. She'd give Halikarnassus that. When it wasn't knee-deep snow or tree-shaking thunderstorms, the weather was pretty amazing. Like today, when the bright blue of the sky matched Liam's eyes.

Whoa. That was weird.

Well, so what. He had nice eyes. And nice legs. And nice arms. All of his appendages were nice. And he was a nice person. And he was a nice kisser.

Nice.

"Gah, what am I doing? I'm turning into some kind of Halikarnassus Stepford lady." Starr kept her feet firmly planted on the grass, moving only enough to sniff delicately at what her nose could reach.

Joanna gave the leash a gentle tug. Starr tugged back. Joanna gave it a harder tug. Starr barked.

"Dog, we have to walk, okay? The sooner you get used to the idea, the sooner you can go back to sitting on the couch and judging me."

"Are you talking to the dog?"

"Waa!" Joanna hadn't meant to yell so loudly. In her defense, she hadn't seen Liam run up—in his shorts, she was pleased to notice once her heart stopped threatening to beat out of her chest.

"Sorry, I thought you heard me." He was still jogging in place. Joanna was mesmerized by the flex of his quad muscles as each foot hit the ground.

"Are you okay?" he asked. He looked down at his legs. Crap, she was caught.

"Yup. Totally okay." *Totally not talking to the dog and sexually harassing you, Nice Liam Man Who Kisses Real Good.*

If she wasn't turning into a Stepford wife, she was certainly turning into an idiot.

"What are you doing here?" Her tone was a little more abrupt than she meant it to be. But then, her tone was often more abrupt than she meant it to be. "I mean, don't you usually run in the mornings?" Because, like all Halikarnassus Stepford wives, she knew the hot library director's workout schedule.

"I overslept."

"Ah," she said, because she knew why Liam had overslept that morning, and it had to do with his appendages.

Starr, apparently done sniffing the grass around her feet, started pulling on her leash.

"Oh. Apparently we're walking," said Joanna. She ignored the disappointment she felt that her conversation with Liam was now over. This disappointment was tempered by the fact that she'd get to watch him run away.

"Mind if I walk with you?"

But then I can't ogle your butt, she almost said out loud. Instead, she just nodded.

All of a sudden, Joanna felt weird. She didn't

know what to say. She didn't know what to do with
the hand that wasn't holding the leash. She was way
too aware of Liam, a bead of sweat running down his
neck, over his Adam's apple, into the neck of his
shirt.

Her mouth was very, very dry.

"So . . . how was work today?" Joanna said, which
was boring but was much better than "Hey, can we
stop walking for a minute? I really want to lick your
neck."

"Fine. Good."

"Convincing."

He shrugged again, but less in a no-big-deal way
and more in an I-don't-want-to-get-into-it way.

"So you're running to clear your mind after a
crazy day."

"Mm-hmm."

"Most people just drink."

"That's for after."

They walked on in companionable silence. Joanna
was thinking about running, and clearing her mind,
and how she was a terrible person.

"How's Peggy?" Liam asked.

"Hmm? Oh, great. She's at Phyllis's. Playing bridge,
or so she says."

"What, you don't think they're playing bridge?"

"All I heard on the phone was *Magic Mike Two* and
a lot of seventy-year-old giggling."

"Wow."

"Yeah."

"Still . . ."

"Still what?"

"I'm not sure. I was trying to remind us to be nice

about older women and their sex drives, but I can't stop picturing Phyllis and Channing Tatum . . ."

"That's what you get for trying to be a good person."

"Duly noted. Poor Phyllis."

"Poor Channing Tatum." They kept walking, and Joanna fought the urge to reach out for his hand. She did not hold hands.

"Are you okay?" Liam asked.

Just obsessed with touching you. "Yup."

"Convincing. So what did you do on this fine Saturday?"

Well, I spent the morning pining after your naked body, she thought. "I went over to Trina's. We played."

"That's great! That is great, right?"

"Yeah. Yeah, it was really fun."

"But?"

"But . . . I learned some uncomfortable truths about myself."

"Oh?"

"I always knew I was a bad person, but today I learned that I'm a bad person in a different way than what I thought I was."

"Oh."

"Kristin Klomberg was there."

"Huh."

"We don't get along."

"I heard."

"The thing is, she's really good." When he looked confused, she added, "She plays bass."

"Wow. I had no idea. People will surprise you, I guess."

"You're telling me." She couldn't help but think of last night.

"So . . . the band?"

"Delicious Lies. It was Trina and me in high school. Now it's Trina and Kristin and me."

"Fun."

"God, we really gelled, you know? Like we'd been playing together forever. We talked about trying to get a gig at Chet's."

"That's great! Wait, that is great, right?"

"Sure."

"Cuz you don't sound like you think it's great."

Joanna stopped and looked around her. This was the street she grew up on. She remembered when the Matarazzos moved out in fourth grade and the Kielys moved in. She remembered talking Kevin Kiely out of the oak in their front yard when he climbed too high and got scared. She remembered spending every summer barefoot, running through sprinklers during the day and catching lightning bugs at night.

The more time she spent here, the more she lost touch with why she was in such a hurry to get away.

Starr sat down in the middle of the sidewalk with a heavy sigh.

"I think your dog's done walking."

Joanna leaned down and scooped Starr up. She may have taken a moment to nuzzle her little doggy ears.

She was officially a softy.

"I'll see you later, okay?" Part of her wanted to invite herself over to Liam's again, to see if the sparks they'd created last night were just a fluke. But she was feeling too soft, and if he was too nice to her . . .

"Are you sure you're okay?"

"Yeah."

"I'll call you tomorrow, okay?"

Before she could tell him not to, he leaned over and kissed her, short and sweet. She still had her eyes closed when she heard his footsteps running away.

Chapter Twenty-Two

Joanna couldn't believe that Liam had passed even one summer in Halikarnassus without visiting the lake.

In the weeks that followed that last walk with Starr, Liam did call, and often. He didn't crowd her or insist they spend time together. He didn't try to get in her pants every time they did meet up (much to her chagrin). He seemed to just genuinely like spending time with her. He was gentle with her. She didn't know what to make of it.

She still was not entirely convinced he wasn't using her for her cooking.

But the man appreciated a good meal, and she appreciated being appreciated. She didn't question it too hard; she'd be gone soon.

But when she found out that he'd never been to the lake—

The lake was a massive reservoir formed when some river was dammed up some time way before Joanna was born. When she thought of her misspent youth—which was often, now that she was in

Halikarnassus—she couldn't not think about the lake.

Getting to the lake involved a pain-in-the-ass hike through the woods that made the water seem all that much sweeter when you finally jumped in. That was the easiest way in—climb out onto the diving board (aka a tree that grew sideways over the water) and jump in. It was the only way in unless you wanted to hike clear across to the other side to the small but much flatter beach. Of course, that involved risking the wrath of Mr. Shaughnessey, and he liked guns.

So even though it was autumn and probably too cold to swim, she was leading Liam on a hike through the woods to the lake.

Well, she had been leading him. He overtook her pretty quickly.

It was those stupid legs. They were longer than hers. That was why she could barely keep up as they hiked up yet another hill.

"Remind me again why I like you?" she asked his back.

"Because I'm so cute?" he suggested.

He was right. He was cute.

She must be experiencing some kind of belated hometown regression, coming back home and experiencing the stupid teenage stuff she'd never experienced when she was a teenager here. Well, she'd experienced some of it—that old feeling that the world was against her and everyone around her was dumb and judgmental and Hal Klomberg was a completely useless human being.

Except she felt different when she was with Liam. She didn't feel like a screwup. She felt like walking away from Bunny Slippers was the right thing to do.

She felt like, yeah, she knew a lot about music and about the kind of music she wanted to make, and not compromising on that was not the same thing as failure. And she felt smart when she was with him. She didn't think she'd ever felt smart before.

She stopped to tie her hair back. Not at all because she was completely out of breath and maybe they were lost. She didn't remember the hike to the lake taking this long. Of course, it had been a while since she'd done it. And she didn't think she'd ever done it completely sober.

Meanwhile, Liam took to the trail like he owned it. Him and his shorts. What was it with this guy and shorts? These were nothing like the running shorts, though. These were cargo-style hiking shorts, with lots of pockets for survival tools, she guessed. God, he was such a Boy Scout.

He put his hand in his pocket, which had the pleasant effect of pulling his shorts tight across his butt, which she appreciated because this Boy Scout had an amazing butt. A butt made for squeezing. A butt made for holding onto while he . . .

"You coming?"

She shook her head. No time for shenanigans. She had to figure out how to get to the . . . oh. There it was.

"How do you get down there?"

She peered over the steep hill into the lake.

"There used to be a tree here," she said, pointing to the gnarled pile of roots at the bottom of the hill. "That was the way in." All that was left was a steep slope that ended in a bed of rocks.

Liam kicked a rock into the pond, where it landed with a plop.

"It's hot." Liam squinted up at the sun, and Joanna watched, fascinated, as a bead of sweat dripped down his neck. Her mouth felt suddenly dry.

"Yeah," she agreed. It was damn hot.

"You used to swim here?"

"All the time."

"God, a swim would feel great right now."

"Hmm," Joanna said, but she wasn't really listening. She was mostly sweating. Well, sweating on the outside and melting on the inside.

"There's probably an easier place to get in, right?"

"There's a beach, sort of." More like a tiny bed of mostly smooth rocks, but, hey, it was flat.

"Where's that?"

She pointed across the lake.

"That far?"

"Mm-hmm."

"Psh. Too hot to go that far."

Joanna agreed, but she was very hot and sweaty and melty, so when Liam took a step over the edge, she didn't really register what he was doing until he was sliding down the hill.

"What are you—?" she asked as he took the last few feet at an unsteady trot and landed inches from the water.

"Come on!" He waved her down, then sat on a rock and started taking his boots off.

"What are you—?" she asked again, but then he tore his shirt over his head and she took a step, then another step, then her feet slid out from under her and she took the hillside down on her butt.

"Are you okay?" Liam asked, helping her up.

"Yup," she might have said, but she wasn't sure, so distracted was she by the magnificence of his chest.

And really, it was magnificent. Lean and tan with a sprinkling of light hair across his pecs.

"Race you," he said, and before she could say "Stop and let me lick your neck" he dove into the lake.

"You know," she said when he surfaced like some mythical mer-creature, "you had an unfair head start."

"Sore loser," he shouted at her, and started to swim away from shore.

"I hope you get eaten by a shark!" she shouted back at him. But he didn't turn around, so she toed off her sneakers and socks, and taking one cursory look around to make sure no one was watching—not that it would have stopped her—she tore off her shirt and shorts and ran into the water after him.

She'd forgotten how cold the lake was.

Well, the lake reminded her.

"Bah!" she said when she came up for air. Liam was a few feet from her, floating in circles on his back, completely immune to her feminine distress.

God, she hadn't been swimming in forever. She forgot how good it felt, to feel weightless and cocooned, the languid movements she needed to keep herself afloat. She ducked underwater and pushed off the murky bottom of the lake. She wasn't sure which direction she was going, but it felt good so she kept swimming. When she came up for air, she was closer to the middle of the lake, past where Liam was floating. She treaded water for a minute, watching him, then flipped over to do the same. She leaned her head back and tilted her head slowly, letting the water flow through her hair while it held the rest of her up.

She felt drops of water on her stomach and opened her eyes to see Liam smiling at her, his hands cupped just above the water. He squeezed them together and she got splashed again.

"Ha ha," she said, and flicked her foot, splashing water on him.

She heard him go under, felt the water underneath her move; then he resurfaced on her other side. She looked out of the corner of her eye to see him tilt and float on his back.

She moved her hands lightly, spinning herself in lazy circles, watching the clouds move across the sky.

Her hand bumped something, and it was Liam's hand, which was so much better than a fish. They continued to float in their independent circles, but when they bumped again, he hooked his pinkie with hers, holding them together, a floating island. She smiled, too relaxed to make a joke or move away. She didn't want to move away. She wanted to float here with Liam, connected by their fingers, spinning slowly as the clouds.

He tugged her, gently, and her body floated closer, close enough that he could lace all of their fingers together. Another minute of floating, her mind drawn to where their hands were connected, drifting toward the idea of other body parts being connected, of feeling his arms around her, of her body being held up by the water and by him. She lifted her free hand and ran cool water across her face. Liam tugged again, hard enough to dislodge her, and when she turned to him, he was treading water, his eyes dark, and he pulled her toward him, his hand going around her waist. Hers instinctively went to his shoulder, cupping water and rolling it down the muscles there. They treaded water together for a minute, their legs tangling, heat radiating from their bodies, so much she couldn't believe the lake didn't just evaporate around them. His eyes roamed, and so she let hers, over his shoulders, his jaw . . .

She couldn't resist anymore, so she leaned in and ran her tongue along the side of his neck. He shivered, so she grazed her teeth along the pulse there.

"Shit," he muttered, but he meant it in a good way because he pulled her closer, his hands tight on her ass, and kissed her.

Yup, he could still kiss. He tasted like sunscreen and lake water and summer, and she straightened her body, aligning her chest with his, clutching his shoulders, his hair, as he growled and plundered and devoured her. She wrapped her legs around his waist, and the kiss deepened. He pulled her even closer and she moaned into his mouth. He kicked his legs to keep them afloat, and every movement of his thighs shifted her and she could feel him through his shorts and holy shit, she wanted him, so she clutched him closer and bit his shoulder. He cursed, and coughed as he swallowed some lake water.

"You gotta keep swimming," she teased him. "Or we're both gonna drown."

"Then quit biting me," he said.

"Okay," she replied, and started to pull away.

He tightened his grip on her, reached down and wrapped her legs back around his waist. "I didn't really mean that. Hold on."

She did, and he started kicking his legs, propelling them closer to shore. She felt his abs flex against her, his shoulders flex under her hands, and she couldn't handle all this hotness so she surged up and kissed him again, nearly taking both of them under.

He straightened, and she felt his legs stop moving as his feet touched the bottom of the lake. "Tiger," he murmured into her lips, then kissed her again. This time she had the best of both worlds, the floaty of the water and the leverage of his legs planted firmly on the ground, so she took advantage of it and climbed so her head was above his. She looked down, her wet hair forming a curtain around their faces, and watched his eyes get even darker, his face more serious. His hands moved from her thighs up her sides, then they were cupping her breasts through her soaking bra, his mouth sucking on the fabric, tugging on her skin. His hands moved to her back and she felt him fumble with the wet clasp but he did it, his crafty hands pulling the bra off her shoulders, his mouth not even hesitating, and she gasped and leaned back farther, her scalp hitting the cool water, her man licking his way across her breasts.

Everything felt amazing. The sun, Liam's arms, Liam's mouth . . . she wanted to stay in this lake forever.

She shifted to sit up—that boy deserved a kiss— but she must have thrown off his footing, because before she could reach his mouth, she had a mouthful of lake water.

They both came up sputtering. "Are you okay?" he croaked and she had to nod because she couldn't stop coughing and laughing, which made her cough even more.

It was very attractive, she was sure.

He ducked underwater, then came up again and shook his hair out. "Holy crap."

"Yeah."

"We should . . . do you want to, uh, do that on dry land?"

"Hell yes. Wait. Where's my bra?"

"Oh. Shit."

Well, it was a crappy old sports bra anyway. She put her hands over her breasts and waded to the shore. Liam, with his strong, long legs, beat her there and handed her her shirt. She pulled it on, then thought about her wet underwear and putting her shorts on over it.

She was already braless. Why not?

She pulled down her panties, fast so they wouldn't stick to her legs, then stepped into her shorts.

She looked up to find Liam, his head half in his own shirt, staring at her.

"What?"

"Nothing," he said. "Nothing. That's just, uh. That's gonna be distracting."

She smiled at him, the big goof. She smiled a lot around him. What was this magic power he had over her? It made her feel all warm and . . . she didn't know, appreciated. She didn't usually go out with guys who told her what they liked about her.

It was hard to hike holding hands. But Liam was determined. Even though Joanna was laughing at him.

"I don't see what the big deal is," he told her.

"It's just . . . it's lame!"

"It's lame that I want to touch you?" *And that if I don't hold your hand I'll grab you and rip your clothes off because I know you're not wearing underwear.*

Fortunately, their argument was ended by the sudden appearance of his car. This was good because the sun was going down and he was starting to get cold. It had been a pretty dumb idea to jump into the lake in his shorts.

Although it worked out okay in the end.

He hustled Joanna into the car, since she was wearing even fewer clothes than he was.

"I should get you home so you can change."

"I don't want to change," she said softly.

"I should get you home so . . ." But he couldn't come up with another excuse because Joanna bit his lower lip.

"Don't you want to make out in the backseat?" she asked, climbing over the center console and onto his lap. The horn honked. She leaned down and found the seat lever.

"Oof," Liam said as his seat back dropped, and Joanna dropped with it.

"Better?" she asked, kissing his neck.

He loved it when she kissed his neck. But her knee was digging into his hip and it was seriously distracting. He nudged her leg a little, but that threw her off balance, so the whole thing ended with her elbow in his chest and the windshield wipers on.

"Sorry!" she shouted, scrambling off him. "Sorry. Here. Come back here. Backseat."

He looked at her in the rearview mirror, looking all disheveled and kissed and not wearing a bra and he really, really wanted to climb in the backseat with her.

He let his head drop to the steering wheel. "I don't have any condoms."

He heard her sigh. "Worst Boy Scout ever."

Chapter Twenty-Three

"Whose idea was it to play outside?" Kristin asked, teeth chattering.

"Baby," Joanna said, and Kristin stuck her tongue out at her.

"Glad to see you guys are maturing," Trina said, adjusting one of her cymbals.

"Is it normal to feel like you're going to throw up before a show?" Kristin asked.

"Yes," Joanna and Trina said together.

"It'll be fine," Joanna reassured her. "Nobody will be paying attention to us anyway."

That was a lie, but Joanna didn't see any reason to make Kristin worry any more.

She was actually starting to like the woman.

Damn, she really was getting soft.

She blamed Liam. If he wasn't so nice to her, she wouldn't be so soft. And she'd be long gone by now. She didn't know where. Someplace where there was actual stuff that was happening.

Not that she particularly wanted to be anywhere else at the moment. It was Halloween, Trina and Rick had dragged the drums down from the barn loft, and Delicious Lies 2.0 was having its informal debut concert.

If Joanna from six months ago could see her now, playing with Kristin Klomberg, in daylight, wearing a Halloween costume.

That was Liam, too. He'd insisted since everyone else was dressing up, she had to, too. He was dressed as a scarecrow, with hay poking out of his too-short jeans and plaid shirt. He looked friggin' adorable.

He only very briefly suggested that she dress like Dorothy, but that was way too much. She was never going to be the kind of woman to voluntarily wear a couples costume.

She was dressed as a librarian.

She'd baby-powdered her hair gray and Granny dug out one of her dowdy maternity jumpers, which Joanna paired with a festive and terrible turtleneck with pumpkins on it. Liam said he was offended by her perpetuation of stereotypes. She told him she wasn't wearing underwear.

And he was right, everyone was dressed up. Granny was dressed as Charlie Chaplin, twirling her cane around so much Joanna thought she was going to have to take it away from her. Skyler showed up, dressed as a mime, *bien sur*. Rick had on a very fancy Iron Man costume, Trina was rocking a red wig as the Black Widow, and Max was painted green and stomping around as the Hulk. Hazel refused to participate in the Flunderman superhero theme, though, and she was wearing her red snowsuit with the hood pulled tight.

"I'm Peter," she told Joanna when she arrived. "From *The Snowy Day*."

The girl was obsessed.

And she was bouncing-off-the-walls excited when Kristin showed up with Kale, who was also wearing a red snowsuit.

Kristin was wearing Lycra, because of course she was. She turned and waved her cat tail at Joanna and Trina. "I'm Josie and the Pussycats!" she said proudly.

And now she was standing on the makeshift stage, trying not to throw up.

"You guys ready?" Trina asked, sitting down at her drum set. "You're not going to run away, are you, Joanna?"

"Ha ha ha," she said, hiking up her skirt so she could get to her effects pedals easier.

"Oh, God, Hal is here! I can't do this!"

Joanna squinted out across the yard, and sure enough, there was Hal, standing at the beer cooler talking to Liam. He wasn't wearing a costume. Or maybe he was. Washed up, entitled loser.

Hey, maybe she wasn't totally soft.

She stepped in front of Kristin, blocking her view of her husband and the rest of the town, who all seemed to be crammed into the Flundermans' yard. "Look at me," she commanded.

Kristin looked at her.

"You are going to rock, do you hear me?"

Kristin nodded weakly.

"You can throw up after."

She nodded again.

"Good. We got this." Joanna stepped back in front of her amp. Trina pulled down her mic.

"Ladies and gentlemen," she shouted. "We! Are! Delicious! Lies!"

* * *

"Big, cute costume."

Hal slapped Liam on the back, hard. He dislodged some of Liam's straw.

Liam clenched his jaw.

"Mayor, nice to see you," he lied. "What are you dressed as?"

"A goddamn adult," Hal said, taking the beer Rick handed him.

"You know this is a costume party, right? I could kick you out," Rick teased.

"And I could call the cops on this noise violation."

Okay then.

"Just joking, Klomberg, you're welcome any time." And with that, Iron Man slunk away.

Liam looked around for any excuse to be standing anywhere but next to the mayor. But he didn't want to be rude. He wasn't sure how Hal would take it out on him.

"You come to see the band?" Liam asked.

"Band," Hal scoffed. "I thought Kristin and Joanna hated each other, and now they're in a damn band together?"

"I think they buried the hatchet. For the sake of rock and roll."

"I can't decide which is worse, Kristin bitching about Joanna all the time or her being gone all the time for this stupid band."

"I've heard they're pretty good."

"Who'd you hear that from, Joanna?"

"Well, yes."

Just then, the band in question started up, loud and fierce. Liam watched Joanna hike up her skirt and bear down on her guitar. He couldn't help the goofy smile he felt forming on his face.

She fucking rocked.

"I always had a thing for her," Hal said. Liam had forgotten he was still standing at his elbow, sucking all the joy out of the party.

"She's like a caged tiger, you know?"

Liam looked at Hal. It occurred to him that he was not talking about his wife. He was talking about Joanna.

He clenched his fist. He was not going to engage in this, not with the man who was responsible for signing his budget.

"I bet she's great in bed," Hal said, making vulgar gestures with his hands. "I bet you like that, don't you, sinking into that—"

And then Liam's clenched fist connected with Hal's jaw.

As Hal sputtered and flailed, Liam kissed the library's budget good-bye. But it had been worth it.

Chapter Twenty-Four

"Auntie Jo Jo!" Hazel came running at her full tilt, waving her arms in the air like a red-suited alien. Joanna lifted Rosetta out of the crash zone as Hazel careened into her middle.

"Oof."

"Auntie Jo Jo, you are so good at the guitar!"

"Thanks, Haze."

"Are you going to say more bad words?" The kid looked up at Joanna hopefully.

"Only if you promise to stop calling me 'Auntie Jo Jo.' Where did you get that from?"

"Daddy said you would like it." Now the kid looked like she was about to cry.

"Uh . . ." Dammit, she couldn't think murderous thoughts about Rick with his daughter's lip wobbling like that.

She did not know how to deal with kids.

"Okay, here's the deal," Joanna said, squatting down so she was at Hazel's level. "You can call me

Auntie Jo Jo." She cringed just saying it. "But only you, got it?"

"Not Max?"

Joanna had never had any siblings, but something in her gut told her there was trouble ahead. "Okay, you and Max. *Only* you and Max, got it?"

Hazel looked at her very seriously. "Got it." She spat in her palm and offered it to Joanna.

"No, that's okay. I trust you."

The lip started to wobble.

Joanna sighed and rolled her eyes. Kids. She fake-spat in her palm and took Hazel's hand.

"You didn't really spit!"

"Holy crap, kid, are you kidding me?"

Hazel's eyes went wide with delight. "You said a bad word!"

Fake-spit forgotten, Hazel skipped off. No doubt to tell her brother that Auntie Jo Jo was there to teach them all the bad words.

"First you corrupt me, now you're corrupting my children?" Trina reached out a hand to help Joanna up from her Hazel-sized crouch.

Joanna wiped her hand on her dress first. Because she was a good friend.

"Who taught her to spit like that?"

"If I blamed my husband, would you believe me?"

"I will if you give me that beer."

Trina handed her the second bottle of beer she was holding. "Cheers. Excellent reunion."

Joanna took a swig. "We weren't terrible, were we?"

"Nope. I didn't think Kristin was gonna make it, but she did okay."

"I know!"

Trina looked at her for a long moment, her gaze strong under that red wig.

"What?"

"I'm just waiting for you to tell me that I was right."

Joanna shoved her lightly. "You know you were right."

"Yes, but I like to hear it."

"Oh, Joanna! That was lovely!" Granny was hobbling over to them.

"Thanks, Gran. I don't think we were going for 'lovely,' though."

"Well, I thought it was lovely. I can't remember the last time I saw you play. You really come alive up there."

Joanna fought back a surge of . . . what was it? Panic? Regret? Whatever it was, it was feelings, and she didn't like it.

"Where did Kristin go? I want to tell her what a lovely job she did."

Joanna was starting to suspect that Granny had gotten into the hooch. Oh, well. It was Halloween. Party time.

"She went home," Trina told Granny. "Hal was in some kind of snit."

"That sounds about right," Granny muttered. Yup, she was definitely buzzed. Granny never said bad things about people when she was sober. Not even about Hal.

"Well, you girls were terrific. But this old lady is tired, so I'm going to have Doris drive me home. Joanna, you'll get home all right?"

"Yes, Gran."

"Maybe Liam can walk you home."

Joanna rolled her eyes. "It's a little far from here."

"Hmm," Granny said, and she toddled off to find Doris.

"Is your grandmother drunk?" Trina asked her.

"I hope so. Otherwise, she's losing her mind."

"So. You and Liam."

"Shut up."

"He's going to walk you home. It totally sounds like you guys are going steady. Watch out, Joanna, or you're going to get yourself a regular boyfriend."

"Ugh. No."

"It's not so bad."

"Regular boyfriends lead to husbands and houses in the suburbs with kids. No offense."

"You don't have to marry him. And medical science has created this amazing thing called birth control? It's cool. If you remember to take it, you totally won't have kids."

"If you remember."

"Just because I was dumb and thought that missing a few pills wouldn't be the end of the world—which it wasn't."

"You just got pregnant."

"Yes. And then I got married! On purpose!"

"You're so weird," said Joanna.

"Not all of us can rock the lone wolf like you do."

"Thank you! Now tell Granny that."

"I'm just saying—"

"I'm not marrying the librarian!"

Several heads swung in their direction. Fortunately, Liam's was not one of them. In fact, she hadn't seen him since the show started.

"Great, now everybody is going to think I'm trying to marry the librarian."

"He's kind of a hot commodity. You should be flattered."

"Flattered that he's chosen me above all the other boring single people in Halikarnassus?"

"Shows he has good taste?"

"Psh. Good taste. And he's crazy."

"Just like you! Your babies will be so cute."

Joanna made a sound like Kristin before the show.

"I'm just teasing you, weirdo," Trina said, throwing her arm around Joanna.

"Careful, you're getting gray hair on your Black Widow outfit."

"You don't have to leave, you know."

"I'm not. Doris is taking—"

"I'm not talking about now. I mean, like, ever."

"Trina—"

"Just don't use Granny as an excuse not to do something you don't want to admit you want to do."

Joanna narrowed her eyes at Trina. "I liked it better when I lived across the country and I could just hang up on you when you were reading my mind."

"Well, I'm glad you're here so I can see the look on your face when I'm right. Man, I love being right."

Liam wasn't so sure that Rick should be trusted with fire. He was having way too much fun building the bonfire in the fire pit. And the way the flames reflected off his plastic Iron Man suit . . . it looked maniacal. It looked dangerous.

But, hey, Liam wasn't gonna begrudge the guy a good time. Especially not when Liam owed him about four thousand favors for separating him and Hal before it turned into a full-on fight.

"How's the hand?"

"Good," he said, though it was a little sore. Hal had a hard head. And Liam probably didn't know how to throw a punch right. Maybe Iron Man would show him.

"Damn, man, I didn't think you had it in you."

"To punch the mayor?"

"No. Well, that, yes, but I mean to defend Joanna's honor like that."

Liam scowled. What kind of guy did Rick think he was?

"Whoa, slow down, Scarecrow. And step back—your stuffing is a little close to the flames."

Liam took a step back. Then he pulled the straw out of his sleeves—it was getting really itchy anyway—and tossed it into the fire.

"I just mean that I thought you were too PC to go all caveman like that."

"You didn't hear what he said."

"Nope. Nobody did, on account of your girlfriend melting our faces." He held up two fingers like devil horns, the universal sign for rock and roll.

She's not my girlfriend, Liam wanted to say, but that wasn't quite true. They spent almost every night together, they weren't seeing other people, they had mutual friends and mutual activities outside of the bedroom (although they also had mutual activities inside the bedroom, which maybe accounted for the lack of sleep that made him cranky enough to punch the mayor). In effect, they were boyfriend and girlfriend. He just had a feeling if he brought that up to Joanna, she would bolt.

He didn't want to think about the fact that he'd robbed her of the chance to defend her own honor.

"So, you don't think she saw?"

"No, man. Sorry."

"No, no, that's good. Listen, ah, do you think you could keep this little . . . kerfuffle to ourselves?"

"Kerfuffle? Dude, you clocked Hal, and he came up sputtering like a baby."

"I know, but . . . look, it's complicated." Because Joanna was complicated.

Also, he really didn't need any more attention brought to the fact that if the mayor was sporting a shiner, it was because of the librarian.

"Seriously," he beseeched Iron Man.

Rick held up his hands. "Okay, okay. I won't tell."

"Won't tell what?" And then Trina was at Rick's side, putting her arms around his waist. And, conveniently, pulling him back from the fire.

"How cute we look in our couples costume and how lame Joanna is for leaving Liam out in the cold like that."

"Hey! I'm wearing a costume!" And there was Joanna next to him. Liam was tempted to step closer to the fire to get those arms around him. But then he thought he'd better not risk it.

"Yeah, but not a *couples* costume."

"But I'm dressed as a librarian. Doesn't that count?"

Rick waved her lack of enthusiastic costuming off. "Babe," he said to his wife. "Did I tell you how amazing you guys were?"

"Yes, but tell me again."

"You looked so hot on those drums." Rick leaned

in to whisper more descriptions of Trina's hotness into her ear. Trina giggled and shoved him away, but he caught her in his Iron Man grip and soon Liam and Joanna were standing side by side at the bonfire, watching their hosts make out.

Joanna cleared her throat.

He wanted to take her hand. He really did have a hard time being near her without touching her. But his hand was also pretty sore.

"Ew, gross!" the Hulk said just as Iron Man dipped Black Widow back for an even more romantic kiss.

Rick lifted his head. "I thought you guys were in bed."

"Grandma Carrington said we could see the fire."

"I want to see the fire!" came a voice from across the yard, and a red streak was zooming toward them.

Joanna caught Hazel before she pitched into the bonfire. "Hey, speedy, watch out." She picked her up and rested her on her hip.

"I almost got burnded," Hazel said.

"Almost."

"Your hair is tickly."

"Do you like it?"

"You're silly, Auntie Jo Jo."

"Auntie Jo Jo, huh?" Trina had disentangled from her amorous husband and was pulling chairs up to the fire pit. Liam put one behind Joanna, then took one for himself.

"Auntie Jo Jo knows all the bad words," Hazel informed her mother.

"I'm sure she does."

"If I put you down, are you going to quit running near the fire?"

"Yes, Auntie Jo Jo."

"Honestly, she listens to everybody but me!" Trina complained, but she did it with a smile.

Joanna sat, and as soon as she did, the wind shifted and smoke went straight into her face. Coughing, she shifted her seat out of the line of fire (ha). She was farther away from Liam, but he could see her across the dancing flames, her black hair badly covered in powder, the neckline of her ugly dress coming unbuttoned. As he watched, Hazel climbed up in her lap, and at first, Joanna looked startled, as if she didn't know what to do with this little red creature invading her personal space. Then Hazel cuddled in, stuck her thumb in her mouth, and tucked her head against Joanna's chest. Joanna put her arms around the sleepy kid, and he saw her mouthing quiet nonsense words to her as she fell asleep.

Oh boy, he thought. He was in big trouble.

"Hey, Liam, come help me in the kitchen," Trina said, disentangling herself from her husband's iron grip.

"Bossy," Joanna said.

"You're busy," Trina replied, nodding to Hazel, who was now asleep on Joanna's lap.

"I can help you," Rick said.

"No. Liam, come on."

Liam looked over at Joanna, who shrugged. He couldn't imagine what Trina wanted him, specifically, for in the kitchen—he was not his best in the kitchen—and neither, apparently, could Joanna.

She didn't say anything as they walked into the house, but he followed her dutifully.

"What's up?" he asked. Maybe he needed her to reach something from a high shelf. Although Rick could have helped her with that.

"I wanted to talk to you about Joanna."

Liam was seized with a sudden panic. "Oh, God, is she breaking up with me?"

"What? No. Why would I want to talk to you about her breaking up with you?"

"I don't know. I actually have no evidence that either you or she would do something like that. Just a knee-jerk reaction, I guess."

Trina shook her head. "Trust me, if Joanna is pissed and wants to break up, she'll tell you."

"Okay. I've got issues. Clearly."

"Well, that's what I want to talk to you about."

"My issues?"

"No! Jesus, let me talk."

Liam mimed zipping his lips closed and throwing away the key.

"Thank you. It's about Joanna. Do not interrupt."

Liam swallowed whatever he was about to say. To be honest, he wasn't sure what that was, only that Trina was going to say something about Joanna that he probably wouldn't like and he really wanted to head her off at the pass. Which would do him no good. He should just shut up and listen.

"Joanna . . . she's not used to people being nice."

"Ooookay."

"She usually dates jerks. Like, honest-to-God ass-holes. I haven't met everyone she's dated, but I've met enough to know. Her type is jerk."

"So . . . I should be a jerk?"

"No. Definitely not. You just be you."

"Good." He was pretty sure he wouldn't be able to be anyone else. No matter how hard he tried.

"I just want to warn you that Joanna has this

habit. Whenever people are nice to her, she gets . . . suspicious. Or defensive. Or, just, weird."

"Okay."

"I don't want you to be weirded out by it."

"By her being weird?"

"By her pushing you away. Because she'll do it. She'll try to push you away, and I watched enough *Oprah* reruns when I was pregnant to know that she'll push you away before you push her away."

He thought about when they'd first met, how every conversation ended with her being abrupt—or downright mean—and walking away. Maybe it was just a defense mechanism. Maybe it wasn't that she didn't like him.

Because she did like him. He knew it. She acted like she liked him. Sometimes she told him. And it was totally, completely mutual.

"I'm not going to push her away."

"Sure, but she won't believe that."

He wasn't sure what he was supposed to do with this information. Wait for Joanna to start being mean to him again? Because she was showing no signs of it.

Anyway, she was leaving. He didn't know when. He was starting to think that she didn't know when. Peggy was much better, and as far as he knew, she didn't have any plans that would take her away from Halikarnassus.

Take her away from him.

And that was when he realized: When she left, it was gonna hurt. He could pretend to be holding her at arm's length, just having fun with a really cool girl while she was around. A really cool girl who bit his head off but was a monster in the kitchen. A girl who held the world at arm's length, but at night, when it was just them and it was dark, she told him her secrets.

If he was honest with himself, he was already way too far gone.

"I'm just saying, be patient with my girl, that's all."

He wanted to ask Trina to say the same thing to Joanna. To be gentle with him, or do something so he wouldn't miss her so much.

But he didn't. He just agreed to be patient.

"Is that why you brought me in here?" he asked.

She pointed to a cabinet above the refrigerator. "Also I need you to get that pitcher for me."

Chapter Twenty-Five

As winter approached, Joanna could no longer deny that Granny didn't need her anymore. She still got sore if she overexerted (which was all the time), but if she didn't walk far, she could do it without her cane. She could drive and cook and walk the dog all by herself.

But winter was coming. What if she slipped on the ice? Joanna stuck around, just to make sure.

Then it snowed.

A lot.

It was one of those weird, pre-winter storms, the kind that comes out of nowhere before the salt trucks are ready and dumps a foot of snow on the ground as if to say, *ha ha, bet you weren't expecting that.*

Joanna sat at the kitchen window, nursing a hot cup of coffee, watching the snow fall.

"It's been a while since you've seen that, huh?" Granny asked.

It hadn't been that long. When you tour around the country, you see all kinds of weather. But this snow was different. This snow wasn't getting between her and her next gig. It wasn't snow she'd have to scrape off their crappy van or wade through to load out. It was just . . . pretty.

She wanted to enjoy the snow, dammit.

"I have your old snow boots in the hall closet," Granny said, reading her mind.

Granny laughed at Joanna's shocked expression. "It's all over your face. You used to get that same look when you were little and you couldn't wait to go outside with the other kids to build snowmen."

"And snowball fights."

"Yes, well. You always did have a good arm."

Joanna stood and put her mug in the sink. She stretched her arms over her head. "Maybe I will go out. Just for a walk."

"Could you use some company?"

"Gran, I don't know if you should be out there in this."

"Not me. And not Starr, she hates the snow."

"Then who?"

Gran took a sip of her coffee.

"Gran. Jeez."

Still, when Joanna got to her room to change into more snow-appropriate clothes, she called Liam.

"Come out and play, librarian."

"Ah, I can't."

"Why not? Too afraid of a little cold?"

"Well, no. I'm at work."

"Work? Why? Isn't the library closed today?"

"No. I got here okay."

"How? The roads haven't even been plowed yet."

"I walked."

"Walked? Liam, that's like four miles!"

"It's closer to three."

"You must have some serious snow boots."

"Yeah. And snowshoes."

She stopped for a moment, one leg in her leggings.

"You snowshoed to the library?"

"Yes. It was the safest way to get here."

"You really are a Boy Scout. So, is it busy? Are you providing warmth to the masses?"

"Uh, actually, no. I'm the only one here."

"Really?" She did not sound surprised at all.

"I'm glad you called. I was going crazy here all by myself. The good news is, I'm all caught up on my e-mail."

"Why don't you close now?"

"Eh, it's fine. Closing is a whole rigmarole with the board and I don't really want to deal with that. Besides, I'm here, so obviously I was able to get to work. There's no real reason not to be open."

"Except that the governor declared a state of emergency and nobody's supposed to be out on the roads."

"I wasn't on the roads. Well, I was, but my car wasn't."

"Yes, but you're the only idiot in town. Nobody's coming to the library, buddy."

She heard him sigh. Poor Liam. He worked so hard.

Poor Liam in that big ol' building all by himself.

All by himself, with no one to keep him company.

And no one to see if his girlfriend walked over to the library and seduced him . . .

Liam's eyes were starting to cross. Maybe putting in a full day at the library when no one else was there was not something he needed to be doing. He thought about his couch, and a fire in the fireplace, and tucking himself under a blanket with a book. Or better yet, with Joanna. Peggy's house was sort of on the way home. He could snowshoe over and . . .

And what, throw her over his shoulder and carry her off to his pink-kitchened love nest?

She would totally go for that.

Just as he was revising his plan for getting snowed in with Joanna, there was a bang from the lobby. That sounded a lot like the front door opening and closing.

Great, patrons.

Well, he had opened the library for a reason. Shelter from the storm and all that.

He blinked hard and walked out from the stacks, ready to greet his patrons with a friendly smile and swift customer service that would have them out the door quickly so he could figure out how to ravish his girlfriend.

And then, there she was.

He didn't recognize her at first, what with the massive plaid scarf covering most of her face. But he recognized that voice.

"Holy balls, it's cold out."

She wiped her nose on the edge of her scarf, and he had never been so happy to see someone in his entire life. What kind of winter magic was this? He just thought about her, and she appeared.

He tried thinking about a pizza. He'd forgotten to bring lunch and he was hungry.

"Hey." He walked over and helped her out of her coat and stepped back as she toed off her snowy boots. "Welcome to the library!"

"Am I the only one here?"

"So far."

She snorted. "So far. You know it's still snowing, right?"

"Is it?" He hadn't looked out the window in a while. He did so now.

Yup, still snowing.

"So." She pulled off her snowy hat and tossed it on top of her snowy jacket. That was probably going to leave a wet spot on the carpet.

Oh well.

She shook her hair out, then smiled up at him. "What have you been doing with yourself?"

"Oh, nothing much. Just getting caught up on stuff. I was just shelf reading."

"What's shelf reading?"

"It's where you look at all the spine labels on the books and make sure they're in call number order."

She just looked at him. He thought he might have to explain it differently. Sometimes he did that, used too much library jargon to explain things to a civilian.

"That sounds terrible."

Yup, she understood.

"It's not great," he said. "But it has to be done."

"So . . . how's it going? Anything good on the shelf?"

"The pregnancy books were totally out of order, but the rest was mostly fine."

"Huh."

"Well, I didn't do the whole collection, so there might be some other problems. I just focused on the sections that are used the most."

"You are such a nerd."

"I know."

"Are you ready for a break?"

"That depends. Were there hordes of patrons behind you?"

"Nope. I had the sidewalks of Halikarnassus all to myself. At least, I think I was on the sidewalks. They're sort of buried."

"Okay, then. I'm ready for a break."

"Good."

She bent down to her discarded shoulder bag and pulled out two thermoses. "Soup, and hot chocolate."

He could kiss her.

But first, he wanted to eat.

"It's weird how quiet it is in here."

They'd pulled the cushions off the chairs and made a little nest for themselves near the science fiction. That way they could eat their soup—which was hearty and delicious and he still wanted to kiss her for it—and watch the snow fall.

Because the snow was still falling. A little less rapidly now, but it clearly was not done with the whole "blanketing the streets of town" thing.

"Imagine that, a quiet library," he said.

She nudged him with her shoulder. "You know what I mean."

He stretched out on the floor with his happily full belly. "It is nice. I mean, I don't think the library needs to be a quiet place anymore, you know? The noise means people are using it."

"Hmm," she said, and he thought she was lost in

the peaceful view from the window, but when he looked at her, he saw that she was looking at him.

"What? Am I being a dork?"

She shook her head. "You really love this place, don't you?"

He wanted to tell her that he didn't really care that much one way or the other, that he would gladly follow her anywhere. But he'd never lied to her, and he wasn't going to start now.

"Yup."

She sighed and looked out the window. He wanted to ask her if maybe she was changing her mind, if these few months they'd spent together had made her see that Halikarnassus wasn't such a bad place or such a boring place. When they were together, it could be great.

But he didn't, and when she turned back to him, she had a wicked grin on her face.

"How much do you love this place?" she asked.

"Uh." He was confused. But that grin was doing things to his insides. Sexy things. "A lot?"

"A lot?" She got on all fours and crawled over toward him, then over him so her body surrounded his.

"Have you ever had sex in a library before?" she asked.

He gulped. He watched her eyes move to his throat and she licked her lips. No, he hadn't had sex in a library. He couldn't think of a more unsanitary place to have sex. Actually, yes, he could, but still. Sex in the library felt . . . well, it didn't feel wrong. It should feel wrong, but Joanna was shaking her head, the ends of her hair tickling his face; then her hands were unbuttoning his shirt and her hair was tickling his chest.

He decided that now was not the time for an ethical quandary. Not when Joanna was reaching for his belt buckle. So he just gave himself over to the fantasy and let Joanna show him how much he could really love the library.

Chapter Twenty-Six

"First thing on the agenda is a special commenda-
tion to the Halikarnassus football team. Boys?"

The first town council meeting of the new year
was usually a slog. Folks were still coming off of the
holiday high, and voting on building permits was a
surefire way to kill any remaining festive spirit.

This meeting was different.

Liam watched as several dozen boys of varying
shapes and sizes—well, mostly big—lumbered up to
the podium. Hal looked like he was vibrating with
pride and glee.

Liam had been to a lot of town council meetings, and
he'd heard Hal present a lot of official commendations—
Girl Scouts, church choirs, war veterans. Once there
was even one honoring a cat who dialed 9-1-1 when
her owner was having a heart attack. (There was a
minor scandal when it was discovered that the owner
had, in fact, dialed the phone himself before losing
consciousness.) This was definitely the most excited
Liam had ever seen Hal when doing his civic duty.

"WHEREAS," he began in a very Mayoral Voice.

"the Halikarnassus High School football team represents the highest standards of sportsmanship, athleticism, hard work, and competition—"

"Except for girls' lacrosse, which actually wins," Doris only sort of whispered to Peggy, who was seated on the other side of Liam. Her granddaughter was on the lacrosse team. It was a big bone of contention.

"WHEREAS, the Halikarnassus High School football team surpassed the win record of any other HHS team in recent memory and achieved a spot in the New York State High School Football Tournament Quarterfinals—"

"Where they promptly lost," Doris whispered.

"Hush, now," Peggy whispered back.

"I'm just saying, this is a whole lot of proclamation for nothin'."

"The boys worked hard."

"That Dylan boy had a growth spurt. That's not working hard."

Liam just leaned back and let the two argue over him. He didn't want to take away from the team's achievement—the quarterfinals was a big deal considering they hadn't been good enough to be invited to the tournament in years. But a good football team—which Halikarnassus High was not, but had the potential to become—meant the library's funding could once again be in danger. This made the already painful annual budget process even more fraught. He didn't want to suggest efficiencies since the library was already running on a bare enough budget. And he didn't want to ask for an increase because he didn't want to make Hal mad. And Hal would be mad if he thought Liam was trying to take any money away from his precious almost-good football team.

"NOW, THEREFORE, LET IT BE PROCLAIMED by the Honorable Mayor and the Town Council of the Town of Halikarnassus that today is Halikarnassus High School Football Day!"

A great, grunting cheer went up in the council hall. Liam clapped dutifully. The boys lined up to shake hands with the council, and there was more cheering and cell phones were clicking away their blurry photos to be posted on the town's Facebook page later, the one that Liam had helped the council set up.

Bitterness was not going to win him points with anyone on the council, so he stood when everyone else stood. Not even the (alleged) 9-1-1-dialing cat got a standing ovation.

"We're very proud of you boys," Councilman Maguire said over the din. "I think this could mean some big changes for your facilities up there at the school, don't you, Mayor?"

Liam looked up at the dais, where Hal was still standing, a triumphant smile on his face.

"That bad, huh?"

It was hard to feel like the situation was hopeless when Joanna's naked body was pressed up against his, her fingers tracing lazy circles on his chest. But he was pretty sure it was hopeless.

"Hal's got it in for the library for some reason."

"He's just mad because he doesn't read."

"Maybe I should do some kung fu reader's advisory on him, turn him into a reader."

"I don't understand half of what you just said, but I wouldn't waste too much time trying to get Hal to change. Especially not when it involves football."

"I don't get it. Why can't we have both? Why do we have to choose between sports and the library? A lot of athletes use the library."

He felt Joanna shrug. "Hal's always been competitive like that. He doesn't just want to win, he wants to annihilate the competition."

"That's how he was in high school. You hate it when people think you're still high school, Joanna. Maybe he's changed."

She propped herself up on her elbow so she was looking him in the eye. "Yes, but Hal hasn't been getting naked with you, making him all soft."

He tucked a wayward strand of hair behind her ear. "You're not all soft."

She kissed him, sweet and gentle. Maybe she was a little soft. Not all soft. He still felt she might bolt at any time. There was still a part of her that he didn't understand.

She put her head back on his chest and resumed her lazy circles, this time on his stomach. "What are your parents like?" she asked.

Liam felt a sudden pang of guilt, remembering that he was supposed to call his mother back. But he kept getting distracted by Joanna's sexiness, and that really didn't put him in the mood to talk to his mother.

"They're, I don't know, my parents." That painted a nice picture for her. "They got divorced when I was in middle school, and they still pretty much hate each other. They say that they keep it polite for the kids, but, well, they don't."

"They fight a lot?"

He wasn't sure if his parents' very communicative noncommunication could be called fighting. "More like a lot of passive-aggressive teeth gnashing. It's pretty exhausting. Especially when the new husbands are there."

"Husbands? Like sister wives?"

"No, no. My mom left my dad for her tennis coach—"

"Wow."

"I know. Might as well have been the pool boy. But now they've been married for longer than my parents were."

"Well, I bet that shuts the haters up, at least."

"You obviously don't know my family."

"Once a cheater, always a cheater?"

That was one way of putting it. "I think she got it even harder because she was the mom, and leaving us was seen as unnatural. Even though she only moved across town. We still saw her all the time. Hell, we still took tennis lessons from Dan."

"Dan the tennis instructor?"

"Dan the tennis instructor-husband."

"I didn't know you played tennis. Tap dance and tennis."

"That's because I suck at tennis. And I hate it."

"There's something deep in there."

"You mean my subconscious hates tennis because it tore my family apart? Probably."

She pressed a kiss over his heart. "You said husbands. So, what, your mom has another husband?"

"No, my dad. He came out when I was a senior in college."

"Whoa."

"Yeah. My mom was pissed."

"Even though she had Dan?"

"I think she still thinks Dad came out to get back at her for leaving."

"Is that how that works? I'd always wondered." She flattened her palm on his abdomen.

"And then Dad had the nerve to also marry a guy named Dan."

Joanna threw back her head. "Oh my God. That's amazing."

"The thing is, I like spending time with the Dans. It's my parents I can't deal with."

"My Two Dans," she said, giggling.

"Okay, I showed you mine. What's your cuckoo parental story?" There must be something there, since she'd been raised by her grandmother.

He felt her stiffen. He tightened his hold on her, just a little, in case she decided to bolt.

"Mine are dead."

"Oh." Well, Liam was officially an asshole. He loosened his grip again. She could bolt if she wanted to.

But she didn't.

"They dropped me off at Granny's so they could build an orphanage in Laos."

"That's very . . . humanitarian?"

"They told me they were going to bring me back a baby brother or sister, or maybe both."

"Weird."

"Yeah, except they went with this hippie bootleg Peace Corps group who used essential oils and herbs instead of actual medicine and my parents died of malaria."

"Oh. Geez."

"They weren't even religious. Just stupid."

She sounded mad.

He didn't know what to say. He couldn't really disagree with her assessment—I mean, there were treatments for malaria. He was no doctor, but he was pretty sure it could be cured.

"Were they out in the country? With no access to medicine?" he asked, trying to understand. There must have been some explanation, surely.

"No. I mean, yes, they were in a rural area, but there was a clinic there and UNICEF people and everything."

"Why didn't they go?"

"Because they eschewed modern medicine. It's poison, they said."

"Unlike malaria."

"I remember how pissed they were when they found out Granny had me vaccinated. She told me that she did it when it became clear that I was going to be staying in Halikarnassus for the school year. No vaccines, no school."

"But your parents were upset?"

"Pissed. I remember watching Granny on the phone with them. She was holding the phone away from her ear, and I could hear my mother shouting and screaming like a crazy person. I've never seen Granny cry so hard in her life, not even when they died."

"God."

"And it took months. The malaria, I mean. Granny was doing everything to try to get them back here, but she couldn't afford to go get them herself, and they wouldn't listen to her pleas over the phone, and then they just stopped talking to her."

"God," he said again, because what else could he say?

"Yeah, and Granny tried to shield me from it. I was only seven. But I knew. They chose their stupid principles over me."

He squeezed her now, tight to him.

"So now you know where I get that from."

It was true. She was stubborn. "But music isn't a matter of life and death."

"Hey now," she said, sitting up. Her eyes still looked sad, but he knew she was done talking about it. This was Joanna. She didn't like feelings.

And even though he knew showing any sign of pity would be a death wish, he couldn't help but feel bad for that little girl she'd been, abandoned by her parents. Even if, in the end, it had been for the best, it still must have hurt.

No wonder she hated this town.

He wanted to tell her that he got it, that he wouldn't hold her here if she didn't want to stay. But he didn't really mean that. If he could, he'd tie her down and never let her leave. But he knew if he tried, he wouldn't have Joanna. She wasn't compliant. She wasn't meant to be tied down. And that was why he loved her.

He wanted to tell her, but he couldn't. If he told her, he'd lose her. So he just pulled her head down closer to his and kissed her. He rolled them so he was on top of her. He couldn't tell her, but he could show her.

Chapter Twenty-Seven

Joanna was in big trouble.

The more time she spent with Liam, the more time she wanted to spend with Liam. He had a way of wringing painful truths out of her and then loving her so sweetly afterward that she hardly felt any pain.

He was going to be hard to leave behind.

Not that she particularly had anywhere to go.

Her phone rang, and she dug in the couch cushions for it. How had it even gotten down there? Starr gave her a lazy growl as Joanna dislodged her pillow throne.

"Did you bury my phone?" she asked the dog.

Starr just put her head down on her paws.

"Don't look all innocent on me," she said as her hand made contact with the phone. "Aha. Hello?"

"Joanna?"

"Who is this?"

"It hasn't been that long, bitch."

Joanna rolled her eyes. Mandy. Bunny Slippers Mandy.

"Hey," Joanna said tentatively. The last time she'd

spoken to Mandy, her former bandmate had told her that she never wanted to speak to her again and she hoped her fingers froze off in a snowstorm. Their professional relationship, such as it was, had not ended smoothly.

"How's it going?" Mandy asked, her tone suspiciously innocent.

"Fine."

"You still in that shitty hometown of yours?"

Joanna wanted to defend Halikarnassus, say it wasn't that bad. Then she realized what she was about to say. Of course it was bad. It was terrible. It was boring. It was . . .

Well, maybe it wasn't terrible. There were a lot of terrible, small-minded people here, but there were a lot of people she really liked, too.

Not that she thought Mandy particularly cared.

"Yup."

"Good. Listen. Calliope's out."

Great, Joanna thought. A sarcastic thought, though, because she had no idea what Mandy was talking about.

"She and Jeff," Mandy explained, clearing up exactly nothing.

"What are you talking about?"

"For reals? Ugh, Joanna. Head out of ass, please. Calliope is—was—the guitarist who replaced you when you *abandoned* us onstage."

So, Joanna was not entirely forgiven.

"The good news is, she sucked, so it's no great loss. Except that now we are without a lead guitarist."

"I thought you said Jeff wasn't going to let me within ten feet of you guys." *Joanna, are you trying to screw this up?*

"That's the other good news. Jeff did a runner with Calliope. I talked to a lawyer, and since he broke the contract, it's null and void. Basically, whatever Jeff said, we can forget."

"So . . ."

"So come back on the tour, bitch! We need you. And you owe us."

Joanna's hands started sweating. She held the phone away from her ear for a minute because all she could hear was the beating of her heart.

". . . not so bad. I mean, their music sucks, but whatever. We get that money, no more Jeff, we can do what we want. Meet us in Minneapolis, bring Rosetta."

"And my fluffy tail?"

"Listen, the fluffy tail. I kind of like it. But Deb and Harlow won't wear theirs, so I guess you don't have to either. It can just be my thing."

No tail, no Jeff, playing the music that she wanted to play.

Opening for a band she hated with people whose judgment she questioned.

"I gotta think about it," she told Mandy.

"Are you kidding me." It wasn't so much a question as a statement that Joanna was once again not acting in her own best interest.

"I can't just drop everything, you know." She had a lot going on in Halikarnassus. Her grandmother—who didn't need her, a band—that was just for fun, a guy—who, well, he'd be fine without her.

And she'd be fine without him.

Right?

"Fine. You think about it. Your big important life

in that shitty town that you hate is a lot to give up,
I know."

"You don't know my life," Joanna said, instantly
defensive.

"No, but I know you, and I know you live to play.
So quit pretending you don't want this."

She did want it. She was pretty sure she wanted it.

"I talked to the guys and they are totally on board."

"The guys?"

"The Penny Lickers, obv. And their management.
They want to make a big deal about it, like you're
so badass and punk rock you just up and leave
whenever. Except that you can't do that again, okay?
You can't just run off whenever you don't agree with
something."

"Got it. I still need to think about it."

"Don't think too long, bitch. We found one Calliope,
we can find another."

"Bye, Mandy."

"Call me tomorrow."

Joanna hung up without committing. She flopped
back on the couch and threw her arm over her eyes.
Starr jumped off her perch on the back of the couch
and onto Joanna's abdomen.

"Oof." But Joanna ran her hands along Starr's
fluffy back, finding comfort in the feeling.

This opportunity was what Joanna wanted, handed
to her on a silver platter. The chance to get back with
Bunny Slippers, to reclaim the band's rightful place
as an actual, hard-rocking punk band that did
not answer to the whims of the corporate music
machine.

But what about when the next Jeff came along?
How could she trust that Mandy wouldn't jump on

the next record contract? Because that was what
Mandy wanted, to be big. She said otherwise, but
could people really change?

Joanna had changed, though. She wasn't the same
person she had been when she'd first come back to
Halikarnassus, just like she wasn't the same person
she had been when she was in high school (and thank
God for that). Now she was happy with Delicious
Lies, screwing around with her friends, playing whatever the hell they wanted with no endgame other
than making really great noise. And Chet had asked
them to play. Their first real gig, with people who
would pay a cover to see them. A five-dollar cover,
but still. Five dollars to see three women play real, authentic, no-holds-barred rock.

Even Kristin was starting to panic a little less at the
thought. And Joanna felt like she couldn't let Kristin
down by leaving before the gig. And if anything
could prove to her that people could change, it was
the fact that she was considering Kristin Klomberg's
feelings before making a decision.

And if she went out on the road again with Bunny
Slippers, what about Liam? Joanna was not a total
idiot. No relationship survived the separation of the
road. And she had nothing to hold him to her, nothing to give him to make him stay. And he couldn't
come with her. Even if he didn't have an actual, important job, she had a feeling he wouldn't want to
leave this stupid town.

She should talk about it with him. Maybe they
could work it out. But then he'd choose Halikarnassus over her, and she didn't think her ego could take
the blow.

"What am I gonna do, Starr?"

Starr just snored on.

She needed to clear her head. She needed space to think. Granny's couch was way too comfortable for her to do anything but fall asleep thinking that staying here for the rest of her life would be a great idea.

"Okay, Starr," she said, sitting up. "We're going for a w-a-l-k."

Starr looked at Joanna, her ears perked up, and she tore down the hall, headed, Joanna assumed, under Granny's bed.

Starr did not want to walk.

And apparently she knew how to spell.

Well, Joanna didn't need company, anyway. In fact, she was probably better off without company. She picked up her coat where she'd tossed it on the floor (because old habits die hard) and wound a scarf around her neck. She shut the door behind her and stood on the front steps, thinking idly about which way to walk. It didn't really matter. She wasn't going anywhere. She'd just walk and see where she wound up.

She shouldn't have been surprised that, twenty minutes later, she was on the steps of the library.

"Mayor's here again."

Liam looked up from his computer, where he'd been fighting with a spreadsheet. The budget spreadsheet, to be specific. And not just fighting. It was more like tearing his hair out.

Of course Hal was here now.

"I don't suppose he's just a regular patron again today," he asked Dani, without much hope that that was true.

"Big! How's it going?"

Hal appeared behind a surprised Dani, who scuttled out of the way and, he hoped, back to the circ desk. Although she was probably going to the break room to tell the others that the mayor was in Liam's office.

He wouldn't blame her if she did. Everyone was worried sick about their jobs. He had assured them that every possible measure would be taken to keep staffing at its current level, but if they cut the budget, he'd have to cut hours, and he couldn't really justify having more people on staff than they really needed.

Not that he said that part. But he thought about it. A lot.

"Hi, Mayor," Liam said, standing up to shake Hal's hand. "What can I do for you?"

"Nice hair," Hal said, and Liam quickly smoothed down his hair. One of the hazards of pulling out one's hair while looking at a budget that might or might not be cut in half. "How is the world of the library treating you?"

"Oh, just fine. Swell. Lots of people out there, as you can see. Gearing up for spring break." Babbling. Sentence fragments.

"I see. Anything major happening?"

"Nothing major. Just the usual. Toni and I are starting to talk about summer reading."

"Summer! You really do plan ahead."

And this man was the mayor.

"I came to drop off these books." Hal put a paper bag on Liam's desk and started to empty it.

Books.

Not great books.

Hardbacks with dinged-up corners. Paperbacks with the covers bent back. Lots of yellowing pages.

Spines slashed with a black marker—ah, the remainders bin. C. J. Box, Lincoln Child, Danielle Steel. All stuff that was really popular, and all of it at least five years old, and all stuff Liam was sure was already in the collection.

"Thanks," Liam said, as he did to everyone who donated crappy books that wouldn't even get fifty cents in the used book sale.

"Guess how much I spent on this pile of books here," Hal challenged.

Liam considered. Ten hardbacks, fourteen paperbacks . . . "Twenty bucks?" Probably less than that, but Liam rounded up so Hal could prove whatever point he was trying to prove.

"Close. Thirty-five."

Wow. Mayor got ripped off.

"You know how much these books would cost new?"

Liam did some math. Twenty to twenty-five for a hardback, fifteen for the trade paperbacks . . .

"Three hundred eighty-nine dollars and seventy-six cents."

"Great. Thanks. We really appreciate—"

"That's less than ten percent."

"Yup." He wondered if Toni had any "Good Job" stickers in the children's room. Hal looked like he could use one.

"So what I'm saying is, why do you have to spend so much money on books?"

If Liam didn't value his brain function so much, he would have slammed his head on his desk. It was preferable to slamming his head against Hal's face.

"True, but you don't get that kind of discount on new books."

"Sure, but Kristin told me she always has to wait for her turn with the new books, so why not just wait and buy them later?"

Because five years was a ridiculous amount of time to wait, and the reason Kristin had to wait was that there were other people in front of her in line who had to wait a little less.

Liam was not sure explaining all that would work.

"Yes, but we already get a forty percent discount from our distributor."

"Forty percent is a lot less than ninety percent."

"Yes . . . but shopping like this is time-consuming, and I'm sure the selection is limited. You probably picked out the best books in the bunch." Flattery, to be sure, but also probably true.

"If you don't want to take my suggestions, fine. I'm only trying to make it easier."

"Make what easier?" A time-consuming, not-very-money-saving idea for adding books they didn't need to the collection . . . that didn't seem like it would help Liam out much.

Hal sighed, as if this was the hardest thing he'd had to say in a long time and he really pitied Liam for being the one who had to hear it. "I really didn't want to do this, but, well, I figured I'd better tell you in person."

"Tell me what?" Liam asked, a sense of dread creeping down his spine and cementing him to his chair.

"It's just that the boys have worked so hard, and we want to reward them. And I think you'll agree that more people come to football games than come to the library."

"I wouldn't agree with that, no." In fact, it would

be a pretty easy thing to disprove. Aside from the fact that the library was open year-round, Liam was pretty sure his average door counts would be higher than attendance at a regular season football game.

At least, it had been. Now that the team had gotten good-ish, Liam wouldn't bet his budget on that.

"I just think in the spirit of doing what's best for the community, we're going to go ahead with the stadium construction project."

Now it was a stadium? "You mean the lights?"

"The lights, for starters. I'm thinking about a state-of-the art venue that can be used year-round. The best technology, the best facilities, everything our boys deserve."

"And girls."

"Huh?"

"Surely a year-round sports facility would involve some of the girls' sports."

"Yeah, yeah, fine. The point is, money doesn't grow on trees."

"No . . ."

"But paper does. And you know what's made out of paper?"

"Money?"

"Books!"

Liam wished he was holding a pencil so that he could break it in half. But then Hal would probably cut his supply budget because now he had two pencils.

"We also have CDs and DVDs and other—"

"I'm just here as a professional courtesy, that's all. Tonight we're having a special session where we'll hear public opinions, then we'll vote."

"Voting on rearranging the budget that the council

already passed?" Tonight? Could he rally enough people to come support the library by tonight?

Yes, of course he could. He just had to activate the gossip train of Halikarnassus.

He wished Hal would leave so he could start making phone calls.

"There is one thing . . ."

Oh, God. Liam didn't think he could take one more thing.

"I might be persuaded to . . . postpone the vote."

"Postpone it? What, like, give me another day?" Liam couldn't help the sarcasm that crept into his voice. Because he couldn't imagine what he could give Hal that could compel the man to give up his dream of a useless football stadium in Halikarnassus.

"It's this band of your girlfriend's."

"What does Delicious Lies have to do with the town budget?" If he was going to ask them to play a special show, maybe he could beg Joanna to do it. If he begged really, really hard.

"My wife has been spending an awful lot of time with that band."

"Sure. I mean, she's in it, right?"

"Big, I'm gonna level with you. I love this town and I love my job, I really do. But I've got my eye on bigger fish. I'm talking Albany, I'm talking DC. And I don't think performing in this lunatic band with a psycho bitch—no offense to you and your taste in women—is the right image for a future First Lady, you know?"

Liam took a moment to imagine a country where Hal was the president. It did not compute, so he focused on the matter at hand.

"So . . . you want me to talk to Kristin?" They were

friends, sure, but he really didn't think he'd be comfortable with that. Of course, if it meant securing library funding, he could certainly try.

"No, no. I've tried that. Talking doesn't work. I need action."

"Uh . . ."

"I need you to get your girlfriend to cancel the gig."

The gig. The one the three of them had been looking forward to with such anxiety and excitement. The one that Joanna couldn't stop talking about, and the one that was keeping her in Halikarnassus.

Basically, Hal wanted him to choose between the library and Joanna.

And by the smug look on his face, the bastard knew exactly what he was doing.

That made him want to punch Hal. Again.

Instead, he took a step back. This was the budget of the library. This was people's salaries and the life of the center of the community. Maybe Joanna would do this as a favor.

God, he hated that he was even thinking that. If he gave Hal this inch, who knew what kind of mile he would be after next?

But he had to try.

"I'll think about it," he said, and as soon as the words were out of his mouth, he knew he wouldn't. Canceling one show was not going to make Hal give up his dream. But at least it might buy Liam some time until he could figure out something better to do. Maybe Hal would postpone the council's vote. Maybe he'd give them another year's reprieve.

"Good man," said Hal. He stood up, shook Liam's

hand. "I know you'll do the right thing. Oh, hi, Joanna. Didn't see you there."

Liam looked up at his doorway and, yup, there was his aforementioned girlfriend, the one who was a bad influence on the mayor's wife.

And she looked pissed.

Chapter Twenty-Eight

"Joanna! Wait!"

Joanna heard Liam running behind her, but she didn't slow her pace. But even with her head start, he caught up to her. Him and his stupid long legs.

"Joanna," he said, but she didn't stop. He grabbed her arm and turned her, but she shook him off, hard.

He held his hands up. "Joanna, I don't know what you heard . . ."

"Oh, I heard plenty. You're going to sell me out to your new friend, Hal."

"That's not what—"

"What, you're *not* going to ask me to cancel the show? You're gonna let the library go down in flames for a stupid rock band? That's pretty dumb, Liam."

"No, of course I wasn't—"

"Don't touch me!" She knew she was making a scene, and right outside the library. But she couldn't help it. If he touched her, she would forgive him, and if she forgave him, he'd just dump her at the next big opportunity.

"I heard what you said," she shouted. She shouldn't be shouting. There were kids in the parking lot. Parents watching with interest. If she wasn't driving Granny's car, she would hop in and drive off, but no matter how comfortable she was driving it, there was no way she was zooming anywhere in that thing. Not with other people in the parking lot.

Although maybe she could run over Liam. Just a little. Just so he could feel how it hurt.

"I didn't say—"

"Don't lie to me! I heard you say you would think about it."

"I didn't mean that! I wasn't going to ask you to cancel the show. That's ridiculous. That's not how this whole process works. I was just buying time. I thought if—"

"I don't believe you. I think you had a split second to choose between me and the library, and you didn't choose me."

"Joanna, that's not fair."

"Don't tell me what's not fair! What's not fair is always coming in second, is everyone having a perfectly reasonable explanation for why they're screwing me over!"

"Please, just calm down."

"Don't you be all reasonable with me! I know you had to do it. Of course you'd make that choice. But don't come after me, all reasonable and shit, and expect me to like it!"

"I don't think you understand—"

"Oh, I understand." She stepped up to him, put her finger in his face. She hated when people put their finger in her face when she was arguing, but she did it anyway. "You get it both ways, don't you? You get your stupid library, and you got me. Well, I'm not going to let you use me like that."

"Use you? How am I using you?"

She could see that she was finally getting under his skin. Good. It almost made her feel calmer.

Almost.

"What could I possibly be using you for?" he shouted.

And now she was totally calm. Dead calm. Her heart was a stone. It could not be broken.

"Wait, hold on," he pleaded. "That came out wrong."

She wanted to say one more thing, throw something in his face before she turned and walked away. But she didn't have anything. He was right. She was nothing to him, just a warm body and a pleasant diversion while she bided her time in this shitty place.

So she didn't say anything. She just got in the car, slammed the door. But there were too many people around, so she got out again. She slammed the door again. And she marched across the library lawn.

"What about your car?" she heard him ask, but she just gave him the finger and stomped toward home.

"Well, you're certainly in a mood."

How very astute of Granny to notice, Joanna thought, as she stomped into her bedroom and slammed the door. The force knocked over a pile of CDs. She kicked them.

She knew she was being childish. But she was just so pissed off. Pissed at Liam, yes, but she couldn't really blame him. One show for a not-very-good band at a bar they could play at any time, versus half the funding for the entire library. She knew she was being stupid. She shouldn't feel angry or hurt. But she did, and that made her even angrier.

It was that same thing all over again. Liam, and Bunny Slippers, and her parents. Why was the right thing to do always the thing that involved shitting on her?

Someone knocked on her door. Granny, obviously. Unless Liam ran those stupid runner legs over here. And Granny would let him in. She loved Liam. She would choose Liam over Joanna.

"Sweetie?"

That was definitely Granny. Liam would never call her sweetie. He'd called her baby a few times, but not in public, and not in a context that was at all similar to this situation.

Good thing she hadn't gotten used to it, because she wasn't going to hear it again.

The doorknob turned—so at least she hadn't broken the door when she slammed it—and Starr bolted in and made a beeline for her pillow. Granny followed, limping just a little bit.

"Do you want to tell me what's going on?"

"No." Joanna crossed her arms over her chest. Well, if she was going to throw a temper tantrum, might as well go all the way.

"Is it the girls? Are you having a problem with the band?"

"What? No, no, the band is fine."

"Good. I'm looking forward to that show tonight."

"You're going to the show?"

"Of course I am! I was at the first Delicious Lies show when you were in high school. I plan on being at the revival."

At least she had Granny.

Then she remembered what Hal had said, about the council meeting being tonight. Granny would want to be there. Granny should be there. It was the right thing to do.

Again.

Granny sighed, and Joanna was once again convinced that her grandmother was a mind reader.

"When you came to live with me, do you remember that?"

Joanna nodded. Of course she did.

"At first it made you so happy, when you used to visit me in the summers."

"Your cookies were better than Mom's." Granny wasn't the best baker around, but at least she didn't use vegan carob chips in her cookies.

Granny laughed. "You were so skinny. I was happy to fatten you up a little."

"Thanks, Gran."

"Then one month turned into two, then the summer was almost over, and it became clear that your parents weren't coming back. I think you knew before I did. You were so angry."

Joanna remembered that, too. Remembered telling Granny that she didn't do things like her mom did, that she didn't read stories like her dad did. Remembered this force inside her, pushing to get out, and she just wanted to fight everyone.

"Here's what I don't think you understand. I wanted you from the moment you were born. You were my precious grandbaby. Of course I knew I couldn't have you, I couldn't take you from your parents. But I wanted to. And then they left you, and part of me was glad." She wiped the corners of her eyes. Joanna looked away. She wasn't going to be able to stay mad if Granny was crying. "And then they died and I thought, is this my fault? Did I somehow will this because I wanted you so badly?"

"What? Granny, no. No, of course not."

"I know that. Of course I do, it makes no sense." She was really crying now, and Joanna could feel the lump in her throat. But she knelt down in front of Granny anyway. "I think I just needed someplace to put my feelings until I could deal with them properly. That's why I got you guitar lessons, you know. I thought it would be a good outlet for you."

"It was. It is. Thank you."

"But I wonder if it isn't good enough, because I don't think you understand. Your parents left you, yes, but I didn't take care of you because I had to, dammit!" Joanna sat back because Granny was crying and yelling and she wasn't really sure what to do with that. "I did it because I love you! You are the most precious thing in the world to me, and to see you holding on to that hurt your parents caused you . . . did I not love you enough?"

"What, Granny, no. No, of course not. I always knew that you loved me."

Granny wiped her eyes and let out a watery chuckle. "Sorry. I know you did. I know you know I did the best I could, though you sorely tested me. I just . . . I sometimes feel a little sorry for myself, you know?"

Joanna sighed. "Yeah, I know a little bit about that."

"So please, whatever is wrong, don't bottle it up. Don't take it out on people who don't deserve it."

Joanna hung her head. "I won't," she promised, even though it was already too late. But maybe she could fix it. She'd have to apologize to Liam. And she'd have to . . .

The house phone rang, and Granny got up to answer. Joanna heard her talking from the living room. "Oh, Liam, how nice of you . . . what? Well, all right, I'll see if she wants to talk to you."

Joanna panicked. She wasn't ready. She had to be sure of what she said because she didn't want to mess it up. Then a car honked from the driveway, and it was Trina in her badass truck, to pick her up for the gig. Shit, it was all happening too fast. What was she going to do, walk off the stage? Not again, she couldn't do that again. She needed to stop and figure it out. But Trina honked another time and she heard Granny coming down the hall with the phone, and she just grabbed Rosetta and brushed past her and got in the truck with Trina.

Chapter Twenty-Nine

"I'm so sorry I'm late."

Kristin rushed toward the stage, bass in hand, and squatted down to unpack it. "I had to find a sitter at the last minute. Hal said he had a 'thing.' I don't know what kind of thing it was, but it was clearly more important than paying five dollars to see us blow the roof off this place."

Joanna knew what the thing was. It was the council meeting, the one that Hal said he would cancel if they would cancel their gig. The one that would decide the fate of the library.

No, that was too optimistic. The one that was going to put the nail in the library's coffin.

And on Liam and Joanna.

She shook her hands out, trying to get them steady. Her hands never shook before a show. She was never that nervous, just antsy to get on stage and start playing.

She looked out over the tables around Chet's. From the tiny stage, with the lights in her eyes, it looked like they were all full. She saw Rick in the front row, his phone poised to take video. She saw Gus serving people at the bar, stopping to give her a wave. She saw Phyllis, of all people, chatting up the sound guy who was trying to do Kristin's mic check.

The last time she'd been on a stage, it had been in front of thousands of people, and it was all wrong. This time, there were maybe a hundred.

It was still wrong.

"I can't believe he's not coming," Kristin said. "I mean, I know he doesn't like this whole music thing, but it's important to me, you know?"

Joanna knew. Joanna knew how important music was, to Kristin and to Trina and to her. She also knew what it was like to choose between two important somethings.

"Hey, Joanna, you all right?" Trina asked from behind the drum set.

"Yeah," she said, even though she wasn't. But they'd just play the gig, and then she'd sort it out.

"You don't look all right."

"I'm fine! Let's just do this. Are you ready, Kristin?"

"Hold on. Band selfie!" She grabbed Joanna and held her phone out at arm's length. "Oh, that one's terrible. Joanna, can you smile? Come on, one more time."

She held out the phone again. This time, Joanna smiled.

"Yikes. Can you smile like you're happy?"

"Kristin," Trina said. "We can take selfies after."

"Okay, okay! I'm too excited." She bounced up and down a few times on the balls of her feet. "I'm ready. Are you ready?"

"I'm ready," said Trina. "Joanna?"

"I'm ready," she said without thinking.

Trina counted off and they slammed into the rhythm, the noise loud enough to drown out the shouts of the crowd.

But not loud enough to drown out Joanna's thoughts.

If she waited until after, the deed would be done. The library would be gutted . . . and Liam. What if Liam left town for a better job? That shouldn't matter, right? Because she was leaving, too. She was going to call Mandy tonight and tell her.

"Joanna!" Kristin's urgent whisper broke into her thoughts. Joanna realized that she had stopped playing. And that everyone was staring at her.

"She's gonna do it again!" someone shouted from the crowd.

"No, I'm fine." She looked at Trina. "Sorry. Can we start again?"

Trina rolled her eyes, but she counted off again.

For a few seconds, Joanna got lost in the music. It was like it always had been, nothing but her and the vibrations of Rosetta. Nothing could replace this. Nothing was better than this.

But some things were just as good. Liam, when he held her close and called her baby. When he dorked out about giving a kid some book he'd read when he was younger. When they argued about what the perfect record was for a Sunday afternoon. When he loved her.

He loved her. And she loved him. God, she loved him so much, and she'd been acting like a child. She'd thrown a fit because her parents were idiots and the world didn't always go her way, so she'd taken it out on Liam before he realized that the people of

Halikarnassus were right, that she was nothing but trouble.

But he didn't think that. And Phyllis was here, wasn't she? And Kristin and Trina. Trina didn't put up with her shit, and she stuck around. And a bunch of people they'd gone to high school with were there, and Gus, and people from all over town. Maybe they were just there to see if she had another meltdown, which was fair. But imminent meltdown notwithstanding, people didn't hate her. They didn't like her when she acted like a crazy fool, but, despite her best efforts, they had made her feel welcome back to the community.

And now she was going to thank them by throwing a hissy fit and costing them their library.

Well, if they came here for a meltdown, they were in luck.

She stopped playing. Again. She heard Trina curse behind her, but she didn't care; she just walked over to Kristin's mic. She winced at the feedback, but she grabbed it anyway.

"Thank you all for coming tonight. It means a lot to us." She indicated Kristin and Trina, both of whom were staring their own version of daggers at her. "Listen, something's happening in this town tonight, and I think it's more important than rock and roll. So, ah, does anyone have any paper?"

Liam felt much better with Peggy by his side. Sure, he would have liked Joanna there, at the Town Hall meeting where the fate of the library and his livelihood and reason for being in Halikarnassus was about to be decided.

It felt ironic, somehow, that as soon as he was about to be untethered from the one thing holding him in Halikarnassus, the woman he loved, who really, really hated that tether, had also untethered herself from him.

Had they ever really been tethered, though?

Yeah. Yeah they fucking had been.

God, he missed her.

But he had always been a good reader, and she'd laid it out pretty plainly for him. She was done with him. He had been thoughtless in his panic, but making a mistake did not mean that he didn't care. One dumb thing did not erase months of love. And if she refused to believe him, what could he do? She'd told him she was damaged goods. He was a fool to think that in a few months, he could erase a lifetime of self-doubt.

Of course he couldn't. He knew he couldn't. But he was really interested in spending a lot more time trying.

Really, really interested.

But what could he do? If every time they disagreed, she took off and left him beating his head against a wall—not a great way to live. Besides, he didn't know if she was the kind of girl to come back. Which, now that he thought about it, was kind of the wall he was beating his head against.

But he needed to be beating his head against Hal's wall.

That didn't sound right.

But you know what, he thought, *neither does slashing the operating budget for the library to install a state-of-the-art PA system on the football field.* Especially not when the football team sucked. No, it was never okay, but it felt like an extra special slap in the face to pour money into facilities for a team that wasn't very good. And money for things that would not necessarily make them better. Would they suddenly get better if Coach Simonetti's Jock Jams played over a better loudspeaker?

Liam had never been one for team sports, but he was pretty sure that wouldn't matter.

Also, Coach Simonetti probably needed some new music to pump up his team.

If only he would come to the library, Liam could look into it for him.

Damn, he should have thought of that earlier, maybe gotten Coach S on his side.

Well, that was unlikely. But Liam was a fool today, so why not.

Peggy squeezed his forearm and he looked over at her. "You'll be great," she told him, and he wanted very badly to believe her. She reached for his notes, which he had been unconsciously turning into a wrinkled pulp, and flattened them out on his lap.

"I'll go up before you, real nice and slow. Work on their sympathy a little."

Peggy was perfectly capable of walking without assistance, especially for the short distance from the car into City Hall, but she'd decided to break out the cane, the one her insurance covered but that she insisted she would never need again. She was not a helpless old lady, she had told him and Joanna. And, with the volume of her declaration, half of the town.

But she, like many of his patrons, had decided they would do their part. Parents coached kids on the art of public speaking. Business owners talked about the ways Liam had helped them find information on loans and services and entrepreneurship. The girls' soccer coach talked about the value of the public library in the life of the student athlete.

The library was not just a place for homeless people to check their e-mail, one of them insisted. Although homeless people in Halikarnassus did check their e-mail there, but why shouldn't they? Liam had more behavior problems with the knitting circle, who had a tendency to get real loud over the advantages of different fiber arts.

"This is all very moving, and thank you for it," Councilman Maguire said. "But there's only, what, a dozen of you here? We have to think about what's good for the entire town."

"There's only a dozen people here because you tried to sneak in this meeting without telling anyone," Doris shouted, earning a bang from the gavel.

"Be that as it may," Councilman Maguire continued, "we have to look at this responsibly. Mayor Klomberg has brought forth some very compelling figures on the benefits of improving our athletic facilities."

"For the football team. What about the rest of the school teams?" the soccer coach shouted. She got gaveled, too.

"All right, all right. We've heard what you all have to say. Shall we move to close public comment?"

"Wait!"

The doors to the council chambers swung open, and Liam blinked, hard, not sure that what he was seeing was real.

It was Joanna, wearing torn jeans and runny eye makeup, marching toward the podium, waving some crumpled notebook paper.

"Hold on a second," she said, and she sounded out of breath. Had she run over here from Chet's?

Then he heard more commotion at the door, and he turned to see Trina and Kristin. Ah, they must have canceled the gig and come over here instead.

That was sweet of her. It wasn't going to help, but it was sweet.

Then there were more people at the door. He recognized Chet, and Phyllis, who stormed to the empty seat in the front row and stared daggers at Hal. Then more people, folks he recognized from the library, some he didn't. But as the room filled with people, it felt as if the entire town of Halikarnassus was in there with them.

"Just in time, young lady," Councilwoman Hopson said. "State your name so this can go on record."

"Now, hold on," said Hal. "We were just about to close comments."

"We were," agreed Councilman Maguire. "But now we're not. I'd like to hear what this young lady has to say."

"Thank you, Councilman Maguire. Uh, hi. Okay. My name is Joanna Green. Most of you know my grandmother, Peggy." She turned to Peggy, who waved with one hand and squeezed Liam's hand with the other.

"Oh, I think we know all about you, too," Councilwoman Hopson said with a smile. "You were quite a troublemaker when you were younger."

"Yeah, about that. Sorry. I was not a very good kid.

And I'd like to take a moment to apologize to my grandmother for putting up with my shit. Oops, my, uh, stuff."

"Oh, pish," Peggy said, but her smile widened.

"I know that my reputation precedes me, and I'm not entirely proud of that. But here's the thing: People change. And things change. When I was a kid, the library was not a place where I felt welcome. I had too much energy and too much sass, and anyway, there was nothing for me there. Now kids like me are actually going to the library of their own free will. Liam has them putting their energy to good use. And little kids—my God, have you been there when story-time lets out? It's like every kid in Halikarnassus is there. It's kind of annoying, actually."

Liam laughed, in spite of himself. He looked down the end of the row at Toni. She mostly looked nervous.

"But, hold on. I'm getting off track. Okay. So, Frank Russell." She pointed to one of the men who'd come in with her. He was wearing dirty coveralls and a ratty ball cap, and Liam tried to place him, but couldn't. "Frank went to apply for a job at that big new hotel in Schenectady, you know the one?" The council nodded. "But even though he was applying to be a janitor, he had to fill out an online application. Online! Even though his job had nothing to do with computers! So you know what he did? He went to the library. And now he has a steady job with good benefits. And what about Molly Sprouse? She's just like I was, kind of a pain in the ass, right?" Molly's mother, who had come in with Joanna, nodded. "She goes to the library every day after school, and Liam taught her how to shelve. So now she does that instead of getting into all the shit I used to get into. Sorry, stuff."

"And she made the honor roll!" Molly's mom shouted.

"And she made the goddamn honor roll," Joanna repeated into the mic.

"What is your point, Joanna?" Hal asked.

"My point, Hal, is that people in this town love the library. And they need the library."

"But they had the chance to come out—" Councilman Maguire started.

"Bullshit. Sorry. No, you know what? I'm not sorry. Because that's bullshit. Nobody even knew about this meeting. The only reason anyone is here is because Liam probably called them personally."

She looked back at Liam for the first time. He wanted to run up and grab her and squeeze her and kiss her. Instead, he just nodded. Because he had called those people.

"What's this?" Councilwoman Hopson asked. "An emergency council session must be advertised in advance. That's why we put it in the paper."

"It wasn't in the paper!" Doris shouted.

"But we gave the notice to—" Councilwoman Hopson stopped and looked pointedly at Hal. He had the decency to look sheepish.

"That doesn't change—"

"Despite that," Joanna said, cutting off Hal's excuses. "I have six hundred signatures here that say they support continuing to fund the library."

There was a buzz in the crowd as Joanna waved the mess of papers around.

"Six hundred?" Hal asked, incredulous. "How did you—"

"Two hundred and seventy-five of those six hundred are actual people who live in town. The rest are . . . well, let's just say it's a bunch of words not real flattering to our mayor."

"Give that to me," Councilman Maguire said. Joanna approached and handed over the papers. As she walked back, Liam saw her wringing her hands together so hard her knuckles were white.

"Is that . . . does this smell like beer?"

"That's the finest beer you'll find in all of New York State," Gus said from the back of the room, and a cheer went up around him.

Councilman Maguire banged his gavel. "Well, in light of this petition . . . I'm not really sure if this petition is even allowable, is it?" He turned to Councilwoman Hopson, who shrugged.

"Whether or not it's legal," she said, "clearly this whole session was a farce. Improperly advertised, out-of-control peanut gallery." The peanut gallery booed and stomped their feet. "Nonetheless, I say we vote. Gentlemen, all in favor of maintaining current library funding and seeking outside funding for the football stadium, say 'aye.'"

As each "aye" was mumbled into the chamber, Liam walked over behind Joanna. "Hey," he said.

"Oh my God, pay attention to the vote!" she said, her eyes wide.

"We got this," he assured her.

"And the ayes have it. The library funding will remain intact. Thank you, gentlemen!"

There was another bang of the gavel, but Liam didn't hear it. Most likely nobody heard it over the roar of the crowd bouncing off the walls of the council chamber.

"You did it," he said, looking at Joanna in wonder.

"I know. I mean, you're welcome."

"But your show."

"Psh, the show. There'll be other shows. In fact, Chet booked us for this weekend."

"That's great."

"Yeah, I had to promise to actually play this time, but I think I can handle that."

"Good." His hands felt useless at his sides as people churned around him, thanking Joanna and slapping him on the back. He nodded a few times, but he couldn't take his eyes off her.

"So, listen," she said, taking hold of the end of his tie between her fingers. She studied it like it had all the answers. "I'm so, so sorry. I was stupid. I mean, I was mad, but I shouldn't have taken it out on you."

"No, I'm sorry—"

"Liam, you didn't do anything wrong. Of course you were going to choose the library over the band. Even if it was your band, you'd choose the library. I shouldn't have even questioned that."

"Well, regardless. The library thanks you."

"Well, please tell the library you're welcome."

"I will." She wouldn't look up from his tie. He wanted to put his arms around her, but he wasn't sure. He wasn't sure what was coming next.

"Here's the thing," she said to his tie. "I'm very glad about the library. Very glad. That was stupid— football lights instead of a library? Come on."

Finally, she looked up at him. "But the truth is, I did it for you. I did it to prove that I'm done running away. This is my home, and I'm going to fight for it."

"What will you do?"

"I don't know. Maybe I can get a job at the library?"

"Hmm. I'm pretty sure that will be a conflict of interest."

"Oh yeah?"

She smiled, and he put his arms around her. It felt right. She let go of his tie and leaned into him, and that felt right, too. "Yeah. It's not a good idea to manage the person you're in love with."

"It's not?"

"No."

"Wait, I mean . . . you are?"

"Yeah." He smiled at her and watched the emotions cross her face. The joy, the fear, and, finally, the love.

"Me too," she said.

Good, he wanted to say. Finally. But she reached up and pulled his head down and kissed him, right in the council chamber, in front of a crowd of hooting patrons.

Man, she was trouble.

He loved trouble.

Epilogue

Two years later, give or take . . .

Liam hung the last panel of soundproofing on the wall and stepped back to admire his handiwork. Well, it wasn't great, but it would muffle the sound enough to fend off some of the complaints from the neighbors. Joanna had a bad habit of waking up in the middle of the night when a song idea came to her, and just playing. Liam was glad she had her creative mojo back, but he wasn't crazy about the close personal relationship they were developing with the cops.

He climbed up the basement stairs, thinking of how Joanna would react. *Honey, I built you a soundproof room! In the basement!*

Oh, hell, he knew she would love it. She would love it because she needed it, and she would love it even more because he'd done it for her. She was definitely a softy, especially when it came to him. He knew that, and he also knew that she hated it when he made her cry from happiness, so he tried not to be too goofy about it.

Of course, he was counting on her softness to counterbalance some of the disappointment she might feel if the room turned out to not technically be soundproof. But, hey, every little bit of noise reduction would help.

He looked up at the kitchen clock and realized he was late. Whoa, way late. He grabbed his phone on the way upstairs to the bathroom, and saw he had a whole mess of texts from Joanna.

> Hi.
> I'm nervous.
> Why did I agree to this?????
> Granny keeps crying! It is not helping!
> Can you bring Rosetta? I can't play, but I need to.
> I'm dying.
> Hello?
> I hate you for making me do this.
> I love you.
> I love you more than I hate you.
> Ugh, I gotta go shake hands.

He smiled as he wrote back.

> Love you. No matter what happens.
> But it's gonna happen.
> And you'll be amazing.

When he got out of the world's fastest shower, he had a message from Rick. He listened while he threw on some clothes. "Hey, man, I'm at the courthouse. It's still early, but I'm hearing that they might call it soon. I tried phoning Trina to tell her but she yelled at me. I guess because I don't have any actual news?

I don't know. Anyway, I just wanted to tell you that and to say good luck when you get over there. It's some kind of mess of nervous energy and you'll probably get yelled at for nothing."

Liam smiled and grabbed Rosetta and his keys. He drove over to Chet's, their unofficial and highly inappropriate headquarters, and nodded at Chet on his way in.

He still wasn't quite used to seeing the place in daylight, but there it was. Someone had been decorating—he suspected Peggy—and there were balloons hanging from the seams of the ceiling tiles, streamers covering the bar, and several of the more memorable posters tacked up over years of band stickers.

Liam saw Joanna right away. She was standing next to the stage, fiddling with her engagement ring, which she always did. He told her she didn't have to wear it, that it was enough for him to know that they were going to get married. But she insisted. Part of him was glad, if he was honest. He liked that she wanted to show the world that they were for real.

"Hey."

"Hey! You're here! And, oh my God, you smell good." Joanna put her arms around him quickly, then let go just as quickly. She was trying to be all professional, which she said did not include her hanging all over her hot librarian fiancé. But when he took hold of her hand, she didn't let go. So he stood there while she finished her conversation with a reporter from the *Halikarnassus Herald*, and, when asked for comment, said that he knew the citizens of Halikarnassus would see that Joanna was the only one for the job.

"Oh, God, I'm so nervous," she said once they were alone. Well, alone in a bar swarming with her supporters. "What if I don't win? Oh my God, what if I do win? Is this a terrible idea?"

"Too late now, babe. You're going to have to live with the fact that you made the right decision."

"But what if I screw it up? What if—"

"Joanna." He took her head between his hands, even though it didn't look very professional. But he had to make sure he could look her in the eyes. "You can do it. If I didn't think you could do it, I wouldn't have voted for you."

She kissed him then, just quickly, but enough to let him know that she heard him and she wasn't running (well, she wasn't running away), and she loved him.

"That's Rick!" Trina called out as her phone rang. "Hello? You better have news or I swear to—" She stuck a finger in her ear so she could hear better. "Uh-huh. Are you sure? The commissioner? So it's official?" She started squealing and bouncing on her heels, still on the phone. "It is? And you're definitely sure."

"Oh my God, Trina, what is he saying?" Joanna shouted in a very professional way.

"You did it!" Trina shouted back, and the bar erupted. That was the only word for the cheer that went through the crappy ceiling tiles, and Liam was caught up in a sea of people coming to shake Joanna's hand and congratulate her.

"She looks surprised," Peggy said, coming up to his side and giving his arm a squeeze. "She shouldn't be surprised. I knew she could do it. And so did you."

"I think she's more stunned. Now she'll have to stop talking about it and actually do it."

"You'll be there for her."

"You know I will."

"Well," Peggy said, stepping away from him. "She promised I could make the announcement."

He handed her up the short step to the stage, where she stood at the mic. She gestured for Joanna to join her onstage. Joanna blushed, but she did it. She had to.

"Ladies and gentlemen!" Peggy shouted into the mic. "After a long, hard campaign and an even longer adolescence—" Folks in the crowd laughed while Joanna rolled her eyes. But she rolled her eyes with a smile. "I present to you my granddaughter, Joanna Green, the new Mayor of Halikarnassus!"

Don't miss the next book in Sarah Title's
Librarians in Love series, coming soon!

LAWS OF ATTRACTION

It's taken law librarian Becky Schrader a long time
to stop comparing herself to her family of
overachievers and home in on what she really
wants—a normal life, white picket fence and all,
Mr. Dream Guy included. But before she gets
ahead of herself, her girlfriends convince her
she needs to let down her hair for once,
meet a hot guy and let the moment take over . . .

After graduating from an Ivy League law school
and practicing in New York for a few years,
the plan for Foster Deacon was to return home to
Denver and join the family firm, marry the right
woman, shoulder his responsibilities.
Except Foster's always been a bit of a rebel, and
he's decided to suit up with his family's rival firm.
What better way to celebrate than to spend a night
with a gorgeous blonde who leaves before he can say,
"Good morning . . ."

Becky feels she did the right thing, leaving her
lover's bed and not her number. After all, she
needs to focus on her job at Glassmeyer & Polak—
until the new hire walks through the door . . .
with a bad case of happily-ever-after.